Maid of Turpin's

by

Derek Hayes

Bretwalda Books, Unit 8, Fir Tree Close, Epsom, Surrey KT17 3LD
info@BretwaldaBooks.com
www.BretwaldaBooks.com
ISBN 978-1-910440-43-8

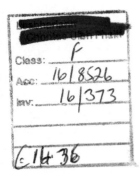

Printed and bound in Great Britain by
Marston Book Services Ltd, Oxfordshire

ACKNOWLEDGEMENTS

To Jenny for her magnificent art work and
my Norfolk friends for their encouragement
Thank you

CONTENTS

PROLOGUE

The long delicately carved oak table took up most of the floor space in the room. Around it sat twenty men in solid high backed chairs. The same ornate carvings extended to the well worn arms and a head rest which Thomas Sharingham felt was distinctly uncomfortable.

Tall, narrow-pained windows were barred and shuttered against any possible connection with city life in the streets of the capital. The walls of the room were Oak panelled up to waist height and then decorated with hand painted murals of naked maidens frolicking in a forest paradise. Upwards and across the high ceiling, the gods, twice the size of the maidens, took erotic pleasure admiring the maidens and behaving mischievously. The light from two large candelabras, one at each end of the room cast flickering shadows on the ceiling giving the distinct impression that the figures moved. Bizarre thought Thomas. He had no interest in this freakish taste but marvelled that someone must have commissioned the work; someone with vast wealth.

None of the men at the table were identifiable, apart from a doctor who carried a gold topped cane, an emblem which marked him out as a physician. All were uniformly dressed in sober black. They may have known one another in their business connections; they certainly all exhibited the behaviour of a ruling class, but intimacy was not evident. Every man had his head covered in a loose black silk hood pulled so far forward that faces were just shadows. Each was addressed on a name plate by his own letter of the Greek alphabet. Thomas knew they were amongst the wealthiest and most influential in the city of London. They were bankers, traders, and politicians. They had one further thing in common which brought them together. It was the driving force behind this criminal enterprise; the singular obsession, the one feature above great wealth coveted by them all. It was power and influence.

In this respect Thomas Sharingham was the odd man out.

Alpha at the head of the table spoke in a cultured, aging voice. The sparsity of the furnishings and high ceiling distorted his voice to a reverberating echo. Thomas thought, in his particular circumstance, an indistinct voice was a clear benefit.

"It's been a number of years in the making but the Company will soon be in the best position ever to complete its task."

There were murmurs from around the room.

"The Company has taken over the National Debt of thirty million pounds and made a loan to the government of seven million pounds. We will receive a five percent annual return."

Epsilon interrupted, "Already the greedy population of the country are clambering to purchase shares."

He looked across the table to the rotund figure opposite, "Look Omicron can hardly contain himself."

Omicron was certainly jigging around in his seat.

"Gentlemen, decorum if you please," said Alpha.

Omicron spoke, "When do we start to sell Alpha?"

"It's imperative that we all hold our nerve, no one must sell yet."

Alpha was clearly a man accustomed to being obeyed. There were nods and grunts around the room.

"Beta you may report."

A rather nervous young man began speaking of share prices and the treasury's interest in the company. He spoke of the Wig government's efforts to raise money for another war. Another voice interrupted with a snort.

"The sooner we clear away this rotten crowd the better." The words were delivered with such venom. There had not been a Tory government in Britain for many years and it was the dearest wish of most of the men around the table to change that situation. Thomas Sharingham had no interest in government; but the corruption of power, was a different matter.

Alpha spoke again, his voice carrying such authority," We have a guest present who shall be named as Zeta"

"Thank you gentlemen. The Spanish government has already pledged ten million pesetas to your cause."

The thick rather course accent seemed quite out of place around the table of largely aristocratic gentlemen.

Thomas knew the Spanish had their own agenda which would be well served by seeing a new government in power. Encouraging a British war with France would suit them very well.

"However in return for," he hesitated, "certain assurances I am permitted to offer a further ten million."

There was general approbation around the table with murmurs of praise.

No doubt, thought Thomas, there were numerous different aspirations and loyalties around this table. His own though was clear and simple enough. His master was none other than his own father the Duke of Sharingham and his loyalty was to the government of Sir Robert Walpole.

"That completes our business for this evening gentleman," said Alpha. "However there is a final matter concerning Kappa."

All eyes in the room turned toward the name place of Kappa who was indistinguishable from any of the other hooded figures present. Before he could move, he became locked in his chair.

Thomas thought the arms of Kappa's chair turned and captured the man's arms, but perhaps it was an illusion. In fact Kappa's arms had become encased in iron sleeves which extended from wrist to elbow and held him fast.

Thomas was so intrigued by the gadgetry that he hardly noticed the servant standing behind Kappa's chair.

"I have constantly reminded you all of the need for obedience to the brotherhood's rules."

Alpha's voice had dropped to a whisper and he spoke slowly as if pronouncing sentence,

"Rules of secrecy and loyalty. Kappa has broken every rule and thus put us all at risk." There were murmurs around the table.

"In return for wealth and power you promised to keep the rules and accept the penalties."

Kappa struggled helplessly in the chair but all he could move was his head. He began to cry out in protest. Alpha nodded to the servant who took a piece of cord and placed it around Kappa's neck. He threaded it through two holes in the back of the chair. Every time the man cried out the cord tightened.

"Hear me out," cried Kappa. The scheme is doomed to failure."

"Will any man speak up for this traitor?" Alpha's voice defied anyone to do so and there was a deadly silence in the room. The servant tied the cord behind the chair and slipped a wooden bar in the loop. It became a turnbuckle which he screwed up slowly forcing the neck against a protrusion on the back of the chair. As the spinal cord snapped with a jerk and his head flopped on to his chest. Kappa's screams suddenly ceased.

Thomas reflected on the manner in which he had contrived to be present at this meeting and pondered on the identity he had borrowed for this occasion.

CHAPTER ONE
THE MAID OF TURPIN'S

"Is that she…; up there?" the fuzzy-bearded youth muttered to his older companion.

He spoke quietly with his face in a tankard of ale. "She's a beauty and no mistake." He was peering nervously at the young woman sitting in the tall chair, on the far side of the half empty parlour. The atmosphere in the cavernous room was already malodourous but the sweet smell of hog roasting on a spit softened the odour of unwashed bodies and wood smoke. It went unnoticed by most of the early evening tavern customers.

"You best look away," spat the older man sternly, nudging his neighbour roughly with his elbow and causing a slop of ale to splash, a warning of the peril of even casting an eye toward the Maid of Turpin's. He directed a discreet squint himself, through narrowed eyes, at the infamous beauty. Sybil Turpin, the owner of the tavern, was already a legend in this part of the capital city.

"She's a Turpin and you don't mess with no Turpins."

The young man turned away. They both had the unmistakeable appearance of Dockers; thick necked, hard-callused hands and ragged scraps of clothing barely covering muscle bound bodies, ingrained with coal dust.

The Maid of Turpin's, sat, head and shoulders, above the customers, listening to the hum of conversation and missing nothing. She saw everything happening inside the parlour, from the far corner of the servery to the front door. Sybil's sharp hearing missed nothing of the tittle-tattle. She knew the river traffic had been busy since the high tide at noon. It had brought in three ocean-going vessels. The entire neighbourhood of the rookery already knew the cargoes. By tomorrow morning contraband goods will have found its way into the shops and businesses around this part of the river port. Some of the liquor was already on its way in to Turpin's cellars, thanks to the two Dockers now being rewarded for their trouble in the parlour.

The maid, a slim willowy creature, thought herself to be about twenty-three years of age but she could not be sure. The simple long pale blue woollen dress left little uncovered above her ankles. A matching bodice gave the, figure-hugging dress, a degree of modesty. So striking were the long golden tresses framing her high cheek bones and a strong jaw. If the complexion of peaches and cream was a smidgeon less than stunningly beautiful, it gave the clue to her determined character.

Sybil was distracted this evening, her pale blue eyes darted restlessly about, but it did not prevent her from collecting snatches of conversation, mostly quite insignificant, drifting around the room. Collectively they revealed the history of the past twenty four hours in the neighbourhood of Cheapside.

"You 'ear about Wiffy Wiseman? 'It by a runaway carriage in Bread Street."

Two shopkeepers sat in a corner grimly discussing the demise of the pawnbroker. "Took both his legs clean 'orf, I 'eard."

On another table apprentices discussed the excitement of their day.

"You seen the booty come in off that Brig from the Americas?"

The other nodded, "I seen some grog come ashore. What else?"

"Tobacco! Some came over this way, I 'eard."

In Huggin Lane, not a quarter of mile away, there had been a fire in one of the clap- board houses which overlooked the Thames.

"Whole family perished," said a shopkeeper.

"Tis a wonder the whole street weren't lost," said another.

The stench of living so close to the river was a dreadful burden but it had its compensations when fire threatened the city.

Amongst some of Turpin's wealthier customers there was something close to hysteria about the continuing rise of shares in the South Sea Company. In a cubby two well-dressed businessmen spoke in what they thought were hushed tones.

"Even the likes of Palfrey, in Lombard Street, has taken his savings out from under the floor boards to buy shares in the company."

"Wife's father is in the exchange," said the other, with a hand over his mouth, "he's already doubled his investment in three months. If he keeps his nerve he'll be worth ten thousand by Christmas."

Little of this interested Sybil Turpin. She had something to do this night and it was a most unwelcome task. One she felt ill-equipped for. In matters of the heart Sybil was, despite everything, almost an innocent. Her slender hands moved restlessly over the polished arms of the tall chair and her feet beneath the blue woollen dress, fidgeted on the well worn step. A commotion at the entrance drew her attention; a beggar, not a local, pushed his way through the front door in to the tavern. He made straight for the log fire in the hearth. An imperceptible movement of Sybil's head and the ragged creature was hauled bodily back in to the street. Hardly anyone turned to watch.

Her young foreman, Ned Church, approached the chair. She questioned him with a wordless glance.

"No one of consequence Mistress," shaking his head. "Just a beggar, not one of ours; offering to sweep the floor for morsels he might find."

"What else?" in her quiet voice, looking directly at her trusted foreman in a way which did not invite idle talk.

"Busy night ahead," he looked confidently up at her. "The cock-pit promises brisk business. I've offered Mr Strutt some help with the baying rabble, but he refused it."

He knew Sybil hated the cock-fights, but was obliged to let them continue. Strutt ran the Pit on his own. He was an unpleasant reminder of the Tavern in her father's day.

"I've taken in two doxies for the evening and sent the rest away," he looked up for her nod of approval.

"The gin cellar's been busy all day; I'll keep Josie in there till we close it. They'll still be busy in the brew house for a while. When they're done, Obadiah and his boy can change the barrels then help out in the kitchens." She nodded again.

"Tyburn's been busy today so we can expect a riotous evening."

"Thank you Ned," she held his eyes. "Was there something else?" she said sharply. He hesitated. "No nothing really."

"Tell me," she said firmly.

He turned his head away momentarily as if still not sure whether to say.

"It's just that, it's… good to have you in the chair." Sybil lifted her chin slightly and allowed a thin smile.

"I'm here to stay Ned." The young man visibly relaxed and smiled back. He knew his boss well enough, but was relieved she had not taken umbrage at his comment.

Turpin's was the most notorious tavern in the city where in an average evening more crime was planned than in the rest of Cheapside. Like her infamous father, so many years before, she sat above the noisy rabble and controlled all that happened around her. Everything about the place, from the enormous open fire drifting wood smoke across the high timbered ceiling, to the sweet smell of pine sawdust on the floor, was like a drug to her.

When Sybil took over from her ailing father, she had no desire to change anything. Neither could she; for Turpin's had become synonymous with every conceivable sort of outlaw. A criminal fraternity had become established around Cheapside and Turpin's was at its heart. In an average evening it was likely to serve criminals of every persuasion. To Turpin's came people planning crimes; from counterfeiters to horse thieves. Vagabonds of every description. Rufflers; bullies who begged from the strong and robbed the weak. Curtsey men who pretended to be well-to-do fallen on hard times. They were all here.

In Turpin's, seafarers from the river port came and regularly had their wealth removed by some means brutal or other. Then there was the organised crime. The leaders of villainous gangs; ironically called Upright Men, were the most corrupt of all. They traded on the fear of others, fought one another, and terrorised the local population. Around the Tavern a notorious legend had grown and this attracted people from across the city who would risk their purse and perhaps even their life for the opportunity to be associated with its esteemed criminal reputation. It was bravado which brought wealthy young blades to drink ale in the tavern; and there perhaps to take a doxie or seduce a wench or just cast their eyes on the celebrated Maid of Turpin's.

In his day Turpin had been personally involved in most of the crime. From a baby Sybil had been nurtured in the company of criminal folk. Without ever knowing her mother she was weaned by hired workers and brought up by a succession of nurse maids. Her accession up the first and then the second step of the tall chair to become mistress of Turpin's was as predictable as growing up itself. As doted-on and beloved daughter she inherited the mantle of mistress. She retained control of this malevolent kingdom by virtue of her quick wits and the consent of a criminal fraternity for whom she provided a haven of safety.

***

Sybil was distracted by other matters this evening but she glanced around the room. There were fewer than thirty early evening customers in at present. Across in the far corner a group of local traders gambled with dice; while a half dozen room guests, congregated at one table were enjoying an evening repast. Several young apprentices, heads down over a table, lamented their troubles to one another. Sybil watched Ned ambling around the tavern floor; a word with the traders and on to the guests; more food called for; another glass of porter. On to the apprentices. Walking the patch her father called it.

"Know your customers Peaches," he would say, "and never trust a soul."

Sybil admired Ned's easy going style and had begun to trust him to sit on the tall chair in her frequent absences of late. Too often she thought, but that will change.

A busy night Ned had predicted and he had ten staff on duty for the evening. There were serving girls, pot boys and the two heavies, who presently sat quietly alongside the door, their staves resting in the corner. When the place was filled to capacity Sybil would direct the activities of her staff from the tall chair. They watched her constantly and would be ruled by the glance of her eyes or a gesture of the hand.

***

Sybil's thoughts drifted back to the first time she met with the young Thomas Sharingham. Six months earlier; it had been an evening such as this. He had come to the Tavern with a group of gentlemen friends to drink and wench the afternoon away having attended a public hanging at Highgate in the morning. Well liquored before they arrived the group were behaving boisterously in a cubby.

The conduct of the young privileged gentry was not a problem for Sybil, however, she had never seen Sharingham in the tavern before, and it became clear that the event was a celebration of someone's coming of age. All his friends, she observed, seemed determined to get drunk. Around the parlour other customers took a more sinister interest in the playful group. They were thieves, all waiting for their respective opportunity to steal. Sybil recognised two Upright Men; each ensconced in separate corners of the tavern surrounded by groups of their own followers. Two doxies drifted over to the group of gentlemen and lounged against the cubby like a pair of book ends. The riotous behaviour grew worse; jugs of ale began flying. All eyes in the tavern were on Sybil but she minded little that they wasted their ale as long as it was paid for. The tavern staff watched her and waited. The villains around the hall watched her also, waiting for their opportunity. They knew better than to make a move in the parlour of the tavern. It was a rule of Turpin's that no crime is committed inside the tavern, but once the drunken group were outside they would be fair game. Suddenly amongst a frenzied mass of arms, legs and petticoats the two girls disappeared in to the cubby. There were cries of protest and Sybil had watched the activity unfold, in a rather detached way; another human drama where the end of the story was inevitable.

Thomas Sharingham had not seemed to enjoy the riotous behaviour of his friends and although he was as intoxicated as the rest, the effect on him was different. He sat quietly on the end of the settle in the cubby doing his best to stay awake.

She had admired his fresh smooth face and the aquiline nose gave him majestic appeal. She wondered what sort of person he would be. She imagined if he spoke to her that his courtly elegance would be matched by a pretentious stuck-up turn of phrase. She had laughed at herself and blushed at the fleeting thought of him without his clothes.

**

Her own experience of men had been limited to the youths who frequented the tavern. There had been short-lived affairs with a number of young men.

There had been an apprentice waterman who had his own wherry on the river. On Sundays when the water-taxis were officially banned from accepting fares he would take her up the river. Once they went up as far as Vaux Hall stairs where they visited the Spring Gardens.

There had also been a youthful highway man who her father thoroughly approved of, but whose life was foreshortened by the gallows. When Pa was alive no self respecting villain would dare to pursue Sybil for fear of retribution from Turpin himself. For his part Turpin set tough rules for the girl living in the midst of such a promiscuous society.

"Keep your drawers on Peaches," he would say "and sleep lonely in your bed."

A slit throat might be the reward for paying court to Sybil. Since her Pa had gone, Sybil judged that none of the men who frequented Turpin's had the gumption to make them a worthwhile catch. A fine looking young man with the boldness to engage her might be asked,

"What is the nature of your business, my handsome?"

"I, Mistress Sybil," the aspiring suitor might say, with thumbs tucked in to his waistcoat, "have the honour of being an artist of most exceptional talent."

"My sort of man," She might say admiringly.

"My hands," holding delicate fingers for her inspection, "are the assurance of wealth beyond your wildest dreams," says the suitor to stir the impressionable young woman.

"So you're a pickpocket or forger with a wish to entertain at Tyburn one fine day."

"Mistress Sybil, you wrong me."

"Have this ale with my compliments, for if you had a brain as well as beauty, I might invite you to my home."

***

The young gentleman had stood to leave the cubby and swayed his way towards what he hoped led to the privy. Sybil looked at the fresh faced callow youth and felt tenderly towards him. Several of her regular rogues slipped out from amongst their companions and followed him outside. It seemed likely that the unwritten rule in the tavern was about to be broken. Sybil acted quickly. She might not normally intervene when young and foolish of the nobility chose to risk their lives in the slums of the city. They knew the risks and came all the same. But something about the boy brought out dormant feelings of tenderness. This was a rare thing for the normally hard hearted woman and it was an emotion she scarcely understood about herself.

The young man and she were much the same age but that was where similarity ended. For the rest, they might just as well have come from different worlds. He the son of a Duke and heir to an estate of unimaginable size; and she the daughter of a notorious criminal whose birth right was the ramshackle pile of brick and timber surrounding her. She beckoned one of her doorman and followed him out in to the back yard. Ned also appeared armed with a cudgel kept beneath the bar.

They followed the foul odour to the privy from where there were already noises of a scuffle, grunts of hard hitting ruffians and the sickening shouts of a falling body broken with pain. It was all over in a thrice. Two unrecognised shadowy figures scrambled away. They might be discovered later from the damage done to them. The dim light of the candle lantern showed Sharingham tipped head first in to the earth closet; covered in human waste from the dregs of humanity. Blood poured from wounds to his head and arms. The stench made Sybil retch. Her men dragged the body out on to the flag stoned courtyard and sluiced it down with pails of water from the well. Sybil had been tempted to leave the body there to recover and drag itself away.

***

From her seat on the tall chair Sybil's mind ranged over the romance of the past months and the anxiety she felt about the task ahead gave way to feelings of sentiment. It had been an impetuous and passionate affair which they had both enjoyed.

"You're still wet-behind-the-ears," she could heard her father say, "and that goes for him an' all." Turpin might not have discouraged an affair with a member of the gentry. He would just as likely have had his mind on the main chance. What sort of pay-back might be possible from a liaison with a nob such as he.

***

After the young gentleman was rescued from privy they dragged the unconscious body back in to the scullery. Ned advised caution.

"This one's well connected Mistress, If he's going to croak we'd best be rid of him now; far enough away from Turpin's."

Sybil replied casually enough, "We'll give him a chance first Ned. You get back to the tavern, find out who was responsible and send me Josie."

So weak was the poor fellow, that he was unable to leave the sick bed in the Tavern for three weeks. His wounds healed quickly but the midden caused a sickness which at its worse left him delirious with a plague like fever. Sybil arranged for a maid to tend him throughout the day and night, but soon took over the task herself not trusting others to do it well enough. There were no words between them. She did not even know his name. At the height of the fever he raved like a mad demented creature.

"Better off in Bedlam," Ned had said, making no secret of his disapproval.

The patient thrashed around in the wooden straw-filled cot. He perspired excessively and the sweat smelt like the mire they had dragged him out of. A quack Sybil found in the tavern said this was good; the putrification was coming out. He wanted to bleed him but Sybil said no and sent him packing. It was out of sheer desperation that she concluded to Ned.

"It can't be right to take his blood while he's so weak and sweating."

So she made a potion of Box and Burr-Marigold to dispel the fever. Sybil spooned boiled water in to the semi-conscious man. For a week she did this, lacing it with good French brandy, for she reasoned that it would restore goodness to his blood.

Days later Ned finally discovered who the two villains were and Sybil invited their leader to talk. She climbed down the two steps from the tall chair late one evening. She always chose neutral ground for occasions such as this: a sop to the sensitivity a person might have against craning his neck upwards in public gaze to speak with her.

Fearless Friar was an Upright Man; and a most disagreeable one. She walked over to the large fireplace where only a huge pile of glowing embers remained. Two children who had been turning the spit all evening scampered away. The small remains of a hog was skewered above the embers and the succulent aroma of the pork still wafted cross the large room. Always a popular spot around the hearth but people moved away as Sybil stood leaning against the stack.

"To what is the honour I might 'av?" said Fearless Friar showing a mouthful of blackened teeth. She raised a foot on to a fire dog and Fearless admired the promising sight of her slim calf even though it was well covered in woollen stocking. Mucous dribbled from the side of his mouth.

"Fine team we would make mistress," the voice gurgled from the back of his throat like a drain. She could smell his fetid breath even though she had positioned herself to be out of the line of fire.

"Your connections and my brains," he rubbed his palms together ingratiating himself to her favour.

Sybil tried hard not to look at the teeth which were so decayed at the gums that she wondered why they did not all just fall out. A narrow bladed knife appeared in the palm of her hand from somewhere around that shapely leg and Fearless Friar was momentarily taken aback.

"I could refashion your mouth with this little blade Mr Friar, it would do you the world of good, and you wouldn't need to pay someone to chew your food for you."

She turned before he could speak and with remarkable speed, sliced a strip of pig's ear from the remains on the spit.

"Woo hoo," said the Upright Man leaning forward with two grubby fingers to lift the gift from the tiny blade. She held it out but as he took it the blade twisted so quickly it was difficult to see what happened, but blood began to pour down his hand.

"Oh, my," she said. "How did that happen?" There was an inch long gash across his palm. The smile froze but the putrid mouth remained half open and the eyes abandoned all suggestion of pandering to her.

"Turpin's rules were broken Mr Friar," said Sybil still holding the blade. "They were your men."

Every eye in the tavern was on them.

Before he finally recovered consciousness and registered her presence at his bedside Sybil had become very familiar with her compliant young patient. At her leisure she had enjoyed gazing on the graceful good looks and boldly admired his lean strong body. A kind of intimacy developed, initially encouraged, by Thomas's total helplessness. Once whilst he was dipping in and out of the delirious state and she had been wiping his brow with a moistened towel, his eyes opened to see her clearly for the first time. It was, for her at least, a momentous occasion, suddenly her intimacy was shared, and it became a relationship – of two people. When their eyes met she blushed uncontrollably at being discovered; caught out in the very act of enjoying that old familiarity. Another time when cradling his head and spooning thin soup in to his mouth, she allowed the soft skin of her bare fingers to caress his mouth. His lips suddenly closed on her finger and she felt trapped; discovered, and guilty until his eyes gave all away.

When he was fully recovered, every moment between them was filled with chatter as if talk became a device to overcome the awkwardness they both felt. The talk was mostly trifling, teasing and of little consequence.

"You pulled me from the Privy?"

"Not me, we used a donkey with no sense of smell."

"How long was I unwell?"

"It seemed like years."

"Did anyone come asking for me?"

"Oh yes, there was a queue of doxies all claiming you were the father of their children.

"You're teasing."

"When you started to recover they all lost interest."

"And my friends?"

"Only those you owe money to."

They became inseparable. Thomas became quite at home in the tavern. He could often be found standing behind her in the parlour; leaning against the wall, feet on the back rail of the tall chair which brought his head level with hers. From this position she talked with him about the clientele of the Tavern. He could soon recognise the gentlemen of the road from the horse thieves, the rufflers from the curtsey men.

"The bald head in the corner by the door," she whispered confidentially to Thomas over her shoulder. "He's a dommer, pretending to be a deaf mute; but watch his technique."

He was a big man, dressed poorly, but he moved with agility between the tables gesturing with his hands so customers understood his affliction: And then when he had their attention; with the dexterity of an artist he cut away a purse which disappeared with such ease.

Sybil and Thomas laughed together at the performance. Then Sybil signalled to her doorman who returned the purse to its rightful owner before dispatching the dommer through the door amid shouts of abuse.

Sybil increasingly entrusted her authority on the tall chair to Ned, and spent more and more time away from the tavern with Thomas Sharingham. Some thought the tavern suffered from her absence. Certainly the customers felt less comfortable in the presence of the young gentleman in whom Sybil confided so much. The likes of Fearless Friar and his ilk, watched and waited. Sybil had crossed the line the day she took on Fearless and bettered him in front of his own.

Finally the chatter between Thomas Sharingham and Sybil gave way to a harmony where words were no longer so necessary. Fondness gave way to passion. Sybil and Thomas became lovers and the Tavern at Cheapside ceased to be the hub of her existence. The tall chair was no longer the place to share one another's company. She felt herself drawn towards an unfamiliar and not entirely unpleasant life style far removed from the nefarious world of her birth right. They journeyed away from the Tavern, short distances at first, to be away from the old familiarity. There were picnics, boat trips and the Theatre. They went to Drury Lane to see a play.

"It's a bloody tragedy," said Thomas, the connoisseur of theatre, trying to explain to Sybil the intricacies of the plot.

"It's an average evening at Turpin's," confided Sybil.

One day Thomas arrived with a coach and pair, and after that the trips went further afield. Such was the intensity of this relationship that neither thought much beyond the feelings they shared for one another. On an outing to Windsor they took food and drink for the day and walked so far out till they were sure the crowds were left behind. They hid themselves away in the forest and the honourable Thomas only heir of the Duke of Sharingham read from a little book of poetry. Sybil sat against a tree listening. She understood very little of the words but fairly swooned at the sound of his voice.

She said to him afterwards, leaning on her elbows, "you could have read me a news sheet and I would have loved it as much."

On one such an occasion that they were rudely reminded that their growing affair was not just a matter of interest between the pair of them. Footpads found them in the heat of an embrace.

"Well what 'av we 'ere," a voice said from the darkness of the trees.

"'Ow lucky what our timing is," said another. Sybil buried her face in Thomas's coat and held her breath. Thomas rolled her over, lifting her skirts high up above her thighs. It had the desired effect of distracting their attention. At the same time he slipped his hand in to the bag in which their picnic had been carried.

"You think we might join in or just watch 'till things gets 'eated up" cackled one of the rufflers. Thomas fired clean through the bottom of the bag and killed one man stone dead.

"I have another barrel in the bag and it is aimed at which ever of you moves," he said calmly. The remaining ruffians quickly disappeared in to the undergrowth.

"Customers of yours?"

Sybil nodded. "I recognised the voices they were trying to disguise."

"You think perhaps this was no accidental discovery?"

"Mr Friar's men, I suspect," she said sheathing her knife which had appeared during Thomas's diversionary tactics.

"And that's for lifting my skirts," she said smacking him gently across the face.

"What?" he exclaimed in mock alarm.

"While there where strangers looking," she added playfully.

***

The Tavern was filling and through the smoky haze from the blazing log fire Sybil watched her regular customers relaxed and at ease in the fellowship of friends and preferred company. The worst of it was that she was beginning to feel distanced from these people. She no longer shared their secrets. It had always mattered to her that she was respected and admired by them, the dregs of society. She had a place in their hierarchy. There was a bond between them. Thomas had taken all that away and what he offered in return was no match.

I can never be part of his world. I'll only ever be the outsider, his kept mistress, his doxy.

***

"So, the son and heir is summonsed to the holy of holies," said the young man looking about him. "It must at least be that the country is going to war or plague has reached the estate."

The honourable Thomas Sharingham leaned back against the door of his father's study closing it with a slam. His eyes cast around the walls of the room as if to avoid looking at his father.

"Sit down sir," his father said wearily. Thomas crossed the room to the large bay window and stood looking out across the estate with his back to third Duke of Sharingham.

"I care nothing for your opinions of my behaviour; your politics or your reputation, for that matter."

He turned defiantly to face the most powerful man in the south-east of England; friend of King George and one of the wealthiest men in the country.

"Thomas, we must talk," the old Duke said, heaving himself up in the seat behind the large ornate desk piled high with matters of state and the debris of a recent meal.

The Duke looked at his son and for a brief moment was detached from reality to see himself in his beloved son's shoes.

I made him what he is, thought the father. Gave him an appreciation of great power and influence. A mind and an intellect to reason and argue for the better. I set him above others and now as my father did to me I must disabuse him of thoughts that he can set aside responsibilities and chose a different passage.

"I have no desire to discuss my friendships with you now or ever."

Overbearing and pretentious thought the Duke, looking directly at the young man. Was I so different?

"You are aware of the reason for this meeting then?" said the Duke tiredly.

"Yes Sir, how could I not be? But as long as I do not allow friends to interfere with my work...."

The Duke interrupted. "There are people that would do me harm by injuring you."

"I can look after myself, you must know that much. You taught me how to. I want no part of your lifestyle. My birth right is like a millstone round my neck. I would rather…."

"Rather what; rather not have been born? Rather relinquish your inheritance for the sake of a whore?"

"She is no whore," Thomas shouted.

"She single-handedly rules Turpin's; the most notorious tavern in the city of London. She is as infamous as her father was. She's involved in every imaginable sort of crime."

Thomas was shaking his head furiously. He leaned over the desk with less arrogance;

"That is not so; she is none of those things."

"I remember Turpin's when the old man ran it himself. They were carefree days."

"That won't do father, you must let me choose."

"If only that were really a gift I could give you my boy. You have no choice just as I had no choice."

"I… love… Sybil," he said it slowly as if it was being drawn out of him like a barbaric practice once seen at Tyburn after a hanging.

The conceit and bluster had gone but there was a sense of decisiveness in his voice. He had not even said as much to Sybil; but it was like a heavy weight being removed.

"Tommy," there was a great sadness in the Duke's eyes.

"Your life is no longer your own. It was ordained on the day you were born. If it were otherwise I would joyfully acquiesce."

"She is my life," Thomas crumpled in to the chair across the desk from his father.

"Peaches is my life."

The older man hesitated

"Peaches; is that her name?"

"It was her father's special name for her," Thomas said quickly and immediately regretted saying it.

The older man smiled at something; a memory.

"Peaches," he said again. "Turpin had a daughter called Peaches." The Duke's countenance changed, as if withdrawing from reminiscence.

Turpin's daughter, he said to himself. When the long silence was broken it was a steely voice which addressed the boy.

"You must never enter Turpin's again; you must never see this woman again; ever. That is my final word. If you were to disobey me, and it would be easy to do so, there would be a great likelihood that your beloved Peaches would suffer the consequences."

***

The honourable Thomas Sharingham was expected in the Tavern this very evening. Sybil had rehearsed what she would say to him a dozen times already. She felt resigned, even philosophical about it. After all, her love affair with the nobility had run its course and had been played out in the most public of places. From the tall chair their romance had been conducted and Turpin's rag tag patrons had seen it all. It was only right it should finish here in this place where it started. She leaned forward in the tall chair as the front door opened again to blow in bitterly cold air and several more wet and bedraggled waifs looking for temporary refuge from the hostile streets beyond.

Where is the boy, she thought. I must do this now, and I can't do it without him. The atmosphere in the Tavern seemed to reflect the rising apprehension she felt. It was as if everyone waited.

What if he doesn't come, what if he never came again?

Another icy cold draft announced the door had opened again. Sybil suddenly became aware of a hush over the whole parlour. The talkers fell silent, the ballad singer stopped, even the gamblers ceased their gaming. All eyes in the room looked towards the door where the Honourable Thomas Sharingham stood momentarily framed in the entrance; like sentinels the two doormen stood either side; and then he slipped slowly to his knees.

Despite the dread she felt about ending their affair, Sybil's initial sentiment had been of tenderness and excitement at seeing him again. The silence in room was broken by a crash as the tall chair smashed onto the floor and Sybil Turpin was brought down, with horror. She ran towards the door as the body slid to the ground. From the amount of blood, he must have been walking in this injured state for some time. Thomas had been struggling to reach the refuge of Turpin's. She tightly held his corpse and felt the icy cold fingers of despair, with the growing realization that someone else had ended her love affair.

CHAPTER TWO
TURPIN'S RULES

Brutality was a commonplace event in the rookery but never had Sybil Turpin felt so personally involved. Even the death of her Pa had not affected her so. In his case it had been a long lingering affair in which he turned yellow with the jaundice and died a little by little every day till she wished him gone for his own sake.

"It was my fault," she told Ned. "Thomas was killed because of me and I'll find out who."

She applied her best efforts to discover who was responsible for Thomas's death. Her highly effective intelligence network around Turpin's had been working constantly but with little success. Her customers, it seemed, had closed ranks or at least it appeared that way.

***

The tavern was quiet in the early afternoon. There was little or no conversation between the few customers leaning over trestle tables, dulled into slumber from the effect of too much drink or too much food, or both. In several of the curtained cubbies soft murmurs could be heard and the occasional playful feminine squeals told that not all passion was gone from the cold afternoon. In the hearth new logs emitted copious smoke but little heat. Clem the pot boy wandered aimlessly around the tables collecting jugs, his ever shifting eyes were alert for a prize. A coin carelessly dropped and lost in the sawdust, a purse unattended by a customer too drunk to notice; a discarded and forgotten coat which might make sixpence in the pop shop. However this was a dangerous game for the young man to be playing, for Turpin's rules applied within the tavern and if there was the slightest suggestion that he was thieving from his employer, he wouldn't just be dismissed. Clem would be thrown back on to the streets, from where he came, but not before he received a severe beating.

The door opened admitting an elderly gentleman, soberly dressed in expensive grey woollen coat and white breeches. He wore an unfashionably long waistcoat and a high parted white wig. He carried a silver topped cane and held it out so that the embossed crown showed. In the doorway he stood and looked around, staring up at smoke stained beams of the high ceiling and from the fireplace across to the serving area and then to the cubicles with their shabby curtains and dark corners. He walked across the room towards the first cubby and sat sideways, on the end of the bench, so that his feet rested on the flagstones of the floor. Another figure, his servant, came through the door and took a seat by the doorway facing towards the elderly gentleman.

"Bring me Turpin," said the man without looking at the pot boy. His voice was commanding but the pot boy looked at him sullenly and with an ignorance which was plainly one of confusion.

"Who's your master," the man said gently trying to rouse the boy.

"Ned sir," said Clem rubbing a sleeve across his dripping nose.

"If you bring me Ned quickly enough there will be a penny for you, but you will need to make haste."

"Are you a Turpin?" said the Duke to Sybil's foreman. Ned recognised gentry when he saw it but couldn't place the man.

High up amongst the smoky beams of the ceiling a small window gave a view of the tavern's main parlour. From here Sybil stood, in her private quarters, watching the discussion between her foreman and the stranger. It was too far away to see much but the bearing of the man, his general features, the way he held himself was familiar to the young woman.

Sybil had not spent much time alone since the murder of Thomas; it was not her way to mourn. But undressed in her own private room ready for an hour of quiet repose she found herself painfully drawn back to the young man with whom she had become so attached. Everywhere she looked, there were reminders of the sad, still unfinished business.

As if by some curious instinct the old man stared straight up, beyond Ned, towards the shadow of a figure in the little window. He was silenced for a moment till Ned spoke again as if to catch the man's attention.

"Mistress Sybil runs the tavern; her father has been gone some years now."

"I'll speak with her in the small parlour," the Duke stood up and walked towards the side room.

"I know who you are," she said quietly, "but I don't know why you have come. This was not Sybil at her most alert, but she had not expected this confrontation and was unprepared.

"I want to know who killed my son," said the Duke, looking at her intently.

Sybil held his gaze.

"You want something more, I know that much."

"Yes". There was a long pause as if he was making up his mind. "But only to see whatever it was that ensnared Thomas; to make him so careless." He showed no feeling of emotion; he addressed her as if she was a nobody.

"I am *it*," she replied angrily, "I'm what he came back for; what he kept coming back for."

The Duke sighed and looked at her tenderly now.

The shawl drawn hurriedly around her shoulders clasped tight about her, by a bare arm. The defiant way she held herself; the confidently lifted chin as she addressed him. Her slender neck caressed by hurriedly attended-to hair, the long golden hair; the complexion of peaches.

"I can see why he did so." He said gently, looking around at the lime washed walls of the small parlour; seemingly distracted by Sybil's closeness.

"You seem to know this place?"

"Yes, I knew it well in your father's day," he said sadly, "when I was Tommy's age." He looked down at the flagstones.

"Will you help me; I doubt I should find the killer without your help?"

"I was about to put a stop to it all," she said more to herself. "But he didn't come; then when he did it was too late."

The Duke looked at the girl. "Will you help me find who killed my son?"

She looked at the old man and for a moment, imagined the suffering he felt at the loss of his only son and heir. "I'll find him." She said confidently.

"I can help," said the Duke, "I have…. resources. One of the benefits of my position."

"Your position won't help here at this end of the city, different rules apply here."

"I'll send someone," the Duke said and walked towards the door. He stopped and then as if an afterthought had occurred to him, he turned quickly.

"How old are you child?"

This was not a question Sybil was asked too often and if it had been by anyone else she would not have hesitated with a reply. However the Duke had put it in such a way.

"Twenty-two years I believe."

He stood looking at her, with ill-disguised admiration.

"Thank God you have your mother's fine looks!"

And he was gone.

The Duke blamed himself for his son's behaviour. He knew he had never spent enough time with him. Matters of state kept them apart throughout Thomas's early years. The present sovereign George I who spoke hardly a word of English and cared nothing for the customs and practice of his adopted country had handed power to rule to a Regency Council so that he could abscond to his real home; to his precious roots where he remained as Elector of Hanover. The monarch spent increasing amounts of time in his native country and seldom attended meetings of the governing Council.

At court Sharingham was a close friend of Robert Walpole and part of a small cabal of ministers who ran the country often without consulting Parliament and never bothering their sovereign king with the politics of the country.

The Duke blamed himself not only because he had neglected Thomas through his childhood but for another more important reason: A reason so sensitive that it distressed him to think about it and when he did it was acutely painful.

Sharingham was the minister who controlled Britain's secret services. He worked directly to Walpole but was personally responsible for all the government's secret service activity. Sharingham ran agencies in Holland, France and Germany. He had contacts in Austria, Spain, and Italy. At the present there was so much division and intrigue at home that he was obliged to keep a number of agents busy in Scotland as well as England.

The father's dread was that he had encouraged Thomas to enter the secret world of espionage.

The Duke walked back to his carriage muttering to himself;

I did no good when I pressured you in to working for the agency. It was a selfish thing I did. Words were said at their last meeting and Sharingham dearly wished he could take them back. But when it came to the protection of his country and the control of its secret services, he worked with a passion seldom seen in the politics of the day. He was in a society where corruption was commonplace; honesty and decency an exception. Yet the nature of his work meant his endeavours usually passed as unremarkable. Only Robert Walpole himself was aware of the Duke's contribution to defence of the country.

Sharingham was provided with a budget of £3000 a year to manage the entire operation. He often paid his agents from his own funds rather than see able men compromised and fail in their endeavours or lose their loyalty to the crown. He seldom had the opportunity to select really capable recruits and often it was left to the integrity of others; his spymasters who handled the agents.

***

Born in to the decaying old tavern in Honey Lane, Sybil's growing up had been a very public affair; conducted in the full glare of the corrupt and criminal patrons of the Tavern.

Turpin's business was running the Tavern, a haven for every sort of nefarious crime. Where thieves and pickpockets would congregate; highwayman gained intelligence for their robberies; kidnapping was planned in the ale house and smuggled goods were brought in and distributed across the city. The list of Turpin's regular customers who ended up at Tyburn, not more than a stone's throw from the tavern, was like a role of honour.

Sybil was cared for by whoever happened to be available. Growing up had been a journey of discovery but a loveless and menacing voyage, where the needs of a small but inquisitive child was an only-just-tolerated distraction.

She leaned back in the shabby leather padded chair with her stockinged feet on the table. This little room, her father once called his Den, no longer held fear for her, but as a child it was the cause of nightmares. Turpin's had been Sybil's now for a number of years but what a legacy, she thought.

A tavern full of thieves and cutthroats where no self-respecting person would come of their own free will. The watchmen of the streets and the parish constables steer clear of Turpin's. Law abiding citizens would rather walk the long way round through Milk Lane and Cheapside High Street, than pass the front door.

Some inheritance.

Her early childhood had been a confusion of warm carefree memories and unspeakable, fearful terror.

They made me what I am.

She smiled remembering Dizzy Nancy.

She couldn't read nor write, but could count and did so when she brushed Sybil's hair: twenty-one, twenty-two, twenty-three……..

Fifty strokes with the horse hair brush and Sybil's tresses shone like burnished gold. Nancy's mouth mimed the numbers twenty-four, twenty-five, twenty-six.

Then Sybil would interrupt, "Is that forty-five yet?" and Nancy would forget and have to start again.

"Twenty-one, twenty-two." Sybil smiled at the memory.

At seven years she had learned very well how to manipulate the people around her. Nancy, as much as she was loved, was a soft touch.

"Are you my mother Nancy," Sybil once asked.

"Goodness no child; how could I be your mother. You only had one mother and she died when you were a tiny baby."

Nancy came, stayed for a while; performing the duties of maid, mother, nurse, and grown up sister; before she then caught the roving eye of Turpin the father and disappeared to be replaced by another beguiled young woman.

Sing-song Mary had been another of her favourites. She had a voice like a nightingale and an Irish lilt; such a joy to listen to.

"Mary, are you going to marry pa?"

"Miss Sybil; now what sort of question is that to be asking of me?"

"But are you Mary?"

"Hold still child; put the cloth over your face while I pour the water."

"Well you go to his bedroom at night sometimes….."

"Now if you don't let me finish the water will be stone cold and you won't be liking that."

"You like him, don't you?"

"Of course I do child, we all do, but Turpin's the master…, and I only do what he asks."

At ten years of age the darkness of the tavern held no fears for Sybil. She awoke one night, long after the candle had gutted, to hear the watchman call the time two hours after midnight. The stillness was suddenly broken by the sound of torturous screams that seemed to go on and on. The Tavern was as black as pitch and silent except for the noise coming from her father's den. Out of her bedroom she crawled along the floor of the corridor; little fingers feeling for every creaky board to a hole in the floor where she could see down in to Turpin's den. The room was crowded with men and she heard one gruff voice crying; pleading for his life.

"For the life of me I didn't know, please stop the pain," a grown up man was sobbing like a child. She saw her father there doing things to him and then the screaming stopped.

She had no understanding of what was going on, but knew fear when she saw it. Sybil stuffed the hem of her nightdress in to her mouth so as not to make a sound and shuffled back along the corridor to her bedroom. At a later time she went back to the room. Her tiny hands reaching up to turn the door handle and was surprised to find it unlocked. The fetid odour of stale gin and pee made her gag. With childish logic she thought – that's why he keeps it closed; to stop the smell from escaping. She had looked around the room but there is no sign of the crying man.

Where could *he* have gone?

Now, twelve years later, Sybil remembered, and put a hand in to her mouth as if re-living the experience.

She looked around Turpin's Den. It had undergone a transformation; the entire room has been scrubbed clean. Still the same table, and space enough for three or four to sit or stand amongst ledgers, bills, lists, and the like.

It was the pure indulgence of the silken Persian rug which signified *Sybil's* ownership of the Den.

She had only the remotest idea where it had originally come from.

From the Nantucket Trader; a four-masted barque moored at Allhallows Stairs; she would most likely say. It was her idea of frivolous luxury. The sensuous pleasure of running her bare feet over the silken pile: tracing the outline of barbarian hunters on horseback, with her toes.

As a child she had never been completely alone. There had been Freddie son of the brewer. Freddie could not speak, he was deaf and dumb; no voice at all but he and Sybil knew how to talk to one another. For a short while, when they were ten and eleven, the Tavern was their playground. In the cock-pit, they played chase in the blood-spilled ring and in the wicker cage suspended over the pit they swung high up in to the roof. The wicker cage in which a cock would be held to show him off and get him wild before lowering him in to the pit to fight. They used the passages and cellars as their playground and crawled through tunnels of the roof space like mice.

Freddie had a brush of blond hair, a shoeless, ragged scruff; he looked like a well- dressed chimney boy.

"Pa says I mustn't play with you any more. He says I might catch something."

He grabs her hand and pulls her along. With grunts and growls he tells her,

"I've found another secret passage, follow me."

They dived off together. Like everything they did it was at full tilt, as if there was not a moment to lose before their childhood ran out of time. And so it was: for Freddie died on Sybil's eleventh birthday.

"I was right," said Turpin to the tearful little girl.

There were other children after that; from the streets and neighbourhood. But when their parents found out, they were taken away.

Pa was always there; somewhere distant but wholly disconnected from the wants of a little girl he never really understood; cosseting and treating her like a small person rather than a child. He would shower her with tokens of a father's affection but was never able to give her what as little girl she needed most.

She watched the way the maids and servants were when he was around.

"Yes Master; No master."

"Pa why do they call you master?"

"Ha Ha, such questions you ask," he boomed at her. "Because," he whispered in her ear, "that's what I am to them, and they're frightened of me." Putting an arm around her, a clumsy show of affection, he laughed conceitedly.

The little girl pulled away.

"And they dare not forget it."

"Do they hate you?" she had said.

But he tired of her childish questions and sent her away.

Turpin never drank his own ale, thought Sybil, only gin. And he died with a gin soaked brain

***

It was commonplace for the aroma of herbs, spices, and even rare perfumes to drift into the dark corners of the Tavern. Brought in as contraband by the regular smuggling customers of Turpin's, small quantities would find their way in to Sybil's personal possession.

When the maid of Turpin's swept by she left the perfume of fresh herbs or the aromatic resins of myrrh or frankincense. While the gentility might carry a nosegay to disguise the odorous smells of the city, Sybil carried the fragrance of whatever aromatic balm she was presently using. She had learned about herbs and their healing powers. She knew, like the apothecary, how to prepare cures for common ailments. She knew how to harness the natural goodness of plants and herbs. She could cure a wart or settle the mullgrubs with a posset. She could cool a fever, stop the flux, and stem the pain of a festering toothache. She could sooth a cough, and ease the passage of consumption. Sybil could discover fancysick from a genuine illness and knew how to prescribe a sham. She knew how the aroma of herbal balms could be used to influence the mood. She had a natural sense; an instinct for their use. Around Honey Lane Sybil Turpin had the well-deserved reputation of an herbalist.

It was mid-morning and two figures stood leaning against the tall trestle bench from where the food and drink was normally served to the parlour. Deep in a hushed conversation, they were an incongruous pair.

He a tall, well built, scruffy fellow with course features, a down-turned grey moustache, and a square jaw which gave the impression of a sad but friendly bloodhound.

She a slight figure half his size and consequently having to crane her neck to speak with him. John Dutch may have been hardly aware of the oil of Lavender which presently wafted between them, or its sublime effect on his senses. Between them on the bench top lay a cone shaped screw of paper.

"This is what you asked for John," Sybil picked up the paper twist in her small hand and held it up.

The Dutchman was a regular at the tavern and like others of his kind planned his criminal business within its confines. She began to untwist the paper and licked the tip of her finger dipping it in to the brown powder.

"Suck my finger," she said holding it under his nose. Without question or murmur he opened his mouth and took the powder.

"That's how you do it John, just a peck on the tip of a finger."

Her hand dropped and grasped his enormous fore-finger in both her hands; smiling she said, "And this is too big. Take the powder three times a day. It's for your kidneys John."

She placed the packet in his hand.

"Will it do for me pissin and all that Miss Sybil?" he said in his broken English.

"It's made from a herb called Love-In-the-Mist; it'll make your waters flow."

"That's a wonder if it do, Miss Sybil." He looked in bewilderment at the twist of paper. Then hesitatingly almost embarrassed to say but remembering Sybil's finger in his mouth, "The love in it, do that work for she also?"

"No John," she shook her head at the big man. "It's not for Betsy your wife; it's just the name of the herb. It's not a love potion."

The Dutchman nodded; he was no more trustworthy than any of his kind, however Sybil had a relationship of sorts with him. He was a gang leader, an influential man in his patch. He controlled the activity of many petty thieves. John Dutch took payment from them in return for his protection but they were his eyes and ears in a city where knowledge was power and in the past he had never hesitated to offer her his help.

"Mind you," Sybil looked up in to his face, "If Betsy gives it to you on the tip of her finger, who can say what it will do for your love life."

"What can you tell me about the murder," said Sybil.

"What I knows, is nothing, Miss Sybil," the Dutchman replied earnestly. "It's just like your man never existed. He never came 'ere and 'e never got killed."

"I don't understand," said Sybil leaning towards him, "how come someone gets spiked outside my door, and no one knows a thing?"

He looked at her sadly.

"You must help me John, There must be someone who knows, there must be."

"There is someone, but he is not a good man to know."

"I don't care John; take me to him."

"I will ask."

***

Clem the potboy stood defiantly with arms folded, facing his accuser. He was a lightly built boy but tough for his sixteen years.

"You came to us from St Clements's workhouse with nothing but what you stood up in and you'll leave the same way," said Ned Church standing before the boy with a long switch of hazel. Sybil thought she had never seen Ned so angry. The boy remained silent. Two doormen stood either side.

"Why did you do it Clem?" Sybil asked the boy. On the table were the paltry contents of the boy's pockets. Silk handkerchiefs, a drawstring purse of leather, and a pair of black gauntlets fashioned of finely cured pigskin. There were a few small coins.

Ned pointed with his rod to the gloves.

"He came in wearing them like he was proud."

"Everyone does it," the boy shouted defiantly. A doorman cuffed him about the ears for speaking out. True he came with nothing but his name.

"We don't steal from our own customers, did you know that Clem?" He nodded sullenly towards Sybil without looking up.

"You're old enough to hang for stealing, do you know that?" She said raising her voice.

"Have you watched the free show at Tyburn Clem? Seen how they dance around sometimes when the hangman doesn't put the noose on properly?"

The boy went white as a sheet as Sybil described the slow death of a convicted criminal who could not afford to pay the hangman to ensure a quick death.

"Do you know why we don't steal from our own Clem?" she went on. The boy shook his head. "Its loyalty, that's what. Loyalty is what you give me."

She stood close up to the boy and he had to look up to her.

"Loyalty is abiding by the rules we all have, and it's about helping me fight my corner when I need you to."

Now listen to me Clem; I have to earn that loyalty from you, but if I treat you badly I don't deserve it. Have I treated you so? Tell me now."

He shook his head.

"Speak to me Clem."

"No Mistress,"

If Clem could have seen the shred of sympathy in Sybil's eyes he might have decided differently but as it was he remained defiant.

He was a stubborn boy and the choice he was about to make would have a profound influence on his future.

"You have a choice." His eyes were alert looking at each of them in the room. "You may leave the Tavern now, with your thievings and never come back this way again. Or you can take a beating from Ned and I'll keep you on. Which is it to be? You're nearly a man Clem and I've given you a grown-up decision to make."

Sybil turned and left before the boy could answer.

CHAPTER THREE
AGENT OF THE CROWN

Richard Hamilton stepped out of his handsome cab on the corner of Thames Street and walked over the threshold of London Bridge. Having disembarked a few hours earlier, he was still in the dull clothes of a seafarer. It was appropriate dress for he blended in to the busy scene as if he belonged. His presence was completely unremarkable amongst the rag-tag throngs in this part of the city. The tottering buildings on either side of the narrow cobbled road seemed to funnel the din of the crowds. The food and drink sellers were the worst of it and in the few yards to his destination he was accosted three times by obstinate traders fighting for his custom.

"Fresh Pies," from a cross-eyed urchin with a tray strapped around his neck, thrusting an over cooked limp pastry in his face from a dirty hand.

"A quaff to put you in good sorts sir." Offered to him from an earthenware bottle, poured in to a chipped and dirty beaker.

"Purest quality, guaranteed curative for every sanitary condition known to man." The vendor with bloodshot eyes and an unwashed odour looked as if he had been sampling his own gin since sunrise.

A tray of cooked meat held aloft on the head of a large woman smelt of rancid fat; but Richard wasn't sure, it might have been the woman's putrid armpits as she wafted a morsel under his nose and smiled at him.

"You never tasted such wholesome food."

But would I survive the experience, he thought.

Just over the threshold of the bridge Richard stopped to peer in through the window of the cobbler's shop. The glass was so dirty it was hard to see anything. He was not surprised that shoes on display shared space with objects quite unconnected with the trade of the shoe repairer. There were candles, an unlit oil lamp, several carpenters tools including an awl and a wooden handled auger. There was a live cat sleeping on a cushion. Placed there for the purpose? He wondered. I suppose it's alive, he thought.

He was looking for the secret signal he had been given. It was in there somewhere amongst all the bric-a-brac. It would signify that it was safe and he was expected. Closing the door, the bell clanged again and the sounds of the London Bridge traffic diminished, for a moment his nose was assaulted by the aroma of leather, and glue heating on a small flame.

Richard leaned over to the window and removed an unclothed wooden doll looking as if it might have been fished out of the Thames. He placed it on the counter in front of the old man. He smiled grimly at the thought that his secret signal was a naked puppet whose strings had been cut.

The old man paused in the act of cutting a leather patten; he looked over his glasses at the tall striking figure of the young man and continued for a moment before gesturing with his sharp knife to the back door. He then leaned over and removed the wooden doll.

Upstairs in a bare stone walled chamber above the shop which straddled the river

Richard met his new handler for the first time. The stench of the Thames penetrated every part of the room as did the roar of water rushing through the narrows between the sterlings supporting the bridge. Richard thought it must be unbearable having to live here in the jumble of houses which leaned precariously over the water.

"From here looking North West," the older man pointed a bony finger out through the tiny widow and across the river, "you can see in to the very heart of the rookery."

His voice was soft spoken and lofty, his speech clipped and authoritative. He was a man accustomed to being listened too and obeyed. They had never met before and Sir Ronald Able-Makepiece was very different person to Richard's old spymaster; a man anyone would travel the extra mile for.

Richard's gazed out. As far as he could see, at least three miles along the length of the Thames, it was heaving with life. The docks were crowded with ocean going vessels and men crawled all over them like ants. Hundreds of small craft filled the waterway and in the most haphazard manner skilfully avoided collisions. On the far side nearest to him coal barges were being loaded from sea going vessels to be taken under the bridge and further up river. There were upwards of a hundred vessels moored around the buildings of the Coal Exchange. On the nearside an even larger numbers of ships from the continent of Europe and ports around Britain, laden with perishable goods, fruit and vegetables, competed with one another to be unloaded. The order of priority was normally decided by the size of the bribe to the stevedore gang leader rather than the time they waited.

Sir Ronald, spoke again angrily, "It's a pity they could not raise the whole rat infested sprawl to the ground."

"You mean fire it?" Richard said. Sir Ronald continued looking at the Rookery.

Even a small fire caused two or three streets to be destroyed, but then they simply rebuilt in the same haphazard manner. Buildings are mostly timber and so tightly packed that they burn like a tinder box.

"They say it's possible to travel across the rooftops for miles without jumping to the ground," said Richard. Useful for escaping from the Watchman, he thought to himself.

Sir Ronald ignored him.

"As far as Black Fryers stairs," the man pointing again, "and almost to St Paul's church yard." His voice raised to make an outrageous point.

"It's become a forbidden area for law abiding citizens. The watchmen won't go in there after dark. No man will serve as a parish constable and even the Justices, rogues that they are, are fearful of punishing anyone from the rookery."

After his briefing they remained looking out of the window and Richard was intrigued by the unrelenting view of grimy rooftops. St Paul's towering up in the distance and beyond that the sinister outline of the Fleet prison.

"Every crime is there and most of it controlled by a few heavy characters who rule the place as if it were their own private fiefdom."

"I was expecting some leave Sir. You'll know I've been out of the country for a year and I was hoping to get down to Dorset to my family," he looked across at Sir William.

"Oh yes your family," Sir Ronald looked at the young man with something bordering contempt. "It's a simple enough task," the spymaster sounded irritated; shouldn't take more than a week to sort. Anyway you weren't my choice."

Richard looked up, what a disagreeable fellow you are, he thought.

"Seems you have a friend in court, Hamilton. So you can thank him that you're not getting leave."

Richard frowned and struggled to understand. He shook his head in disbelief. He must be talking about someone else.

They walked down the stone stairs and left the little shop discretely. On the narrow roadway of the bridge Richard asked.

"Can you tell me what happened to Sir George?"

"He got old, and was making too many mistakes." The hubbub of the street traders competed for Sir Ronald attention.

"He was an old friend as well as my handler." Sir Ronald stepped swiftly across the busy thoroughfare and leaned precariously over the edge of the low wall peering towards the end arch.

"This is where they punish their own," He pointed at one of the twenty foot high wooden water wheels part of a system providing a water supply to local houses.

"They wind the wheel up out of the water, and tie the victim to it and then slowly lower it again;" he looked away, "leaving the watch-keeper of the bridge to find the body in the morning."

The pair walked back across the bridge to Sir Ronald's carriage. "That's where you have to go Hamilton. That's where the answers lie."

Richard followed his gaze along the river bank and thought about what Sir Ronald had been saying. He was struck with the difference between his old mentor and this man.

The coachman, who had been staring at Richard, climbed down and opened the door of the carriage. He whispered something in Sir Ronald's ear.

Sir Ronald turned at the step and spoke again.

"There's a Tavern in the very heart of the rookery. A Tavern with no name.

Locally it's called after the criminal who once owned it. Turpin's."

He hesitated.

My man thinks you may be carrying arms?"

"Yes I have a pistol," said Richard rather surprised by the question. Sir Ronald smiled.

"We'll leave you here then."

"No doubt the answer to all your questions will be found in Turpin's. Run by the daughter now," he said dismissively, as if the whole matter was of little consequence.

"She's said to be a beauty." He looked over at the younger man and there was a thin smile.

"Knowing about your inclination for attractive young women........."

"Sir," cried Richard genuinely indignant. Sir Ronald turned his back on the young man and climbed in to the carriage.

"I have read your file Hamilton," Sir Ronald said wearily. "And I recollect that even in the thick of a scrap you have always managed a regular amorous encounter."

There was a silence and when Richard did not respond, "Spain last year, a dusky maid in French Indies in nineteen. A French diplomat's wife in eighteen..."

Richard had the good grace to colour slightly.

"Only in the course of duty Sir."

"Well I trust your course of duty will serve us. I would not wish to see you on that water wheel one morning." He tapped on the roof of the carriage.

"On your way then Hamilton," He leaned out of the carriage window. "When will you go in?"

"Tomorrow evening Sir."

"Very well. You know what has to be done, get on with it."

As his new master disappeared in his coach, something told him this would be far from a straightforward assignment and he should not expect any help from Sir Ronald who seemed bored with the whole business and knew less about espionage than the cobbler.

***

Richard leaned over the taffrail of the brigantine and stared in to the murky waters of the river basin where the vessel was moored. He had come aboard a whole two weeks ago for a passage back from Spain and was taking advantage of his friend, the vessels captain, to lodge on board before going in to Cheapside to tackle his new assignment. It was hardly luxury accommodation but he was safe from prying eyes and he had the company of a friend who did not enquire about his business. Richard had often travelled on the May Bell; it was used by the British government's secret service for clandestine work. A two-masted square rigger, the ship was small enough to negotiate into tiny harbours around the European coastline and fast enough to leave a pursuing craft behind.

As so often happened during long periods of absence from family, Richard found himself reminiscing about an earlier time in his own life. It was a half-forgotten time of carefree childhood.

"Get along home to your mother," his father had said. "Tell her to make you some warm compresses, and be quick before I change my mind."

There had been rather more disadvantages to having a father who was also the village schoolmaster. But he had loved the man regardless. He smiled to himself at the memory.

"Hamilton," the master had called from the front of the class, peering over his spectacles "read the next line."

Richard hesitated; looked around at the dozen or so pupils crowded in to the little classroom; no help coming from either side.

"Stand up boy," snapped the master. The other pupils looked away.

"Step forward," he opened the high desk behind which he normally sat peering at them like a hungry bird of prey. The head disappeared inside and fished at the back of the desk amid the papers books, chalk and confiscated property. Richard knew the inside of that desk intimately having tidied it on so many occasions for minor misdemeanours. Out came the cane. It was long and whippy, with a bendy handle. It would be laid across his hands unless he could think……. quickly.

"Sir," he had hesitated, "I have blistering pains in both ears, I can't hear a thing." He held his hand out high, so father would not think he was expecting to be let off. Richard had held his breath for a full half minute whilst the master was rummaging about under the desk lid and consequently his face was now as red as blazes. He held a hand over one ear as the final touch. Father hesitated in mid swing and stopped…

Childhood had begun in the village of Cerne Abbas in deepest Dorset where Richard was the youngest of five children and learned, much to his mother's discomfiture, that to get a share of anything he had to fight for it. He was usually last in the line at meal times; accustomed to wearing worn out cloths; familiar with cold murky grey water for washing and always being the one to carry the can. For everything except his mother's love he was last in the line. For that he received more than all of them. Mother was the provider of copious love for her youngest; even when she knew quite well that compress of healing herbs for his 'blistering pain', was just not called for.

Human Activity amongst the ships on the dockside decreased as the evening light faded. The gentle waves driven by a breeze and the sluggish current of the Thames gave the silhouette of a hundred or more masts, a natural swaying movement; a vibrancy unrivalled in the absence of human activity. There was no unloading of ships after dark unless it was undertaken with stealth and deception; without the usual rowdy exchanges between dockers and the ever present threat of bloody retaliation between competing gangs. Richard raised his eyes from the foul water to follow the shuffling watchman as he lit the oil lamp marking the corner entrance of the basin. The old man raised a hand acknowledging Richard's wave. Strange he thought after noticing one-another for the last two nights we greet as if compatriots. He studied the watchman disappearing along the river bank and thought the fellow must have survived in to old age by minding his own business, perhaps being paid not see anything of the illicit trade as he crawled along the dockside night after night tending the beacons.

It was growing up amongst his older siblings, where he discovered that every problem brought with it a chance for a counterstroke; an opportunity to retaliate, gain the upper hand, turn the tables and to learn from the experience. He developed a talent for getting out of scrapes, driven no doubt by the need to survive against heavy odds.

"It's alright Dick," his older brother James had once said, "you can eat woodlice everyone knows that, but you have to be quick before they crawl away." So he did, furiously munching away. If his brother said it was alright it must be. They all laughed at him when he was as sick as a dog.

But when Richard secretly put caterpillars, a whole bowl full, into James' meat pie the next day he asked, "Are they creamier than woodlice?"

The Hamilton children grew up enjoying the patronage of a certain Squire Hallwood, a good friend to their father, whose influence eventually found employment for them all. As a child Richard hated the man for a good reason. Father's gun was a Brown Bess; a flintlock with a rifled barrel. By the age of fourteen when only he and James were left at home, Richard could shoot a rabbit dead from ten yards. But when the pair of them hunted in the squire's lower fields they did it with snares. Cutting hazel sticks, sharpened at one end, and fixing a cord at the other. Hammering the stake in to the ground the loop laid six inches high and the whole trap rubbed with a rabbit pelt to disguise the human smell. They collected a rabbit or two at least once a week and secretly left them at Widow Turner's cottage. They would hide and watch when Goodie Turner came out and discovered meat for her larder hanging on the door.

"Glory be," she cried dropping to her knees, "tis a miracle." Richard remembered how they, hiding behind a bush, had watched, and James fell over laughing so much and Goodie Turner, as poor as a church mouse, shouted.

"Who's there," not in the least bit afraid. "If there's anyone there they'd better watch out for I've got the good Lord on my side."

Richard smiled at the thought of these memories. He remembered they kept it going for three months and watched Goodie Turner get healthier. It all ended when the gamekeeper caught them and the Squire who was also the local magistrate ordered a thrashing for them both and said it was to be administered by the gamekeeper because their father would be too soft. Some time later Richard learned Goody Turner was still receiving visitations from the Lord in the form of a rabbit hanging on her back door. Perhaps, he thought, Squire Hallwood wasn't such a bad lot after all.

When James was packed off to join the navy, their father with Squire Hallwood's support, turned attention to Richard's education. Being the brightest of all the children, he was finally sent off to Oxford to study. He excelled in the academic environment where his intellectual naivety made him enemies and a few good friends.

He discovered the implacable disadvantages of having no ancestral breeding and the sweet pleasure of exercising his intellect over those very same barriers.

"I'm done for Richard; if the Proctor hears about this he'll send me down. You know the rules about mixing it with the locals."

"Conflict between town and gown isn't such a bad crime Thomas. What happens is your wealthy father simply offers a donation to the library or a grant to the Chancellor to fund a chair in something expensive."

"No chance of that and anyway such benefaction only works when you have a doting father who thinks you can do no wrong. You've met the Duke of Sharingham; he's more likely to do it for *you* than his own son."

"I know he thinks the world of you and I know he's a kind and generous man. But it *was* a bit silly proposing to the barmaid."

"Dick she's the sweetest thing in the entire world and I love her with all my heart and soul."

"If that's the case you'll let her go."

"I can't do that either; her father's threatening."

"You've led too sheltered a life to be let out in the real world Thomas. You're a liability."

"Help me Dick,"

"I'll help you for the sake of the poor girl, but listen to me most carefully."

And he did listen and when Richard had finished, Tom went away and proposed to the girl's three sisters and even their mother who was as ugly as sin.

Richard smiled to himself at the memory of his good friend Thomas Sharingham.

Thomas's attraction to bar maids had turned out to be a costly weakness of character. Across the river he could see the ghostly shapes of the prison hulks. Although battened down for the night, the soulful cries of the convicts never stopped.

It was time to leave the May Bell and make waves in the rookery called Cheapside.

***

Richard leaned back in the stern of the small craft and watched the oarsman effortlessly lift the blades to slice the water like a knife through butter; hardly causing a ripple on the surface. He had hailed the water taxi from the deck of the May Bell and climbed aboard with the competence of a time-served matelot.

The man was unrecognisable being partially hidden by a muffle and long greasy hair sprouting like a bramble patch. Richard mused on why the rowlocks were bound up with cloth but the effect was unmistakeable for the craft glided soundlessly through the water with not a scrape of sound.

It was a full forty-eight hours after his meeting with Sir Ronald that he finally stepped ashore in the darkening evening on to Three Cranes wharf, a quiet reach of the Thames. He felt good about finally getting the mission started.

Handing the rower a coin, the man looked up from under the mass of greasy hair and nodded his head; he muttered something quite incomprehensible under his breath. Richard turned carefully on the slippery weed covered steps as the fellow prepared to push off in to the main stream to join the traffic of small craft plying their trade up and down the turgid water way. The air was damp and held that sulphurous odour which assaulted his nose and left a sour taste in the mouth.

From behind, he heard a clunk as an oar struck against the wall; unusual considering the man's skill. Richard stooped low and twisted around just in time to see the oar scythe through the air harmlessly above him. The aim, he thought, had been to remove his head. Then it was swishing through the air again returning for a second chance to clout him a serious blow. Richard grabbed the wooden blade and turned it pushing the boatman backwards. For a moment they were quite motionless on either end of the long pole and then with a thrust Richard pushed hard, and his would-be assassin rolled backwards into the water with all the grace of a lame duck. He hesitated for a moment, thinking to haul the man out and discover his business but thought better of it. If he managed to clamber out of the water, let the message go out, Hamilton was not a man to mess with.

The fog slowly layering itself across the river several feet above the water reduced visibility and made detection less likely.

So much, he thought, for my futile attempts to disguise an arrival. It seemed as if all his precautions for a quiet unannounced appearance in the rookery were for nothing. It seemed now that he was well and truly expected.

This called for a different approach. As he walked along the centre of New Queen's Street towards the heart of Cheapside, he considered perhaps it would be better to trumpet his arrival and flush out the opposition. Past the last of the crowds shopping from stalls along the pavement, candle lamps were already lit on some of the stalls and some of the traders had begun to pack up as the damp in the air became a fine drizzle.

Cheapside well deserved its reputation for being the place where everything imaginable was on sale in the open market. And if it wasn't on sale openly, it could be acquired, at a price.

People stepped aside to let him pass. He walked towards a stall being cleared of its display of sweetmeats and, in a careless manner, snatched a fruit tart to stuff into his mouth. The owner cried a protest but was silenced when Richard turned towards him and threw the remnants on to the ground. People stared with undisguised curiosity but no one stopped him. The signal went out through the streets of the little community, there was a stranger in the area. He had the look of a half crazed man ragged bully, clothed like a vagrant, only the torn remnant of a service uniform gave a clue. Richard stopped at a stall and tried on a heavy grey coachman's jacket, threadbare already and stained about the front with dried blood. He put a dirty finger through a hole above the bloodstain. Well at least he thought the blood is dry.

"Not worth more than five pence," he shouted at the old woman. She was hardly distinguishable from the rags hung around her stall.

She met his stare with gin soaked eyes and cackled, "Gwan then six pence and it's yourn." He put the coat around his shoulders, straight away feeling the benefit. She took his coin and bit on it; bending low she muttered almost to herself.

"So what brings master Dicken back home again?"

"Trust your eyes and ears are still as cute Meg?" Richard muttered.

"To be sure, and they tell me you're attracting singular attention." He smiled down at the woman. "You're late my boy we been expecting you for the last three nights."

"I know Meg but there were things to do."

"There's lodgings awaiting you." She grunted her approval of the coin and shouted after him. "That's bloodsucking at the price you mind."

Richard walked up towards St Mary Le Bow. Along Bow lane there was a short cut; an alley pitch black except for the occasional glimmer of candle lamp from an upstairs window; and quiet as the grave save for the distant cry of traders and the steady flow of sewer water splashing down the open gully in the middle of the lane. Being a large-built fellow was no guarantee that he wouldn't be an immediate target for the street gangs. In fact Richard had to establish his credentials to these people and that probably meant taking a beating at some time or other.

He stopped and backed against the wall. His keen eye noticed a darker outline shifting against the grey sky. It indicated that not all the shadows were as solid as the walls of the houses. Richard sunk both hands deep in to the pockets of the coat and smiled finding that Meg had left him useful small gifts in anticipation of the scrap he would certainly have before reaching his lodgings.

Despite his alertness the first blow about his shins came as a painful surprise. A scything bone cracker with a stave took him right off his feet and leaving him head down in the gully. A heavy body fell on him and pushed his face against the ground. A hand grabbed his hair, lifted his head and began pounding him against the stone. He roared like a lion and kicked up with both feet in the hope of finding a target.

His foot found someone's back and the assailant stopped for a moment.

There was a shout. "Legs, grab his legs."

I've landed with a couple of beginners Richard thought, reaching back in to the pocket of his coat. His hand grasped Meg's little present and with all his might he threw the handful of pebbles back over his shoulder where he thought someone's face would be. A scream signalling he was on target. He twisted over and grasped at the fellow below his armpits. With both hands Richard threw the body over his shoulders. At just this moment the accomplice with the stave tried to join in the affray. In the darkness he began beating his own partner over the head. To encourage him Richard cried out.

"Stop, I can't take no more, take my purse, take anything."

Encouraged by the cries, the mistaken assailant continue the beating with renewed enthusiasm. Richard stood up and grabbed each by a leg and dragged them roughly over the cobbles towards a flickering street lamp. The boot came off one and he scuttled away on all-fours. Richard was left with the cowering figure of boy who held his hand up to his face to ward off Richard's blows. Across the street the night-soil man's cart was parked, the pair of heavy horses waited patiently for the man to return with the contents of a householder's over-flowing cess pit. Richard grabbed the boy to lift him in to one of the barrels full of effluent. The boy saw what was coming and fought to keep his head from being immersed in the barrel.

"Please sir," he begged. Richard stopped.

"You're not a very good thief. Perhaps you're good for something else. He lifted him down.

"Come with me," said Richard walking off down the road without looking back. Then over his shoulder he shouted to the youngster.

"You watch my back boy."

Clem traipsed along behind his new master.

Richard felt hard-pressed not to look round, thinking every moment the boy might land him one on the back of the neck or more likely just disappear into an alley.

But there was something about the lad; a certain vulnerability. Richard's decision to trust him was instinctive; an intuitive feeling born somewhere in his own childhood. A familiarity half recognised and half forgotten.

CHAPTER FOUR
A DANGEROUS MAN

A week after Sybil's conversation with John Dutch he returned to the tavern and held open the door of a small but stylish carriage drawn up in to the courtyard. He tugged the corner of his droopy moustache nervously offering his arm for Sybil to step in. She glanced up at the coachman; a figure swathed in a heavy cloak and broad brimmed hat pulled well down over his face. The inside of the coach was plainly upholstered in dark red leather. The smell of leather and waxed wood had a sublime effect on her senses. It belonged to a person of good taste. Expensively fitted out but not overly extravagant.

"I'm impressed John I didn't know you ran a coach and pair?"

"Neither don't I Miss Sybil, this is borrowed."

She sat down with a jolt and grabbed the leather handles as the coach took off at a breakneck speed. Sybil was swung violently around as it left the courtyard and set off across the city.

"Does he know what he's doing, the driver," as she fell about trying desperately to hang on.

"I'm thinking the man is carried away with the importance of his passenger," said John seriously. He leaned out of the window and shouted something after which the driver slowed to a slightly less erratic pace.

Sybil wondered at the wisdom of coming out with John Dutch but he was one of the few regulars at Turpin's that she trusted. She had asked for his help and he was offering it now.

"Who are we going to see John; can you tell me anything about him?"

"I cannot say Miss Sybil but I promise I will bring you home safely."

He looked at her keenly. "He is a man of great influence but a dangerous man to stand in the way of."

Nothing much to worry about then, she thought glancing over at her fellow traveller.

He sat quietly smiling at her on the opposite seat. If she was to find out more about Thomas's murder she had to do this and if it meant stepping out of the sanctuary of the Tavern, it would be done.

But she felt vulnerable.

John Dutch spoke, almost as if he knew what she was thinking, "Turpin's rules do not apply out here Miss Sybil, but my Betsy would never forgive me if you were harmed."

"The potion worked then John?"

He smiled.

The blinds in the carriage had been pulled down, which was normal when travelling in the city; it safeguarded against having rubbish lobbed in through the window or an opportune tradesman from poking his head in to sell pies, gin or a cure-all for every illness. However Sybil could still see the familiar streets as they made off away from Honey Lane.

After a while John fished in his pocket. He drew out a neatly wrapped paper package.

"This is for you," he said. "It is quite new, never worn I am sure."

Sybil knew this was a code for it having been stolen from a shop; but stolen after it has been so neatly wrapped?

Why on earth would John Dutch go to so much trouble? She removed the paper and was taken aback by the quality of the scarlet coloured silk scarf. The man looked pleased with himself.

"It's beautiful John."

"I thought you would be liking it nicely, you deserve to have nice things around you Miss Sybil."

Sybil frowned.

"Why did you do this John? Such a fine present should be bought for your Betsy."

He leaned forward and took the scarf from her in both hands,

"I am sorry in doing this but," Sybil thought for a moment the scarf was going around her throat.

"You must allow me to cover your eyes for a short while; it is for your own safety." His large hands gently tied the scarf about her head.

"Why is this necessary John Dutch?" she found difficulty in keeping the alarm out of her voice.

"It was a rule set by the man you are meeting," said John reassuringly. "He is a very private man and insists on this to ensure his privacy is protected."

Sybil groaned inwardly. The point was not lost on her; it was intended to prevent her from knowing where she was going; which might make it more difficult to find her own way back, if it became necessary to flee. But more than that, it told her that John Dutch knew this man well enough to be trusted by him and that implied her affable friend was more than a casual criminal acquaintance.

The carriage continued on through cobbled streets and for a while Sybil was able to keep track of the route they were taking, the sights and sounds as well as the smell of the city were second nature to her.

Drop the Maid of Turpin's down anywhere in this part of London, blindfolded or not, and she could find her way home using every back alley and little known route. Soon the cobbles gave way to cart tracks and the air began to smell fresher. The gentle swaying of the coach on softer ground combined to lull the passengers to a sleepy state. Suddenly there was an almighty crash and the coach swayed violently before righting itself. There were shouts from outside and the driver hauled the team of horses to a halt. John Dutch leapt out of the door holding a long-barrelled pistol behind his back. Sybil slipped her blindfold and used the moment to get her bearings. She could see very little apart from the tree trunk which had successfully stopped them on the road.

"You know whose coach you've stopped," shouted the driver in a most belligerent manner. Still the shouting continued.

With the Dutchman's appearance the voices quietened. John Dutch hardly spoke but gestured with his hand beckoning the highway man to dismount and come away from the coach towards the side of the road. In the failing light Sybil watched. His gun still out of sight, the big man put an arm around the masked robber, and led him toward trees, talking to him courteously. Then she heard a shot and the figure dropped to the ground. John Dutch climbed back in to the coach.

"I am sorry Miss Sybil but he won't stop us again."

Beneath the blindfold Sybil shook. The highwaymen had only threatened them. It was seldom that anyone was ever seriously hurt from such villains. She had just witnessed cold blooded murder.

An hour passed before the carriage finally slowed and the Dutchman who had been quiet for the latter part of the journey removed her blindfold as they entered the enclosed yard of a country house. When her eyes became accustomed to the fading light of the late afternoon she thought the large house looked like others she had seen in the area of Hampstead. From the coach yard she was led in through a back door. A glance behind showed they had travelled up a long overgrown driveway. In the distance a gate house and tall iron gates swinging closed.

Sybil was ushered in to a darkened room; she took to be the library. She was not familiar with such grandeur, but was not deterred by it either. The large log fire shed sufficient light for her, left alone, to wandered around examining the contents of the shelves. Many of the books were written in a foreign word she could not understand, but it was a pleasurable experience allowing her fingers to brush across the leather covers,

These books are often taken out and read, she thought. A voice spoke out from the darkened corner of the room.

"You read Latin Miss Turpin?" it enquired patronisingly.

She hoped he hadn't noticed her jump at the suddenness of his intervention which was obviously contrived to make her start.

"Not very useful in my business," she said quietly, "It wouldn't help in conversation with my customers."

She turned to face the shadowy figure.

Please come and sit down," the voice was cultured, "you will forgive my lack of manners, I was keen to watch you unobserved for a brief moment."

"I shall try to get better acquainted with your unusual courtesies, Mr ...."

"Doctor, Miss Turpin, Dr Medici Dearnought."

Sybil raised an eyebrow at mention of the name. It registered something. Not Dearnought, another name

Who are you? That's surly a name I know; mentioned in hushed tones even in Turpin's parlour.

She sat in a comfortable chair on the opposite side of the fireplace. The man's face was still in shadow while Sybil was quite revealed.

"John Dutch said he would bring me to someone who could help find a murderer."

"And for my part," said the shadowy figure, "I was eager to meet the woman they call the Maid of Turpin's."

"But you go to great lengths to hide your identity Dr Dearnought. Now there's a contradiction. You want to meet me yet you'll not show yourself and must guard against being discovered."

He laughed gently.

"You must forgive me Miss Turpin, I had heard you were forthright in your speech but you *do* deserve an explanation."

He stood and moved one of the candle lamps making the shadows diminish but not disappear. Sybil saw a tall rangy fellow in dark dress. He wore a cauliflower wig much favoured by Physicians. It hung down the sides of his face but not well enough to hide the long scar which marked the left side of his face. Sybil winced at the sight of it and immediately regretted doing so.

"I see you understand now."

"I'm sorry Dr Dearnought."

He ignored her and went on.

"As for the secrecy, the nature of my business makes it essential I take what measures I can to confuse my enemies; and believe me I have some very spirited opponents who would dearly like to benefit from knowing my whereabouts."

Sybil was swayed by the man's amiable manner and warmed to his pleasing turn of speech.

"I quite see why the Duke's son was taken with you and I'm sorry he took a drubbing; was knocked out for his trouble."

"You're acquainted with the Duke?

"Only indirectly and he is certainly not acquainted with me."

Took a drubbing, Knocked out for his trouble. Sybil thought this was a man capable of bad things, a doctor who would smile gently at his patient whilst bloodletting the very last drop of his blood.

"Thomas Sharingham was murdered on my doorstep Dr Dearnought."

"Yes but," he held the palm of his hand towards her, "it had nothing to do with him knowing you Miss Turpin. Young Thomas Sharingham was involved in other matters which brought his downfall."

Sybil sensed she might be hearing the truth or at least part of it, but something else about this man made her think she was being led blindly away from the truth.

Was there more to come? She looked across at the friendly figure at ease in his own comfortable surroundings.

"His demise was a matter far removed from the commonplace villainy of Turpin's. I can tell you no more than that."

They were both silent for a while. Sybil spoke first.

"Yours is the name people dare not mention Doctor; even in the quietest corners of the rookery." She had finally placed the man. It had to be him.

"It's alarming to hear I might be mentioned at all."

There was a note of irritation in his voice. "You have a certain eminence yourself Miss Turpin." he added in a hushed tone.

"*You* shouldn't worry; the name you are given offers no clue as to who you are." And to herself she said, only what you do.

If Dearnought was the least bit interested to know what he was called in the rookery he gave no indication.

"None of this explains your involvement Doctor; people are murdered in my part of the city every week but it is unusual........"

"Unusual for you to be personally touched by the death?"

"No, I don't mean that," she stopped to think,

"It's unusual for there to be such a mystery about who was responsible and why it was necessary for him to be murdered."

She sat back in her chair and relaxed, watching the face of the figure before her. Without the scar it would have been a soft and sensitive face. She wondered, if he is who I think, I should be fearful. He's a man who guards his secrecy by brutal means. Seldom does anyone admit to knowing him.

"Am I in danger having come here to meet you Dr Dearnought?"

He looked towards her and frowned.

"Should I be frightened that you will not let me return? You're a man around whom there is so much mystery that even the name is not mentioned for fear it will bring retribution."

She did not feel any fear. On the contrary, in these surroundings; in his presence she felt empowered to say whatever she thought.

"You are a refreshingly frank young lady." A smile played over his face," I think we shall get on very well."

***

In the coach returning from her meeting she sat silently wedged in the corner, deep in thought. Opposite John Dutch sat, his eyes never leaving her face. She waved away his attempt with the blindfold and he did not press the matter. It was as if having come away from a meeting with the man, Dr Medici Dearnought, she had gained a new regard from amongst those who attended him.

What benefit will this have; certainly the coachman treated her with a degree of deference. He opened the door of carriage and assisted her stepping down on to the safety of her own yard.

The information she had gained from Dr Dearnought was, she felt probably the truth, but it simply led her toward further questions. Anyone might have killed Thomas but Dearnought had been at pains to point out that it was not him; that the decision had been made by someone far removed from Turpin's. Thomas was involved in a matter bigger than her world. The answer might never be found in the rookery. She looked seriously at John Dutch.

"If I had known you were taking me to meet Dr Death."

She left the statement hanging in the air and John Dutch did not reply.

**

Richard Hamilton sat sprawled back against a corner of the parlour with his legs and arms stretched over several tables in a gesture familiar to Sybil Turpin. It signified his ownership of the space in that corner of the room. Head thrown back he glared contemptuously at the gawping of other customers.

The attention he created marked him out as a power to be reckoned with. Here was a new criminal face in the rookery; seeking his fortune by any number of nefarious deeds.

Beside him the familiar figure of Clem, Sybil's one time pot boy, supped a glass of ale and behaved like the cocky lad. Here was Clem, as a customer, lording it over the staff he had left behind. Clem had chosen to walk away when Sybil had offered him a choice. He had still taken a beating and was then kicked out the back door. Now he had returned in the company of a new hard man on the streets.

Sybil stepped down from her tall chair and walked towards the stranger. At the far end of the room a group of itinerant musicians were preparing to play. The tables were already full and still people arrived jostling with one another for a seat. There was an atmosphere of anticipation in the tavern tonight. The musicians looked about them apprehensively and so they should. They would shortly be gifted with ale or hounded out of the tavern. It was all the same to Sybil. It kept her customers amused and was good for business.

Sybil sauntered over to Richard Hamilton and around the room watchful eyes gleefully anticipated The Maid of Turpin's confrontation with the brazen newcomer. Sybil stood with hands deep in the pockets of her blue woollen dress.

"You're a new face in Turpin's."

Richard knew she was hard pressed to keep the contempt out of her voice.

"Indeed Ma'am," he replied, "and made to feel most welcomed I should say. Dick O Cerne at your service Ma'am." He stood and gave her a half a bow.

Sybil stared at the worn out coaching jacket and Richard felt disconcerted by her

gaze. He dipped into his ale then fixed her with a most disarming smile. She held his gaze.

"You're very welcome to stay Mr Cerne but Clem has been banished from Turpin's."

"Whatever could the boy have done to deserve that," He spoke softly and she had to lean forward to catch his words. He had almost lost his Dorset accent but knew she was trying to calculate from where this ruffian came.

"He stole from my customers when he should have been serving them; he chose to leave."

"He stole from the hand that was feeding him?" Richard asked slowly looking round at Clem.

"And he's banned from my tavern Mr."

Richard leaned casually over to the fire and took hold of a burning ember. In a flash he grabbed the boy's wrist and held the outstretched hand hard down against the table.

In a gentle voice he said, "If he misbehaves in here again," he was looking in to Sybil's face, "or steals from me," he drew a line of charcoal across two of Clem's fingers. The boy screamed. "I'll cut these fingers off." He smiled at Sybil. "And if he does it again," another mark was drawn across the wrist, "I'll cut there."

Clem was shaking with fright and Richard saw that Sybil shivered at his barbarous exhibition.

"I believe you Mr,"

Richard could tell she utterly despised him now.

"But he's still banned from the tavern."

To the boy he said: "Go and wait for me outside. Leave your ale."

"We have Turpin's rules you see, and I'm obliged to you." She turned quickly away to wander amongst the tables chatting to customers. Few had missed the exchanges between Richard and Sybil and opinion varied about who had the better of it.

***

Outside on the doorstep Clem sat leaning against the wall looking wretched; waiting. Richard called him over and put an arm around the boy's shoulder.

"You behaved well boy," he looked down in to an eager face. "You wouldn't steal from me, Clem, would you?"

The boy shook his head without speaking and they walked on down the dingy street towards their rented hovel.

Walking away from the tavern Richard couldn't get the Maid of Turpin's out of his mind.

He had felt her cold determination. Such a powerful presence he thought; but no room for intimacy.

She's the matriarch in Turpin's parlour but is that all there is? In the tavern no one steps over her line scuffed in the sawdust.

She's a mystery.

But Richard thought there was more to discover about Sybil.

The honourable Thomas Sharingham got through that fierce facade.

Two matters gave him a measure of understanding.

First, the fragrance about her; she had the scent of meadow flowers. Like in the meadows near his family home in Cerne. So unexpected in the grim world of crime she presided over. In his imagination he placed her in the tranquil setting of his childhood. He shook his head to clear the nonsense away.

Then her eyes; there was no disguising the person behind the Maid of Turpin's gaze. Her eyes reveal a more compassionate person.

Passionate even?

It was irritating because Richard prided himself on being good at gauging character. But this woman was a confusion of messages.

Need to see more of the Maid of Turpin's.

***

It was gone nine o'clock but Sybil knew Obadiah Trewfell would already be at work despite the late hour. As the tavern's brew-master he was obliged to keep irregular hours and Sybil was very aware that he put in far more than he was paid for. He brewed a weak ale called 'Boys' which sold for one penny a pint and Porter a darker beer and stronger costing a little more.

Sybil rested her elbows on the open topped mash-tun.

"Obadiah," she called, "did the Cooper come to do those casks?"

"Not yet Mistress, but when he does there's another sprung." The old man was nowhere to be seen but his voice echoed around the building. Finally a grizzly old head appeared above the rim of the wooden vat, and then a hand holding a brush he had been using to scrub it clean.

Reckoning that Obadiah had just finished boiling the wort: "Did you save me the dregs for the pig?"

"As I always do." He could be quite prickly at times especially when the mistress herself took to questioning his memory or method.

"Sorry Obadiah, of course you did," she smiled at the old man. Actually his memory was not so good these days but Sybil regretted upsetting him. She used the dregs mixed with some of the stale beer in a kilderkin to immerse the pork carcase for several days before it was set on a spit for roasting. It gave the meat a mellow malty flavour that customers came from far to taste.

Sybil wandered around between the wooden casks. She loved the smell of the brewery and in her father's day would often help out in here.

"Was there something else Mistress?"

"No nothing."

Leaning over the well cover she helped herself to a cup of the fresh sparkling water from the wooden pail.

There was something else on her mind   but she still hesitated. The old man had been with them since a young man and she wondered if he was still able to manage.

"How's the new boy coming on?" she dallied.

"He's tolerable good but he'll not make a brewer,"

She looked at the old man questioningly; no youngster would ever be good enough for Obadiah. She wondered if her question had reminded him of his own son Freddie who would be twenty four years old now if he had lived.

"He don't mind the detail," the old man said forcefully, "he's a messy worker not seeing ahead."

"He's got the best of teachers Obadiah but if he's not the best pupil, let him go and we'll find another." There was a silence and then Sybil took a deep breath. "Someone complained about the ale last night" she said.

"They never did," Obadiah was alert.

"A lot left on the tables."

"There never was."

He was on the offensive now.

"It tasted foul, go see what you make of it."

"Twas well enough when I put the new barrel up."

"Tasted it myself Obadiah; Ned has a jug kept back for you. Sort it for me."

The old man grumbled his way out of the wooden vat and made for the kitchen. Sybil watched him shuffling off. Was he getting too old for the work and what could she do with him if he was?

Obadiah came to find her a while later in her father's den where she was talking with her foreman Ned Church. A sharp rap on the door and Obadiah waited to enter; old habits died hard for the old man. He would have been kicked out if he had entered without Turpin's consent. Sybil opened the door and nodded to an empty chair.

"The ale's been mixed with something."

"With what," asked Ned? The old man shook his head.

"It could be anything," he held a glass bottomed tankard up to the light. "put in after it was barrelled; after the ale left the brewhouse." They peered up through the amber colour and Ned sniffed at it.

"Smell's like the privy to me."

After the event, a more careful watch was kept on the casks of ale when they left the brewhouse. Even within the confines of the brewery Sybil insisted on more security. Doors must be kept locked when the

Brewhouse was not in use. Barrels of new ale were firmly bunged after being set up in the parlour, so that it would not be easy to interfere with them.

***

In the fresh morning air Sybil sits on the grass bank, protected from the road by a thicket of bushes; she removes stockings and hitches up her skirts to the thigh. She dips a toe in the water and hesitating, as if reminding herself that it was the painful discomfort of the cold pond which kept others away from this isolated spot.

It promised to be a warm day and even though the sun had hardly risen over the eastern skyline it was already penetrating the trees casting bright shadows across the pool. She wades in up to her knees hardly bothering to look around for signs of prying eyes, and stops to watch tell-tale bubbles rising from the gravely bottom to ripple up through the crystal clear water like strings of pearls. She stands breathlessly counting the separate chains of bubbles as if to make sure they are all still there, that none have disappeared since she last visited the pool.

She is a little girl again discovering this natural spring for the first time, and she plays with unrestrained childlike pleasure.

The spring was one of a number feeding a nearby reservoir. Sybil leans forward and puts her foot over a stream of bubbles to feel them tickling as they rippled up between her toes.

No more than a half an hour ride from Turpin's going north out of the city and she is amid open countryside, meadows of pasture, small plots of cultivated ground and dense scrub interspersed with coppice. Here is a place where the Maid of Turpin's relaxes and forgets about the problems of the Tavern. She wades further across to where the pool deepened and the banks were impenetrably thick with shrubs. In this securest of places she pulls the woollen dress over her head and rolls it up with her remaining underclothes. She lays her head back, eyes closed and submerges herself entirely in the tingling cold water.

Sybil knows, as her watcher knows that the simple act of bathing in this manner, even as she does sometimes, in a tub in the privacy of her own home, is completely offensive to most people, unheard of, unhealthy and if it became known she would be considered immoral or even lunatic enough for an asylum. None of this gave her the least concern as she luxuriated in the spring water. So devoted to the practice was she that her bedroom at the tavern had a converted ale cask kept topped up from the well water for a morning dip. At home she would not even be much disconcerted by the occasional intruder; who, if discovering her naked in the tub,   would quite likely be dismissed of with such furious tongue-lashing abuse he would think himself lucky to get away without injury.

However it was an entirely different matter and hardly a coincidence, that Richard Hamilton had ridden out of the city on the same route, not simply for his own recreation, although he might claim it to be so. Richard was concealed in a hollow hidden by bracken and trees watching her.

'Breath-taking,' he whispers at the sight of the lithe figure.

I wanted to see more of you but….

He marvelled at the way she floated so perfectly at ease, her head, toes and breasts just above the surface of the water.

He justifies his presence, by reassuring himself he is there for her security.

He acquits remaining pangs of guilt for staying, with the thought that at any moment she might be discovered and he would need to defend her honour.

He entirely dismissed the possibility that she was perfectly safe without him.

Finally he gives way to instinct and simply watched. Chin resting on his arms and with a silly contented smile he followed her with his eyes backwards and forwards across the pool, marvelling at the sight of such beauty.

'A water nymph,' he thinks, ' or a mermaid.'

She turns on to her back with effortless ease, hardly breaking the stillness of the surface he sees little more than the shapely shadow of pale curves.

He shook his head in disbelief,

I'll wake in a moment and find it's just a beautiful dream.

A mischievous thought enters his head and he eases back from his hide. By a circuitous route he contrives to approach the pool openly. Hands in pockets, walking with measured indifference he whistles his way to the bank of the pool, throws off his shoes, shirt and breeches and crashes in to the water with as much finesse as a man o'

war being launched from the shipyard. Water fowl fly up in every direction and in the ensuing panic Sybil reacts with speed; grabbing a tree root she holds herself beneath the water. Golden hair swirls around but is mostly hidden by a branch overhanging from the bank.

Richard swims backwards and forwards across the pool cutting through the water with all the grace of a duck dropped from the air by a musket ball and sunk amid a flurry of feathers. Anxious blue eyes watch with growing impatience; rising at intervals to take a breath.

He finally tires of splashing around. Richard is no water nymph. His skill in the water has more to do with survival. Sensitive enough to judge when Sybil's anxiety might be wearing thin, he rises, water cascading from him like a wreck recovered from the seabed. He fights the inclination to look back over his shoulder and so does not see curious blue eyes widen in astonishment at the sight of his nakedness. He fails to hear the gurgles and splutter when she opens her mouth, forgetting it was under water. Richard throws on his cloths and walks away from the pool thinking sadly that there was no chance the day could possibly get any better.

***

Riding home Sybil's mind was not on the rough road ahead.

'So much of him,' she thought. Her eyes widen again at the memory of his unclothed frame. She allowed herself just the faintest smile thinking she had outwitted the handsome giant.

CHAPTER FIVE
ALSOP'S

The next morning Sybil was out early walking in the empty streets around the tavern. Despite the spring season there was always dampness in the air. She wrapped herself in a shawl to ward off the early morning chill and walked across the courtyard, past the brewhouse to the front of the tavern. She stared at the heavy pine front door remembering it was the place where Thomas had died in her arms not so very long ago. And now there was another; Richard O' Cerne. Not so aristocratic perhaps, yet there was more to liken them than not. She dismissed thoughts of the pair of them and was pleased to have the tavern's domestic arrangements on her mind. It was not just a matter of keeping busy to take her thoughts off recent events; the pressures of the business including the twenty or more staff dependent on her was an obligation she took very seriously.

The bowed figure of Strutt, always an early riser, hurried away and out through the back yard of the Tavern towards Cheapside main street. She knew he would be making for Pancras Lane where he reared cockerels for the pit. The empty baskets he carried would bring poultry back for the evening's entertainment. Sybil hesitated, watching him curiously as he disappeared from sight. Strutt normally never moved quickly. What was it that hurried him today?

Well named, was Mr Strutt. He had been a lifelong friend of old man Turpin: Involved in many of the nefarious criminal plots during the old regime of power. When Sybil finally took over the Tavern he came with the furniture.

His popular appeal and experience as master of the Cock-Pit made him an impossible character to let go.

The largest amount of her trade came from the custom of shopkeepers, market traders and itinerant wayfarers; some of them seafarers, passing through Cheapside and making for the docks. She stood and looked out through the open doors of the courtyard south towards the river. Already people were moving around opening shops or just hurrying about their business. There was a particular place by the corner of the tavern gate in Honey Lane where she could see all the way down to the river. Along Bread street, past Old fish street and Watling street; a full quarter of a mile away the Thames made its journey through the neighbourhood.

It was just how the streets all lined up giving the smallest glimpse of Queen Hith Stairs and one of the largest docks on the river. It was full of ocean going vessels; their masts looking like a forest of leafless trees at this distance. It was a viewpoint she was often drawn too. Between Turpin's and the river many of her customers lived and worked. Craftsmen, journeymen, and merchants of every imaginable description. Mercers, goldsmiths, jewellers, coach-makers, printers, carpenters, scriveners, cordwainers, waxchandlers, and further down towards the dock there were fishmongers, chandlers, sail and rope makers. The area of Cheapside was a self-contained community within the city.

She watched a waterman winding his way slowly up the street towards her, a sack over his shoulder. She mused. Some locals never left the confines of their community from birth to death. Never even travelled across to the other side of their own city. Despite that, the Thames made them the most worldly citizens.

The man stopped and muttered something to her. She shook her head. The load looked heavy but she was not buying today. She smiled as he trudged on. Take a waterman out of his skiff, Sybil thought, and he was the slowest of god's creatures. However this one she knew well. He was a night plunderer.

Merchant ships came up the Thames from all over the known world and the entire community in Cheapside was familiar with contraband trade; foods, spices and fine cloth. The residents of the neighbourhood saw and tasted such rare commodities which ordinary city dwellers might never hear of in their entire lifetime. Everyone was involved in the reception, storing, distribution and onward carriage of the unlawful goods.

Sybil shouted a question after the waterman, and he replied.

"Tomorrow perhaps … you want some?"

She nodded, "Spices, whatever you can get."

He waved a hand without turning.

In this manner the concept of the Rookery survived; the entire population benefiting from illegal trade and became dependent upon it for their livelihood.

Distracted for a brief moment, Sybil's thoughts returned to work of the present. Soon enough there would be a queue hammering on the door for food; to be eaten in Turpin's parlour or taken to one of the little shops or trades which employed people in the vicinity of the tavern. Eel pie was on the menu today and it was always well received. It could be eaten at a table in the comfort of the tavern or sold from the back door, to be taken away. Bread was baked in-house with sufficient to sell on to local customers. Ale was brewed and that was also for sale through the hole in the wall, in the parlour or delivered locally by one of the pot boys.

***

Mid-afternoon Sybil sat alone in her den, feet up on a cushioned stool staring absentmindedly out of the little internal window which looked down in to the Parlour. It was quiet down on the tables. Ned Church was instructing a new pot boy on how to baste and turn the carcase on the spit. The replacement for Clem was so small and ham-fisted he was hardly able to manage the iron ladle.

So much patience with the boy.

Ned would make a good father. He and Josie should have their own little pot boy…. or girl. Her mind drifted to the worrying matters of the moment.

Hard to keep an open mind, she thought. No doubt someone's poisoning the ale but for what reason?

Fearless must be top of the list of suspects. Trying to get his own back on me. But not a very clever fellow. He wouldn't know how to taint the ale without actually killing us all. Perhaps that's what he was trying to do, and got it wrong. She shook her head. Fearless couldn't organise poisoning in a brewery.

John Dutch was another unpleasant surprise for Sybil.

He had showed himself a trusted disciple of Doctor Medici Dearnought; showed his ruthless side murdering the young highwayman.

She had felt very vulnerable and wondered about her treatment if she hadn't allowed John to blindfold her. The killing didn't follow the normal custom of the rookery.

Richard O' Cerne's the real mystery man. She half closed her eyes to visualise the tall stranger; and she blushed.

What's to know about Richard O Cerne? Was it chance he turns up at Turpin's after a visit from the Duke of Sharingham?

There's more to the man, she thought and then she smiled to herself. That gesture with Clem was pure drama, but the boy was never harmed.

Sybil's continuing survival at Turpin's depended upon being able to keep a step ahead and that meant knowing as much as possible about her customers.

Was the man just another ruffian trying to break in to the area where fortunes were to be made if the the law could be avoided. She thought not.

Was it coincidence him turning up at the pool? Splashing around like a lost whale in the river.

Sybil wished she had never met Dr Dearnought. The man so feared that his name was mythical in the city. If she was correct, he was blamed for every unexplained crime in London Town. She hardly believed he existed until now. But having met Medici Dearnought there had little doubt he was the man commonly known as Dr Death. The worst was, she felt a shy liking for him. Despite everything he had behaved perfectly well towards her.

If he was telling the truth saying Thomas was killed for a different reason than just to get back at her. If that was so, what ever was the reason?

***

Sybil was pleased the routine in Turpin's was unrelenting. It normally gave little time for worrying about matters that could not be influenced. Early the next morning she was in the bakery.

"You've got something on your mind, I can tell."

Josie Church blushed as she turned to Sybil but neither girl stopped what they were doing. The pair stood at the long table kneading dough with their hands and tearing it in to loaf size lumps.

Sybil had several people in the bakery but she often worked alongside them. Josie wiped a curl of hair away with flour covered fingers and whispered in Sybil's ear.

"There's a clever girl,"

Sybil hugged her friend and there was suddenly flour all over them both. "Does Ned know yet?" She whispered back. Josie shook her head.

Faggots had been lit inside the oven and the embers raked out again when it was sufficiently hot. When the dough had risen it was quickly pushed in on trays and the heavy iron door closed.

The enormous bread oven was considered something of a treasure by the local community. It not only served the tavern but on high days and holidays neighbours were permitted to bring their cakes and poultry in to make use of it.

The heat wave as the iron door was cranked open again brought beads of perspiration to Sybil's forehead. The aroma of fresh bread was overwhelming and always at this time staff came from throughout the tavern with some reason to drift in to the kitchens on a pretext of one kind or another. Sybil took a small loaf, still almost too hot to touch, for herself and sent another to the brewhouse for Obadiah who had never quiet recovered his composure since the bad ale incident. Within an hour this batch of bread would be served to her own customers for breakfast. She held the warm loaf to her cheek and carried it away to her own room.

***

The guest rooms were all full and by eight o'clock the trestles in the parlour were full with her guests and early rising market traders who would have opened their stalls an hour or two before but stopped for the small pleasure of hot food and some drink.

The cubbies were set aside for her residents at this time of day and it was from one of them that a roar of disapproval was heard. It was followed by string of curses as crude as they were entertaining.

The culprit was a noisy seafarer; a captain off one of the merchant sloops on the river. The sound of his voice reverberated around the room and brought a pot boy scurrying over to the captain's table. The boy called for Ned the foreman and soon there was a small group standing around.

He held a fresh bread roll in his large fist. Down the side of a whiskery wind tanned face a dribble of blood ran and as he opened his mouth his teeth were stained from the meat in his bread.

"Squab pie," he announced in a voice which informed the entire room. Taking a knife from his boot he sliced the bread neatly revealing a dead rat.

Ned and Sybil were back in the den in deep conversation.

"The captain was just surprised but not much shocked. He said in hard times they sometimes ate rat aboard ship but it was usually better cooked and they always cut the head off."

Sybil wretched at the thought of it.

"It might be acceptable for seafarers but the locals won't tolerate undercooked rat. "

"It must be someone with access to the kitchens," said Ned. "Someone we trust." Sybil shook her head.

"I don't know but it's likely to be the same person who tainted the ale. We must find out who is responsible before I lose all my customers. Someone is trying to put me out of business Ned."

Sybil suffered the disturbances far more than anyone else. Customers, were indifferent to the foul tasting ale and the rumour that Turpin's served rat bread. Sybil returned to her elevated position on the tall chair and most of the regular customers took her presence there as a reassuring sign that all was well. Within a week the incidents were forgotten and all *was* well. Turpin's, Sybil began to think would never be brought down by matters of such significance. However she had not reckoned with the persistence of the unknown villain.

She warned Ned and the most trusted members of her staff to be more vigilant. The sea captain like other temporary residents had come and gone. Most would not be deterred from returning especially when they remembered the illicit benefits of their patronage at the tavern. Local traders had no inclination to withdraw. The tavern was after all at the very heart of their social life.

It came as a great blow therefore when the saboteur struck again. The full horror of the next disaster struck Sybil very hard.

***

"What do you want to do with your life Clem?" Richard led his horse in to the stables having returned from a ride which had taken him away for best part of the day.

"I want a job where everyone calls me mister." He took the reign, led the well lathered horse into a box and began to remove the saddle.

"What is your full name?"

"Just Clem," the boy carried on.

"You must have two names if you want to be called Mr."

"The workhouse don't give two names, just call every boy Clement after the name of the parish."

Richard helped him with the saddle, "Ok I'll give you a second name," there was a pause while he thought and Clem looked at his new master eagerly.

"Clem Applebee," he announced. Clem looked at him questioningly.

"Is that a real name?"

"Oh yes very real, I used to go to school with a boy called Applebee." He looked over at the sixteen year old. "He went on to become a school teacher."

"Stone me; same name as a schoolteacher."

"He wasn't always a schoolteacher, he was a right little tearaway when I knew him," Clem glowed with pride.

"Bit like you really."

"When can we start then,"

"Right away Applebee." He turned his head towards Clem who was grinning so much.......

"Mr Applebee, it is then."

Richard shook his head, "The Mr comes later, we start off with Applebee; you have to earn the rest.

Richard lodged in a small broken down house on the far side of the rookery. It was about a half mile from Turpin's and backed on to a hostelry with a small yard for stabling. He could take his meals there and come and go about without question. Clem served him well and although the boy had not yet figured out who or what his master was, he behaved with considerable willingness. He knew what it meant to watch-out for his master. Over the weeks which followed Richard gave him tasks to do and he watched him most carefully. An allegiance of sorts developed that Clem responded to with enthusiasm.

"Take this message to the man who'll be waiting for it on the east side of London Bridge. Don't break the seal and return with his reply. Don't get waylaid."

The boy returned at breakneck speed. "Funny old cove he was,"

"You weren't long Clem?"

"It's a straight line run across the roofs; don't need to use the streets."

He was hardly breathless.

"Did you read the message?"

The boy became embarrassed and confided, "I don't read so well."

On another occasion: "Deliver this package to the morning mail coach and pay for it to go that address."

Clem bounced out of the room with a handful of coins jingling in his pocket. Richard considered the possibility that he might not see him again.

"He tried to do me out of me change," Clem returned indignantly. "Said I'd only give him a shilling."

"What happened?"

"I played the hard-done-by and some gracious milady waiting for a coach took my side. I think she would have hit him with her stick if he hadn't done right."

The tasks were nothing which could compromise Richard's work but served as a good test of the boy's ability and willingness.

"Take yourself down to Three-Sister wharf, don't speak to anyone, and wait for a man to contact you."

The not-speaking instruction was never achieved, for Clem couldn't help himself. He was wise in the way of a street urchin. He knew the ins and outs of the rookery and was known by many of its ragamuffins. As Richard established trust the tasks became more important.

"I want you to watch Turpin's for me today, from a distance. If you're approached by anyone you must leave; pretend you're up to mischief, but return here straight away. You know how to look as if you're up to mischief don't you Clem?"

The boy nodded grinning widely.

"Tell me about everyone who comes and goes through the back door."

Finally Richard came to a task of real purpose.

"Who do you know who works for Fearless Friar?"

"I know them all," he held up his fingers."

"Ten?"

Clem shook his head and flashed his fingers twice.

"Twenty?"

"Or more," said the boy excitedly.

"What does he pay them for thieving?"

Clem looked startled.

"He don't pay them Mister." He paused as if trying to think his way through this line of questioning. "he feeds them sometimes."

"No questions Clem; but here's coin. Offer to buy some goods off them, you know what's what. Don't pay over the odds and bring back what you get with some change."

Clem grasped at this task eagerly.

"And don't be followed back here, but if anyone asks you can say you work for Dick O' Cerne."

The enterprise was hugely successful and since Clem knew very well the value of goods likely to be lifted by foysters and nippers and taken to the pop shop, he proved to be an astute trader. Soon he had regular contacts with Fearless Friar's gang; but it wasn't long before the man himself discovered what was going on.

"We got rules about poaching," Fearless Friar said standing over him so that Richard was unable to avoid his fetid breath, "and them rules as been broken." His mouth was wet with spittle and it sprayed as he spoke. Behind him Friar's motley collection of supporters stood. Richard leaned back against the wall and moving his tankard of ale aside he lifted the heavy walking stick from the seat beside him and placed it between them so that its ferruled end was pushing gently in to Fearless Friar's stomach.

"Step away if you please, I find your odour too disturbing to bear."

"Disturbing is what I am," Fearless cackled. "There's no room for another Upright man in this place, you should go across the city while you still have both feet willing to carry you there."

"If you paid your boys better they wouldn't want to sell to me Mr Friar."

"You're dead meat Mr,"

"You're a yesterday's man," replied Richard coolly, "but if you ever want to work for me, I could find something suited to your intelligence."

Fearless shook with anger and his hand grasped at the dagger at his belt. Richard felt that his insults might have gone too far.

If I don't let him converse with me he will revert to the only way he knows. Out of the corner of his eye Richard could see Sybil sitting in Turpin's tall chair, head and shoulders above the crowd her watchful eye missing nothing of the conversation between the two men. He did not want Fearless to attempt an attack in the Tavern. He must act quickly.

From his pocket he calmly took a round lead ball the size of a small finger nail. He rolled it across the table top towards the man leaning forward.

"Pick it up Mr Friar, look at it very carefully."

Curiosity got the better of his anger, the man did as he was asked.

"My stick has one the same size in its barrel, aimed directly at your belly."

Richard loved gadgets but doubted that his shooting stick would be accurate over anything but a very short distance. Fearless backed away holding the ball between his finger. Richard stood carrying the remains of his ale and walked across to the tall chair holding the stick over his shoulder as if it were a rifle.

"You'll want a safe exit from the tavern?" Sybil said.

He stood undisturbed by the commotion behind him and smiled at her. For the briefest of moments there was an exchange between them. Like a meeting of minds.

"You're ahead of me Mam," he smiled up at her.

"Go and talk nicely to Ned behind the bar, he will find you a suitable route out."

Richard turned.

"And, since you persist in using my hostelry I shall have to call you something other than Mr."

"I'd like that Miss Sybil," he bowed towards the tiny shoe which was lifted towards him as she uncrossed her legs beneath the woollen dress; and he smelt the perfume of fresh violets.

"Dick O' Cerne at your service." He felt warmth between them; just for a moment.

***

Richard leaned back in his chair and without shame looked upon his elderly mentor with admiration and affection. The man wore no wig but his hair, almost white, was curled in a very fashionable manner. Tiny gold coloured spectacles perched on the end of his button shaped nose. He was erring towards plumpness and sat quite primly in the faded brown leather chair where his feet hardly reached the floor. He always spoke quickly in short bursts and very softly so that Richard had to lean forward to catch his words.

"Oh dear me no I didn't go voluntarily. Ushered out is what I think you might say."

"And it was a sudden move, little warning that it might happen?"

The older man nodded, "I had an inkling that there was a faction to have me removed," he shook his head. "It still took me by surprise is all I can say."

"Lord Sharingham couldn't help?"

"I think he was kept out of it."

Richard's old spymaster Sir George Murray frowned.

"This new man Ronald Able-Makepiece, had you ever come across him?"

"Never in my life, he was the greatest surprise."

"He knows nothing about espionage," said Richard." You weren't replaced by a better man Sir."

Sir George smiled humbly.

"Sorry we had to meet secretly too."

They were in a small room for private gatherings, at the back of Alsop's Gentlemen's Club. Near St Paul's, a more fashionable area than Cheapside, Alsop's was for wealthy gentlemen of the city.

The dark oak panelling and the pale painted walls gave the impression of shabby gentility. A table and four well-worn leather chairs were the only furniture in the room. Richard thought that decayed opulence pervaded the entire fabric of Alsop's and it included the wealthy members who, in the common rooms sat around the tables in small groups, reading, smoking, drinking and dozing.

"I have enemies Richard and it would not do for you to be seen in conversation with me. I'm not worried for myself but it would make your task more difficult."

Do you know what I am about Sir?"

Yes I think I do. I rather think I know the back story better than you know it yourself."

Richard smiled and settled back in his chair. "I feel sure I have intentionally been kept in the dark."

Sir George nodded.

"Thomas Sharingham was put in by his father to discover a plot which threatens to destabilise the country."

"I knew Thomas quite well; we were at Cambridge together," said Richard.

Sir George hesitated patiently. "The South Sea Company was set up by some very wealthy financiers, many of whom are members of parliament. In return for an initial loan of £7 million pounds, the government offered this new company the monopoly on trade in the South Seas. The government went further and allowed the company to underwrite the national debt on a promise of five percent interest. They also promised the company the sole rights to trade in South America."

"That sort of deal reassured the investors across the country that South Seas was a rock solid opportunity."

"It did more than that; it attracted investment from across Europe."

"People thought with government backing it couldn't fail."

Sir George nodded again.

"Across the world in fact; but it's a sham."

Richard frowned and shook his head.

"It's an enormous confidence trick."

"You mean…"

"I mean even as we speak people are investing in the South Seas Company thinking they will make enormous profits," Sir George shook his head. "It will not happen. They'll lose everything."

He sipped his tea.

"Mr Walpole saw through it some time ago but the greed of powerful politicians has made it difficult.

Since becoming Chancellor of the Exchequer he's made some progress. He asked the Duke of Sharingham to use his secret agencies to get at the truth," Sir George hesitated.

"And the Duke lost his son as a consequence."

"That's right Richard."

Sir George looked a tired man.

"There is a small group who will stop at nothing to keep the fraud going as long as it brings in funds from gullible investors. I believe you are considered to be expendable Richard: you've been set up to fail."

The weary spymaster and his protégé finished their tea in silence.

"Good of you to introduce me here Sir George"

"I hope it might be helpful to you dear boy. A stuffy crowd but amongst them there are well connected types, some of whom will be determined to help you fail.

"It really is a joy to see you again." Apart from having put on a little weight he thought his old master looked as fit as ever. "I was beginning to think you'd disappeared completely."

"That, I think is what was intended for me."

Richard smiled.

"But a faithful pigeon told me Richard Hamilton was back home and…….. well let's just say my curiosity got the better of me."

"I am most grateful to you sir; but I think we must get you home now."

More to the point, thought Richard, the man has lost none of the sharpness of intellect which had many times saved me from a drubbing.

"You say I've been set up to fail?" Sir George looked at him steadily. "Yet Sir Ronald Able-Makepiece said that I wasn't his choice? That doesn't fit so well."

Sir George held up his hand.

"Consider this. Having you involved, to take over from Thomas gives an air of respectability to the investigation." Sir George rose heavily from his seat. "One more thing before I leave you here; trust no one until you are sure; least of all those who would appear to be driving you onwards."

"I must see you safely home first."

Sir George shook his head. "There's a back way out of here and my man will be waiting outside."

"I wish you joy of your membership of the club. Hopefully it will lead you somewhere. Give my respects to your dear father when you see him next."

***

CHAPTER SIX
A FROBISHER FOR BAIT

Richard was back at Alsop's the next evening, dressed, as always, with particular care. Tonight it was his intention to see and be seen. His behaviour was more extreme than the night before. He sprawled in a seat in the smoking room and waved his arms about, calling noisily to attract the attention of a servant.

"Take this bilge water away and bring me better, there's a good fellow. Tastes more like the Thames."

He called after the servant: "Bring me a new bottle …and open it at the table."

Like many young men his normal custom was to wear his own hair tied back in a queue sometimes with a small bow. His coat and pants were a black matching material and the stockings a fine white silk. He had chosen a short grey waistcoat with small embroidered flowers around the neck. The shirt, matching his hose, was all frills and bows.

His taste for fashionable clothes marked him down as a dandy, and his behaviour picked him out as a wealthy, ill-mannered lout.

The right impression is everything Richard thought.

The servant returned with a bottle and an empty glass.

Gripping the man's arm Richard affected a loud whisper, "Find me a wench for company," close to his face but loud enough to be heard across the room: "You know what I'm talking about don't you? Better company than these tedious shits hiding behind their boring news sheets."

There was hardly a rustle from the tedious shits.

"I can give you an address Sir," the servant fawned. "There are a number of places popular with our members."

"Never mind," he picked up the gazette news sheet, upside down and began to read.

"Pardon my intrusion sir but I couldn't help noticing; is that a new Frobisher you carry?"

Richard looked up from his paper at the man standing before him.

"It is indeed sir, you recognised it correctly. Might you also be an admirer of the craftsman's work?"

"I am indeed and keen to possess one myself, but they are still hard to come by." Richard carefully passed over his walking stick by the ebony crowned knob for the other man to inspect.

"How kind," said the other warmly.

He twisted the knurled ring but nothing happened.

How ridiculous is this thought Richard. I'm offering my weapon to a stranger, the enemy perhaps. Suddenly eight inches of shiny steel slid silently out of the narrow end of the stick. A click signified that the blade had locked.

The man's eyes lit up.

"Such fine steel too; I do apologise for my manners sir I am Dr Medici Dearnought at your service."

Caught you… now to reel you in.

Richard stood up, "Richard Hamilton sir, newest member of the club I think."

Dearnought replied without taking his eyes off the blade of the sword stick.

"Welcome indeed…. it's the triangular cross-section to the blade which gives it the strength."

He carefully returned the weapon to Richard who retracted the blade and put the stick down beside his chair.

"Might you care to join me in a pipe? They have some very fine leaf in; one of the benefits of this establishment." Richard knew he was referring to the fact that merchant traders used Alsop's and they would often make expensive and rare commodities available to the members. The port Richard was presently drinking was the best quality and would almost certainly have come directly from the hold of a merchant ship. But who was to check if duty had been paid when it was the owner of the vessel who did the removal.

The pair moved to a discreet corner of the smoking room.

"At supper earlier; who was the fellow with the penchant for third helpings of everything and the wish to make everyone wealthy?"

"Don't underestimate Palfrey," said the Doctor. He isn't just an empty vessel. He already owns a fortune with a first class fleet of vessels." He smiled at his small humour but the smile died before it left his mouth.

It was a feature of supper at Alsop's that everyone ate at one long table and the Palfrey character had addressed the entire table.

"I can sir, mark my words, I can make you a very rich man," he had bellowed. Richard had thought the comments seemed to be directed at anyone of a dozen affluent looking gentlemen around the table. Palfrey was a plump fellow with a round face which would have been pink were it not that his periwig had been so enthusiastically powdered; with such effect that he was consumed with talc above his neck and even the shoulders of his coat had a dusting.

Dearnought being a doctor wore a Cauliflower wig which signified his profession.

"Palfrey's talk of making fortunes is true." Dearnought sat alert in Richard's company. Richard was struck by the man's piercing black eyes which seemed to engage him in the most disturbing of ways. On the other hand the conversation was easy going and entertaining.

"Talk in the Club is of little else but the fortunes being made in the South Seas Company."

Richard relaxed down in his chair and tried to enjoy his pipe.

Dearnought's next words brought him immediately to the alert. Outwardly the only sign was a subconscious hand that felt for the ebony handle of the Frobisher. He hoped Dearnought hadn't noticed.

"You are acquainted with Sir George Murray I believe?"

Richard thought quickly. "No more than an acquaintance; he was a friend of my father's but I don't know him well. He was kind enough to arrange some introductions for me."

"A singularly unsociable fellow I find," replied Dearnought.

Richard looked dismissively towards the side door where Sir George had departed the day before. So much for our secret meeting, he thought.

"It's a duty call whenever I am here. I have no idea what his business is. Don't you find that strange sir, we have had supper together twice now, he is obviously well connected, yet I have not the remotest idea about the man."

Dearnought smiled at the young man's eagerness to share confidences.

"For what it's worth I think he is something in the admiralty although he doesn't move in my circles." They sat relaxed in one-another's company. Filling his pipe for a second time Dearnought spoke again.

"And you sir what is your line of business?"

"Ah well it might be easier to tell what I don't do. I've done service with the military; traded a little in the Indies and before that taught in my father's school. In between all that I spent too little time studying at Cambridge." Richard discarded his pipe.

"And now?"

"Now sir I find myself somewhat unsettled. I trifle with this and that." He went quiet as if dreaming, and then grinned. "You might say I've made trifling an art form."

"You seem to have packed more than most in to your young years?" Dearnought studied the young man.

"Perhaps I should like to be a doctor next," as if the thought had just occurred. "Save for the fact that those I know are such stuff shirts and what ever right minded person could imagine that bleeding away a person's vital spark was beneficial." Doctor Dearnought smiled benignly.

"There now I have toppled you with my impudence; I am sorry, it is my failing, I am told."

"Not at all sir you strike me as a fellow able to do anything should you put your mind to it."

That is what I intend you to think, thought Richard.

"But you doctor, are you a regular physician? A successful one I imagine."

Medici Dearnought spoke almost to himself.

"A little like you I find; a successful practice, yes, but a penchant for the extraordinary."

Then looking directly into Richard's eyes; "If you can imagine that possible in a stuff-shirt doctor."

Richard playing the feckless young man fell in with the way of the worthy doctor. He allowed himself to look at the man's scarred face and felt transfixed by the eyes.

"You must come and dine with me, I have rooms in Curzon Street and modest accommodation above," He handed Richard a card; "I can tell you all about how not to become a stuff-shirt doctor."

＊

The modest accommodation turned out to be lavishly provided in a respectable double-fronted terraced house. The ground floor was given over to consulting rooms and the doctor lived above in a very comfortable apartment. Much of this Richard already knew. His own intelligence had provided an encyclopaedic summary of the eccentric Doctor.

There was some doubt about his qualification to call himself a physician; unlicensed too, and constantly at odds with the established Company of Barber Surgeons. He risked prosecution for practicing illegally yet still continued by managing to keep one step ahead of those who would judge him.

Dearnought now had a following; his patients did not just come from the rags and tags of the streets although many did; they also came from the middle classes where word of his success grew.

"I don't deny my approach is unconventional, but it works my dear fellow it works." After a good meal they sat at ease in the withdrawing room whilst with relentless excitement Dearnought expounded on his theories about medicine, the welfare of the poor and wealthy society, of which he considered himself to be a rank outsider.

"I am a disciple of Paracelsus," said the doctor. "Medicine is a scientific matter. That much is undeniable."

Undeniable, thought Richard was the man's passion for the sound of his own voice.

"However," his voice rose as he leaned over and touched Richard's arm, "the human mind is a microcosm of the universe."

Now, surely, he's taking me in to the realms of fantasy.

"Take that as a truth and everything else falls in to place. What others might dismiss as incredible becomes the life-force of our very existence."

Dearnought just stop so I can take a breath.

But his pointing finger pressed home every idea relentlessly.

The man threatens to drown me.

They whiled away another hour during which time Doctor Dearnought ceaselessly talked about himself and his good works with the poor of the city. When Richard thought the time was near when he could politely take his leave a servant entered the room with a note on a silver dish.

"Well my boy, here's your chance. You shall see me in action, if you wish…?"

I'd rather your mentor Paracelsus was attending you.

Richard could not judge the man. Some might regarded him as a charlatan and a quack, but there was no denying he believes in himself.

If applying astrology to the sick mind and body gives relief to some people, so be it. Surely there is enough sickness around, particularly in the rookery, for anyone to make a difference.

They travelled cautiously through the pitch black streets. The sound of carriage wheels on the cobbles and clatter of hooves announced their journey to everyone within a quarter of a mile. Rain had been falling steadily and across the empty city. The debris and noxious excrement of the day was being gently washed away into the gutters. Richard leaned back in to the comfortable red leather upholstery and wondered.

What is it that made this man an infamous criminal?

Why is Medici Dearnought thought of as a threat to the country and what's his involvement in the death of Thomas Sharingham?

Above the shop of a draper they stood in the small bedroom of the doctor's patient. The heat from a fire in the grate made the room oppressively hot. Richard had been introduced as the Doctor's assistant but he had never felt so out of place in his life. In the bed propped up on bolsters of every description a middle aged woman sat red faced and struggling to breath, every wheeze sounded as if it was to be her last and beneath her struggle for breath it appeared as if she were wracked with pain.

I shouldn't be here, thought Richard. He turned to go.

"I'll wait for you downstairs Doctor," he said moving towards the door.

"No stay," the man commanded turning quickly, "I'd like you to see this." He sat on the side of the woman's bed and took her hand. With a cloth he wiped the beads of perspiration from her forehead. He lifted her chin with two fingers and made her hold his gaze. He spoke to her in a soft but authoritative voice which demanded her attention. He spoke slowly and constantly; gradually the woman's breathing eased as if her sub-conscious was helpless to disobey.

She was commanded.

Without turning his head from the woman he addressed Richard standing behind him, "It is only temporary relief, whilst I am present and able to breach the natural tides of her astral bodies."

The woman closed her eyes and lapsed in to a fitful sleep. He continued speaking, disregarding his patient as if she were not even in the room. The gentle voice which had so entranced her took on a hard edge.

"The quality of her life is so diminished," he spoke as if he was the tutor instructing his pupil.

"She has become so weak to the point where she cannot care for herself."

He wallows in a sense of his own importance, thought Richard.

"The awful penalty for my greater wisdom is that I am now elected to make the final burdensome decisions for her."

He's behaves like a celestial deity now, chosen to be the final arbiter over her life and death.

The doctor took a small bottle from his bag and poured a copious quantity of thick clear liquor in to a glass and, with a small ebony rod taken from his pocket, mixed it with wine.

"Give her all of this as quickly as she is able to take it." He looked twice at the dishevelled woman servant hovering in the doorway and changing his mind whispered to his patient who obediently, submissively obeyed. She opened her mouth and took the draft in one enormous gulp.

"There," he said, "it is done. She will suffer no more."

On the return journey Richard asked: "The dose you gave her?"

"Laudanum, a mixture of opium; it was strong enough to send her into an unnaturally deep sleep from which she is unlikely to return."

"You mean you have given her a fatal dose of medicine,"

There was no sign that Dearnought had noticed Richard's horror.

"I first penetrated her life-force," the old arrogance was still there, "and found no energy capable of sustaining life. I gave her the means to exit her mortal coil. Her astral bodies will do the rest."

Richard remained silent in the carriage trying to justify what he had seen. There was no denying the respite the woman had received, but at the price of her life.

The doctor went on. "I am no more than the humble servant of that sick lady. It is my calling which demands of me the duty to make the ultimate sacrifice on her account."

Emboldened by his own erudition and Richard's silence, he continued.

"For the physician, making decisions over life and death it is a great burden; A high price for the privilege of a professional vocation."

He lapsed in to a silence Richard welcomed.

And then a catastrophic admission from the doctor.

"The rewards however are manifest. The dear gentle lady has already changed her last will and testament to favour my good self. She wishes to reward me for the care I have given her."

Richard was stunned. He felt as if he had been dealt a mortal wound. His breath caught in the back of his throat and he stared ahead in the darkened coach. Thank heavens he thought, for that darkness. He fidgeted with the catch on his Frobisher. Medici Dearnought's own outrageous boldness somehow secured Richard from revealing his revulsion.

***

"He has a most elevated opinion of himself; believes he's the final arbiter over the life and death of his patients."

Richard was talking to himself. He had been summoned to a meeting with Sir Ronald and was presently walking along Thames Street rehearsing the meeting with his spymaster. It was a fine morning and he chose to walk the route which was no more than a mile to the meeting place.

He had gone over the details of his recent meeting with Medici Dearnought many times trying to discover if there was some alternative way of interpreting the facts. There was little doubt in his mind, yet he remained concerned his spymaster would judge events in a different light. Sir Ronald was not a man with whom he felt at ease.

He was supposed to be a confidant, a supporter, the person with whom Richard could share concerns. It did not help that there were matters about Doctor Dearnought he hardly understand himself let alone explain to Sir Ronald.

The street running a parallel course the river was crowded yet Richard hardly noticed. It was a lively bustling place where the city met the international world of commerce. Where office buildings looked down on the shipping and wealthy merchants watchfully stood admiring their vessels from the safety of counting houses.

So you think he's a murderer?

The man must be stopped; He is killing people under the pretence of doing them good. He wheedles his way in to their lives, and then collects the inheritance for his trouble."

Well stop him if that is what you think, Sir Ronald would say.

In the large building of the custom house, a stone's throw from the Tower of London, Richard was ushered in to a room overlooking the river. Sir Ronald Able-Makepiece sat looking out of the window his back to the door. Ushered into the room Richard stood facing towards the narrow hunched back of the man sipping tea.

He was ignored.

"Are you finished with this business Hamilton?" Sir Ronald spoke eventually.

"No sir I am not entirely finished,"

"Then what progress?" he continued irritably. "Must I drag it out of you?"

"I have found," Richard hesitated and then hurried on nervously," Sir I hope you will forgive my impertinence but may I speak frankly?"

"Get on with it man," Sir Ronald spun round in the chair, his face, not an invitation for frank speaking.

"So far I have found nothing in the rookery to suggest links with a serious threat to national security. There is widespread villainy, but…"

"Then we shall recommend the matter is closed and done with."

"There is this matter of Doctor Dearnought. He is, I believe an inherently evil man."

Sir Ronald's reaction was much as Richard had expected.

"If we went round locking up everyone with evil intent……."

"I believe he is a murderer."

"Can you prove it?"

Richard shook his head, "Not yet. But if he is connected to the South Sea Company matter, he brings a new and sinister perspective to this whole matter. He is not just a common criminal, there is something else. He possesses some strange power over the mind……"

Sir Ronald shook his head with contempt, "You are saying that he can fix you with a spell?"

"No sir I am saying he has the ability to induce a sleep-like condition in which he can control the mind of his patient."

Richard knew he was losing.

"You've experienced this?"

"I think I've felt the effects myself, yes. Feeling relaxed in his company, to the extent of willingly allowing him to command; thinking the man is the best of fellows and I certainly watched him use this power on one of his own patients."

"Did *you* succumb?" Dearnought mocked.

"Not entirely but I believe the effect was to make me feel his behaviour was somehow *completely reasonable*. I felt obliged to co-operate, to do his bidding because it was perfectly rational to do. I found it so in his rooms and was unable to refuse his offer to accompany him whilst he attended a patient."

Sir Ronald shook his head, "I can give no credence to this Hamilton. It'd be more believable happening at a fair ground."

"But don't you see, if he has this power to influence the minds of others, he might well be able to use it to shape political minds also. His trickery and deception is already proved. But I have yet to make a connection beyond the Rookery. A man of his intellect is capable of far greater damage."

"I've heard quite enough Hamilton. It is time to close this matter. Such evil doings as you have described can be dealt with by the magistrates. They do not require the services of crown agents."

Richard felt he was dismissed but Sir Ronald raised a bony finger. "There is still a matter to deal with. We are called to the Duke of Sharingham; seems he is concerning himself personally with this affair."

Sir Ronald fixed him with a stare,

"He must be told the inquiry is done with, because we both believe it is going nowhere. Do you understand Hamilton? The Duke must be told the matter is closed."

***

The hammering on the door of her den was an unwelcomed awakening for Sybil.

"Master Ned says come quick as you can."

She turned away hoping he would not notice the high colour in her cheeks from a little dreaming of something not entirely unpleasant occasioned by Richard Hamilton's intrusion at her secret pool.

Ned Church looked grim standing beside the well in the courtyard. Obadiah Trewfell was there also, looking angry. Around them a group of tavern staff drifted away as Sybil arrived.

"We're finished this time," said Ned holding her gaze and hardly able to keep the emotion out of his voice.

With an earthen ware jug he scooped water from the pail and poured it. As the water splashed on to the cobbles Sybil could see it was a bright purple in colour.

"The well's been poisoned," said Obadiah.

"We're finished," said Ned again.

"Has anyone drunk from it,"

Sybil sniffed at the remaining water in the jug. They all looked towards a serving maid standing nearby her face a picture of terror. Her hands and arms were stained but she was silent with the fear of what might have happened. She held her throat as if it burned. Sybil's hand instinctively covered her own mouth in sympathy. Comforting hands were laid on the girl but it seemed to increase her distress.

Now she wailed mournfully.

This might be the end for them all. Without a constant supply of well water they would be finished. If the well had been poisoned there was no way back; whoever was trying to destroy her livelihood in the Tavern will have succeeded. Yet there was something wrong with this argument and Sybil's own panic was preventing clear thought. The water stained her hand as she scooped the liquid from the pail but it did not burn. She poured the remains of it on to the cobbles.

Ned's little terrier joined the group standing around the well, sensing there was something going on and wanting to be part of it, he lapped at the water splashed from pail.

"Ratter no," shouted Ned in alarm, but it was too late the animal licked away contentedly. They all stood around and waited.

Josie held Ratter who enjoyed the attention.

They all watched Ratter; the serving maid momentarily forgotten. For the next hour no one took their eyes off the little dog.

Ratter suffered no ill effects from the purple coloured water even though it stained his tongue. The serving girl received less sympathy. She might have been dying but then she always was; from something or other.

Being closely connected to the commercial trade of the riverside had its advantages. Favours were called in from Beswick the Chandler by Queen Hythe Stairs. He supplied a ship's pump. A very inefficient affair of leather and wood it needed three men to operate. Two to hold it down and one to crank the heavy wooden arm. Old Beswick supervised and the well was pumped continuously for the rest of the day till the water began to lose its colour and both Ratter and the serving maid were still alive.

The dog became bored with the attention and went back to his singular occupation delivering a rat. The maid somewhat jealous of the fulsome attention the dog and hoping to extract a degree more sympathy took to her bed for the rest of the day and wailed a little at intervals till all sympathy was lost.

"Mr Condy's fluid," declared Sybil's apothecary neighbour knowledgably. "Someone has put crystals in the well to frighten you," he sniffed.

But didn't want to make the well permanently unusable, she thought.

***

Sybil sat behind the ink stained pine table which served as a desk in her father's old den. It was still thought of as Turpin's lair by many of the tavern staff. Being called to the old man in this room was often bad news particularly for the serving girls. The door was always kept closed and locked. Old man Turpin did not welcome visitors unless it was for his own perverted purposes. Nowadays Sybil kept the door to the courtyard propped open whenever possible so that she could see and be seen by the staff, but memories of the past were not easily forgotten and absentmindedly checking through bills, picking disinterestedly at the platter of fresh bread still warm from the oven she wondered what her father would have done in the present circumstance. In the days following the incident with the well, life in the tavern returned to a semblance of normal order. However Sybil knew she would not find the culprit on her own; she needed help.

That's what father would have done; found an ally. Someone he could use; an accomplice, probably an unwilling one or one who thought there'd be something in it for him, but of course there never was. Turpin only ever used people for his own ends and when they ceased to be helpful he'd just dispose of them.' Sybil was dispassionate about her father. Turpin had been everything she constantly tried not to be.

In the dingy smoke stained room where the sunlight from the open door struggled to penetrate to the cobwebbed corners, Sybil rested her elbows on the table apparently studying the heavy ledger but her mind was elsewhere, thinking about the people who worked for her.

None have anything to gain, less they've been threatened to cause the mischief; or promised a reward: no, that wouldn't serve, she knew her staff too well.

It was like living under a sentence of death she thought. Everyone waited for something else to happen.

The anxiety is so evident amongst them I can smell it, taste it in my throat. Even the regular customers were aware. They came to watch and wait for the next crisis.

A small figure in the doorway threw a shadow in the room and Sybil looked up quickly.

"Mistress," said the whiskery Obadiah Trewfell pulling a lock of hair, in his customary act of obeisance to Sybil.

"New barrel of porter set up in the bar, won't be ready afore tomorrow. Boys is nearabouts finished, I'll tap the new barrel shortly. It's been resting for long enough." Sybil smiled at the old man and was unusually rewarded with a shy grin as he backed out the door. Boys was the most popular and cheapest ale they sold.

She called after him, "Obadiah, you have any thoughts about who might be causing us trouble?"

The Brewer looked at her kindly. "If I knew…; when I find out," he said defiantly, "you'll be rid of 'im soon as that."

He clicked his fingers and was gone again.

She watched the old man shuffle out across the yard.

Sybil's thoughts returned to Richard Hamilton, new in the rookery, wants to establish himself as an Upright Man, a leader amongst these men. His treatment of Clem showed how ruthless he could be. She shivered at the thought of him threatening to cut off Clem's fingers. But there was something about the man; could he have just been putting on a show with the hot charcoal from the fire.

Something *honourable* about Richard Hamilton? She shook her head vigorously as the image of him crossed her mind.

Capable of putting on a show? She inclined her head. I've seen him in the bare, that doesn't mean I know him any better. Richard O' Cerne is quite capable of arranging the accidents so he could take over my business. He's become a regular in the tavern. He faced down Fearless Friar and has everything to gain; it'd make him a powerful man in the rookery.

Dr Medici Dearnought on the other hand behaved quite honourably. Thomas Sharingham had been involved with other matters not connected with Turpin's, that's what the doctor said; didn't say what the other matters were. He must have known why Thomas was killed but cared not to tell me.

Felt at ease in Dearnought's company. Sybil smiled to herself remembering that she had almost drifted off to sleep in the library listening to his voice. What would he have thought if he'd noticed?

But he was holding something back.

She thought about the angry scar down the side of his face and imagined pressing her healing fingers deep in to the disfiguring wound.

Must have been caused by a blade. Was he really the one they called Dr Death? The name strikes fear in most people's minds; a reputation for terrifying acts of cruelty; they say he kills in the Spanish way, with a garrotte.

So quickly the victim hardly knows.

The stories about the mysterious Dr Death were legendary in the Rookery. Mothers warned children in their cots to behave lest Dr Death might visit.

He thinks I have a certain eminence; wonder what that means. She was interrupted from her daydreaming by another visitor to the door.

"Ned, move those papers aside and sit down."

Sybil's foreman the most trusted of all her staff and the only one who could be left to run the place in her absence, although he did not much care to, not often anyway. Ned had a perpetual hang dog expression on his young face which gave the impression of gloominess. Not a true effect, for when his dry naïve humour showed it was all the more potent.

"Josie alright?" Sybil put down the quill knife she had been gripping and relaxed in Ned's company.

"She's better today. I think it was just….," he blushed and shrugged his shoulders, "you know," he patted his own tummy. Sybil nodded looking at his face, encouraging him to go on.

"A woman's thing," he managed eventually.

"I know Ned," said Sybil mocking his modesty, "she's gone six months carrying your child. That's not just 'a woman thing'. Anyway let her rest and keep her out of the cellar. If she wants to do a little work make sure to give her a boy to do the lifting."

Josie normally managed the gin cellar, and although it was not heavy, there were risks of working alone in the little underground room which opened out on to the street. The hole in the wall was a throwback to days before Turpin's had a licence to serve alcohol inside. Gin and ale was served to customers through the cellar door. It could be dangerous. It might just be a child coming to collect a jug of the liquor, but it could be a drunken rogue who thought he could get it free by kicking the serving girl in the face.

"The carpenter's fitted a well top and it's locked. Shall we keep the key here in the office?"

Sybil nodded.

Ned left the office after a while and Sybil's thoughts returned to the problem of sabotage. She fetched a wisp of long golden hair back behind her ear and picked up the pen-knife again.

Richard O' Cerne might be a handsome fellow but he was still a fool, walking away from the pool, water dripping from his graceful frame, nothing was hidden on that occasion. Just a naked fool. Getting involved with such a villain carried a heavy price. It was never worth the effort. They always ended up on the gallows particularly those who thought they were too smart to be caught. She thought to herself; just use him, like father might have done.

CHAPTER SEVEN
MRS MAISY'S TEA HOUSE

Richard woke with a start early the next morning. It was damp in the drab clapboard terraced hovel which served as home for him and Clem. They were one street back from the water front in two rooms, one above the other.

It was cold in the room they shared, but his cloths were wet with perspiration and his mind immediately returned to his recurring nightmare.

So regular it had become that he called it his *Black Brute*. It always returned at the most disturbing times. He could recall every detail. It was a dream based in reality and as real now as when it had happened five years ago.

It was the memory of an assignment, but one he would dearly love to obliterate from his memory if it were possible to do so.

He had woken this time to find Clem sitting on the end of the bed helplessly sharing his terror.

He had been thrashing around, shouting loudly to make himself heard above the din of a bloody battle.

So many times the battle had been fought on the Spanish plains; he wondered if it would ever end.

Still he lived every detail of it.

***

There were the cries of men screaming and then being cut short by death dealing means. Ragged musket fire, thundering hooves, the cut and thrust of sabres. Animals died noisily.

He was the only civilian in the heart of the battlefield. His odds of survival reduced rapidly by the moment.

Life was dependent on the hundred or so British soldiers, all strangers to Richard; hurrying now to form a square. So called haven of safety in the centre; felt more like an execution yard. Red coated strangers of the 37th North Hampshire regiment, yet Richard could not wish for better companions just now.

God only knows a lethal fighting force is what's needed. Men, experts in killing. The front row kneel, musket butts pressed into the muddy earth and bayonets pointing skywards; a deadly barrier against the enemy horse.

The rattle of harness grows louder as the heavy Spanish beasts break in to a gallop. The cavalry roll forward out of the mist towards the Square; driving through the loamy turf disturbed by heavy hooves. Flaring nostrils like dragons breath signify that even the horses will kill beneath their hooves.

An officer screams a command, the second row holding weapons at the shoulder fire in to the solid packed cavalry attacking on three sides. The discipline in the height of raging battle is what makes the square a formidable weapon. Standing near the centre of the square, beside regimental colours Richard fires his carbine weapon at selective targets. Visibility closes down as the smoke from weapons clouds the air. Better to hold fire and chose a target carefully when the air momentarily clears.

An order shouted for the middle rank to fire low at twelve paces cutting down the heavy cavalry horses. But at such short distance, even after being hit stone dead, they charge on to the very edge of the square.

Now officers are screaming orders directing the fire of their sections on all four sides.

In his recurring nightmare Richard suffers the pain of every act of agonising death taking place around the perimeter. Every cut and thrust of sabre and lance he feels.

As the second row reload muskets the third row fires again. The fire is a continuous hail of death dealing lead. A cuirassier, a giant of a man, is thrown from his injured animal and flies through the air to be impaled by his neck on an upturned bayonet.

A lance thrown from a mount splits the face of a young trooper in the first rank. Before the boy stops screaming he's hauled back inside by the legs and another takes his place. The smell of cordite stings Richard's eyes. A heavy horse rears up before the front rank and momentarily penetrates the square. As the horseman dives, bayonets pierce him with casual ease.

A Spanish officer fires a pistol and the random shot hits the young ensign holding the regimental standard. The young man takes the shot in his shoulder but clutches at the flag for he knows it is more precious than his life.

Richard thinks the bullet was meant for him.

I'm a marked man.

That might be so; being the only man in civilian clothes, he must be important. A target for anyone. The slaughter continues relentlessly and the haven of safety fills with the dead and dying.

He was sent to Spain to cause trouble between France and Spain. The sort of task he is good at. Needing to exit Spain rapidly, it turned out to be a bad idea seeking support from the British military.

"If I get out of this alive," he calls to a captain of artillery who'd taken refuge in the square when his guns were overrun, "I'll open a tavern in the Chelsea and serve free   beer to the troops."

"Well in that case," the soldier replied, "let's get on with it."

The British Square was reckoned to be invincible to everything except artillery and it was a chance shot from a twelve pounder found the middle of the square. It severed both legs from the boy ensign. He dropped like a stone hardly making a sound.

Richard knelt beside him looking helplessly at his missing parts.

"Sir," whispered the fourteen year old, now cradled in his arms, "I think I've shit myself."

His face was pale and splattered with his own flesh and blood. The white trousers were stained but it was hard so say what with.

"We'll soon wash them," Richard whispered, "no one will know, our secret." An officer walked over and sheltered from the boy handed Richard his pistol.

"Do it quickly before the pain comes." Richard looked at the boy who was trying hard to suppress a cry.

Surely not Richard thought; no need, his loss of lifeblood will finish it. But the blood vessels exposed contracted as if by the instinct for survival and the blood ceases to flow. But the boy's face is already screwed up with waves of searing pain. Flailing skin and long fractured ends of bone protruded from his once smart uniform. The gunfire diminishes and it feels as if everyone in the square has stopped to watch Richard with this gruesome task.

This was his recurrent nightmare and from the end of the bed Clem Applebee was sharing his Black Brute. Richard sat up on the straw filled mattress and looked about the room.

Hard to say what Clem was thinking. Whether he knew his presence was some sort of singular comfort to the older man.

***

Richard swaggered in to the tavern late in the evening in a manner best suited the image of a heavy handed bully he carelessly shifted several locals out of their seats and sat down where he could see right across the parlour and his back was protected. He placed his stick on the table facing outwards and looked around the room, a familiar place to him now. For over a month he had worked hard playing the role of an Upright Man, a leader amongst the lawless community of the rookery. In this forgotten area of London where there was no system of justice for the common man, it was natural that the strongest and usually the most brutal gangsters held court. The ordinary people of Cheapside had no voice.

It was late and there were no more than two dozen customers sprawled around on tables. Several minor villains watched for their respective masters. Richard's presence was noted. Ned was doing duty on the high chair alongside the fireplace. A child kept the remains of a hog turning on the spit. It was hardly necessary for the fire was reduced to embers and it would not be fuelled again tonight. At ease in the warmth of the room Richard relaxed. It was safer than the darkness of the streets and while he had successfully established himself as an antagonist in this community he was still the outsider. No one trusted the outsider. To the average local resident, an incomer was either the next victim, or a future oppressor. Either way he was someone to be avoided.

A serving boy brought him a tankard of ale without waiting to be asked and stood hopefully at his elbow. Richard threw a coin high in the air and it was caught with a shriek of childish excitement sounding so very much at odds with the disquieting atmosphere in the parlour. The lad hurried off to the servery. The usual welcoming smell of tobacco and wood smoke filled the parlour and another servant of the tavern, disgruntled to have missed an opportunity, slouched his way from one table to another collecting empty platters. Hands covered in grease, he sucked his fingers before tipping the leftovers on to the fire.

Richard looked hard at the face of a customer sitting alone. The man a well-dressed tradesman looked away, not wanting to make eye contact. He risked everything if seen associating with an outsider. What would it take, Richard wondered, to make one of these people change their allegiance from one bullying Upright Man to another; to upset the established hierarchy. He shook his head dismissively.

Why bother with Turpin's? Its connection with my assignment is remote and getting more so. There's no reason to be here at all.

Apart from…

He looked around the room but Sybil Turpin was missing.

His gaze shifted around the customers in the room. In the far corner of the parlour a younger, greasy haired fellow in a stained military greatcoat sat alone at a table. He wore a pair of ancient spectacles; the lenses cracked and dirty. He was a disciple of Fearless Friar. Working for his master he sat with notebook and coin in neat little piles covering the table. At intervals customers would leave their own seats and walk over to the man. Hardly any conversation took place but coin changed hands and the customer returned again to his own table having parted with his dues.

Richard leaned back on the wooden bench and studied the pale liquid in his tankard.

Why do I want to make a difference?

What does it matter to me? These people will always be downtrodden, but she could make a difference if she cared to.

As if the answer to his quandary was suddenly resolved, he stood and walked over to the table.

Greasy Hair ignored him; continued counting the dues. Richard touched the barrel of his weapon on the man's forehead and it left a ring of black grease just above his nose.

"Your master wants you urgently; leave now, and don't touch anything on the table."

The man looked up hardly disturbed by the intrusion.

"Mr Friar's business keeps me here," he replied with a belligerent tone.

"I should leave directly before that mark on your forehead becomes a neat little hole." He smiled at the man, "does he pay you enough for that?"

Greasy hair got up defiantly and left. At the door another joined him and they shouted a warning to Richard and slammed the door.

Richard gathered up the money. By this time every eye in the room was on him. He beckoned to the serving boy.

"Free drinks for everyone." To Ned he added, "as much as they can drink."

Back at his own table he sat waiting. The atmosphere in the room was buzzing with excitement. A sound, a shadow made him looks up. The lone tradesman was standing on the other side of the bench, in front of him, his eyes glued to the barrel of the weapon. Richard nodded for him to sit. Still nothing was said. The tradesman held his gaze now. Richard wondered if this was the moment he had been waiting for.

"I'm paying protection to two different gangs, what're you going to do about that?" The man spoke aggressively; Richard took it as a warning that his action would not bring friends and supporters, just responsibilities.

"What would you want me to do?"

His actions had given hope to some, but he had raised their expectations of Richard O' Cerne.

The man looked at him defiantly and turned away.

Traders, craftsmen, and labourers were all marked by the system of dues. Richard's intervention might slowly change allegiances and as the evening wore on other local characters sidled over to him, watchful, cautious for fear of retribution. Mostly they approached Richard's table singly and always waited for the invitation to sit. There were debts unpaid, theft of property, protection needed, protection paid three times over; matters which in the lawless society of the rookery would be left undone or exploited by others. They came and sat down facing the barrel end of his stick.

It had become his badge of office; widely known the weapon was charged with powder and would fire a half inch lead ball across the length of the room, at the pressing of a concealed button on the ornate handle. Someone who could afford to keep such an unusual weapon was reckoned to be a powerful man and Richard's facing down of Fearless Friar had become legend already.

"He charged me twice over," cried the one.

"He's been cheating customers with his prices for years," claimed another.

Richard listened patiently.

This won't take me closer to Thomas's killer, he thought.

It will just embroil me deeper and deeper into this corrupt society.

How much difference can one man make?

From the concealed window in her den Sybil watched the man deliberating on the problem he had created for himself.

Much later it was Ned who rose from the tall chair and walked over to him.

"Mistress Sybil would like to speak with you Mr."

Richard nodded without looking at Ned.

"Tell her I will attend but not here, not in this place; tell her to name a place and a time; anywhere."

Ned walked away his glum expression signifying nothing.

"No wait," shouted Richard across the room, "tell her I'll be at Mrs Maisy's Tea house over in Westminster at two o' clock on Thursday."

A smile played across Richard's face. There was loud laughter from one or two people close by following the exchanges. The implication of Richard's invitation was clear to all. Sybil would be like a fish out of water in a place like Mrs Maisy's. On the other hand he enjoyed the idea of getting her away from the rookery at least for a short while.

Ned frowned but did speak. A moment later he returned to the parlour.

"She'll be there. Miss Sybil suggests you might want to leave by the back door again this evening?" At last Ned raised a smile as he walked away.

***

They were to meet the Duke of Sharingham in the Admiralty buildings not far up the river at Greenwich. Richard was immaculately dressed looking entirely the part of a wealthy young buck. He felt good too in skin tight black buck-skin breeches and stockings which fitted his leg as if it had been painted on. The coat of crimson velvet was embroidered with metal braid around the front edge, and worn long. He wore a ten shilling shirt, covered by a waistcoat, a favourite;

crème coloured, embroidered with a crimson thread. His own hair was tidy tied neatly in a queue at the back of his neck. He took an extraordinary circuitous route to get there on the assumption that he might almost certainly be followed.

The route took him past the shipwrights yards clinging to the waters edge, across the rope-walk yards toward the Admiralty building. Clem, now enjoying a very trusted position in Richard's employment, had been sent ahead to watch his arrival at Greenwich Steps and notice if anyone took an interest in his arrival. Richard thought it imperative that he arrive undetected by anyone from the rookery; but if he was followed he needed to know by whom.

At Greenwich Steps he walked away from the river in to an open space of parkland.

At the massive mahogany table sat three people. The Duke's secretary who had collected him at the entrance of the great building stood silently at the door. The Duke got up quickly as Richard entered the room.

"Mr Hamilton, how good to meet you at last." Firmly shaking his hand he led him over to the large French windows and out of earshot of the other two continued.

"You've been busy. Some fine work in Spain; the papers you returned with, were very revealing and I believe they were gained at no small price to your own safety."

All the while the Duke pointed with his arm outstretched in the direction of park and down in the direction of the river. His hand waved about as if indicating features of the landscape.

"Before that you were in the Dutch Republic. But that was after the business in the Americas looking at the Massachusetts problem."

Richard was surprised the Duke knew so much about him. He said nothing and since the Duke had an arm around his shoulder directing his gaze, he could only stand there taking pleasure from the comments.

"You know this matter has a personal dimension for me."

"I was sorry to hear about Thomas, your grace. I knew him when we were at Cambridge together."

"I believe so; Thomas spoke warmly of your friendship."

With great composure the Duke continued his deception aimed at the two at the table. The view from the window could never have been given such attention.

"I am pleased you are helping, but I must warn you to be careful Richard. There are those close to this assignment who you might reasonably expect to be," he hesitated, "supportive. But matters are not always as they seem. Keep your own counsel and if necessary do not hesitate to contact me directly."

They walked back towards the table.

While Sir Ronald Able-Makepiece sat quietly, the other person was less patient.

A wrinkled little man, dressed with yards of lace on his collar and sleeves

 fidgeted around in his chair; kept clearing his throat and talking loudly to Sir Ronald about the busy day he had ahead. Neither of the men at the window turned.

Finally the Duke turned, "I'd like you to meet William Chasemeet."

"Your servant sir," said Richard giving him a slight knee.

"Yes yes," said Chasemeet testily, "now can we please get on?"

"William Chasemeet is a Director at the Bank of England," said the Duke. "Or perhaps I should say he is the Bank of England." This introduction was delivered without a glance toward the man.

Chasemeet tittered, waved a lace handkerchief clearly enjoying the introduction.

"He knows as much about this business as anyone and his greater understanding of the economic dimension will, I feel, will be of the greatest value to you."

Richard raised his hands and exclaimed "Goodness I hope so. I must say I know nothing about money; never keep it long enough, don't you know."

By the end of the meeting Richard was only a little better informed about his task.

In front of the Duke, Chasemeet had promised all the help his department could offer. He obviously had not taken to Richard and appeared to be constantly concerned with his own appearance, the need to be somewhere else, far more important and his lace collar which needed constant attention.

Richard was quite distracted by Chasemeet's bottom lip which drooped uncontrollably and wobbled long after he stopped speaking.

Sir Ronald Makepiece had contributed little to the meeting. The Duke had taken much away; mostly the knowledge that the case was safe in Richard's hands.

"I wish you well of the inquiry," wobbled Chasemeet after Richard and Sir Ronald had gone.

"But if that's the best you have in the way of agents….."

"Appearance, I find, is often deceptive Mr Chasemeet. You would do well not to underestimate that man."

***

Although it was no more than an hour's walk away from Turpin's it was a world away from the rookery. Mrs Maisy's Tea House was a highly respectable establishment serving refreshment to the cultivated residents of Westminster. Sybil Turpin was unlikely ever to enter such a place; not even by accident. It was in a part of the city where the upper crust had their town houses, there were watchman on every street corner and beggars were seldom seen. The streets were washed down every night and there were public gardens with seats, where residents could sit and children might play.

Sybil faced the challenge of her outing to Mrs Maisy's with great apprehension.

He thinks to get me away from the tavern she reasoned. Perhaps to shame me in front of gentle folk. Well we shall see.

A full twelve hours before the appointed time she stood in her spacious bedroom facing a long mirror. The door was bolted and even her friend and close confidant Josie Church was not present. On the bed her everyday clothes: the long blue woollen dress, shawl, and a shapeless cotton shift in which she was most at home. Fashion for women demanded, what amounted to stringent uniformity of dress and Sybil, despite her everyday preferences, had a wardrobe here in the heart of the Turpin's which would have been the envy of many a lady from the wealthy parts of the city. Keeping an up-to-the-minute, fashionable wardrobe which was hardly worn, seldom seeing the light of day was the most incongruous circumstance.

Perhaps Sybil Turpin could explain but she was not likely ever to do so. Was it possible she had secret aspirations of an escape from her present life in Turpin's; a time when such clothes would be worn every day?

She selected a mantua of blue French silk and caressed it against her bare skin. In the mirror she fantasized walking in to the tea house imagining what Richard Hamilton would think. Would he notice it matched the colour of her eyes?

Would the silly man be surprised with her transformation? The gown had a deep cut front intended to be worn under a bodice. She chose one of crème silk embroidery at the front to contrast with the gown. Josie would be needed to lace her in. Convention demanded the restricting bodice was worn to mould her to the fashionable feminine shape. Sybil seldom had time for convention however she had good reason to play the role Richard Hamilton had prescribed. It gave her confidence; she would take Mrs Maisy's Tea House by storm.

Josie Church was called. Her friend clapped her hands together and whimpered; there were tears in her eyes.

"Oh Miss Sybil," was all she could manage dancing round her in wonderment. Together they worked, lacing Sybil in to the bodice till her small breasts pressed revealingly to look generous above the bodice.

Josie's excitement was infectious and whilst the knee-length chemise and and underskirt were fitted, they were like children at a dressing up party. Finally the hooped petticoat was donned. When the final garment was fitted, the stunning transformation was complete.

Josie was all fingers and thumbs piling Sybil's hair high under a little white lace cap. It had side pieces, 'lappets', which tied under her chin. Finally silk shoes lined with linen completed the outfit.

It required a carriage to convey her to Mrs Maisy's. Sybil made no concession to fashion when it came to makeup and she knew this would probably single her out amongst the other customers taking refreshment. Ceruse, the white lead paste was very fashionable and so were patches. The effect was a matt white complexion which smoothed the skin hiding wrinkles and smallpox scars. Not necessary thought Sybil although she often wished her complexion was less rosy.

She had a fine collection of jewellery to choose from. Like so much of her wardrobe it had been shipped and smuggled through the port of London to end up in her closet; payment for outstanding accounts. Sometimes pieces ordered on a half-promise to return a favour, like the diamond pin from Brazil. She and Josie spent hours rummaging through the box each item had a different story sometimes she thought, a tale that was better forgotten. They selected and a string of pearls from the Far East the gift of a captain from an ocean going trader who had a winning smile but too high an opinion of himself.

I hope it turns out to be worth the effort, Sybil thought leaving the security of her boudoir. His choice of a venue might have given him the upper hand but the way she felt now, it was all evens.

At least the trip was enjoyable she had a hackney carriage from her neighbour Tom Newton who had a business close to the tavern. He also had a licence for sedan chairs, very popular for short journeys.

Sybil thought his carriages were rather uncomfortable but Tom only charged her one shilling both ways, considerably cheaper than the official set rates. That was how it worked in the closed community of Cheapside. Tom would benefit when he was next in the Tavern.

The trip took her up Ludgate Hill, past St Paul's, along Fleet Street to The Strand. The streets here are very narrow, one carriage wide with passages either side for walkers. The timber houses overhang the streets and the congestion of traffic meant hours of delay. Past the Charing Cross, through White Hall and she was set down on the corner of Bridge Street with some helpful instruction from her driver directing her to Mrs Maisy's.

It was a mild afternoon and she enjoyed watching the activity on the river and behaving like a sightseer for a change. There were wherries carrying passengers and light cargo down to Gravesend and water taxis criss-crossing the river. It cost six pence to be taken by a waterman from London Bridge to Westminster. It might have been more pleasant to have taken a water taxi, but it was a slightly more hazardous journey and no guarantees of getting there dry and in a tidy state.

I wonder if he'll recognise me, she thought childishly and then dismissed the idea, embarrassed at the thought that she might be caught out for thinking it.

Sybil had asked for this meeting and although Richard O' Cerne was making her jump through hoops to get to it, she felt excited about seeing him again and her own singular motive did not altogether spoil a tingle of excitement. Mrs Maisy's turned out to be a double fronted timber framed house. The only shop in the row with two large bay widows, It had that look of decaying affluence which marked out so much of this area. Saved from the worst of fire damage which regularly destroyed swaths of streets it had aged badly. The unpainted woodwork looking like so much tinder. Opposite, across the cobbled street there were no houses just a square of open ground with trees and seats.

Why, I might even take my tea across the road in to the public gardens. Sybil felt she had been transported to a different place except for the ever present odours wafting from the Thames which gave it all away.

Stepping inside the open front door, there was no doubt about the credentials of Mrs Maisy's patrons. It was clearly the place to be seen for those who could afford the latest fashions. Her entrance caused a lull in the hum of conversation, but it did not distress her one scrap. It was the discerning eye of Sybil the business woman who surveyed the scene.

Mrs Maisy is to be congratulated she thought, she has a profitable little business from this place. No more than a dozen little tables packed full with customers wearing the latest London fashions. There might have been room for a dozen more if it were not for the voluminous fashions, she smiled to herself. The place had a *swept clean, airy* feeling about it. Walls were hung with soft lacy drapes matching the table covers.

How well the furnishings and décor match the genteel atmosphere, she thought. The genteel customers were presently gaping with hostility at the outsider but Sybil was in no way disconcerted.

Wonder how they'd cope with sawdust, cursing dockers, and a hog roast on the spit.

She was disappointed to discover he had not arrived; that he was not sitting at an empty table waiting for her. She chose a table in the corner of the window with a view of the pavement and the gardens beyond as well as the interior of the room.

On every table there were neatly written cards describing the choice of refreshment available; tea, coffee or chocolate. There were biscuits and pastries also, and she noticed people around her delicately nibbling as they enjoyed a drink. A bobbing waitress attended her as she studied the menu.

"Tea," she spoke sharply, "and," she pointed to the next table, I'll try the biscuit."

What does Mrs Maisy pay for her tea I wonder?

It was charged by the leaf and cost around six pound a pound for anyone unfortunate to have to pay the real price.

A business opportunity occurred to her. Very few people were interested in tea at Turpin's but it came in through the docks and was available at a quarter of the price.

Perhaps, she thought Mrs Maisy might be interested in some good quality tea leaf.

A tiny china cup was produced and the waitress poured steaming pale grey liquid from a tall bulbous pot which looked more like a burial urn. Sybil lifted it to her nose and caught the faintest aroma of tea. Far greater was the stale acrid smell of a liquid brewed a long time ago. In the bottom of the cup there floated a few pieces of leaf. The waitress turned to go.

"Wait," she spoke sharply touching the girl's arm. Sybil lifted the cup to her lips and let the liquor scald the back of her mouth. There was no taste of tea only of brackish water. They were not tea leaves only hard pieces of grit; the sediment from a pot of tea which, in keeping with custom and practice, had been prepared early in the morning to be heated and reheated throughout the day. The custom, she knew, dated from when the whole day's tea was made up, taxed as a whole, and then sold by the cup. She sipped at it delicately and was hard pressed not to spit it straight out again.

She waved the girl away when realisation dawned.

The biscuit's the thing. She broke off a piece and popped the thin oaty, sugar coated cake in to her mouth and treasured the relief.

Clever Mrs Maisy provides the medicine and the remedy.

She waited and he did not come. She suffered more tea and watched the people around her. She searched the crowded street for the sign of a familiar face. The elegant fashion passing by began to arouse hostility in towards Richard.

Her curiosity was being replaced by insecurity to these foreign surroundings.

But little understood and deeply hidden there was a desire, thwarted by Richard Hamilton, to somehow be part of this beautiful society.

Even if it is a parody of reality, she thought angrily.

"Pardon me Miss," she was roused from her daydreaming and turned to see a young waitress bobbing a curtsey.

"Lady Fanshaw," the girl whispered, looking nervously over her shoulder, hoping no further explanation would be necessary.

"She usually sits here." The waitress was trembling and looked as if she was about to burst in to tears.

Sybil turned toward the formidable features of a tall, grim apparition complete with lap-dog and a ceruse painted face.

Looks as if might have applied with a wooden spoon, thought Sybil.

Lady Fanshaw had arrived and was clearly a person who commanded *the* seat in the window, befitting her position in the social hierarchy of Mrs Maisy's.

"Well she'll have to sit elsewhere," said Sybil, loud enough so that the girl would not have to relay the message and be punished for her trouble.

"Perhaps if her ladyship wants a window seat she'd like to squeeze in beside me, I'm not at all fussy."

Sybil was rather proud of her put-on accent, but it didn't fool the lady beneath the painted mask. She fumed and blustered; the waitress finally burst in to tears and Sybil turned away cursing the name of Richard O' Cerne or whatever he called himself.

At this moment the door of the shop opened and a handsome young man entered in the uniform of a footman. Complete in the livery of the sovereign, King George;

wig slightly askew and the face; where had Sybil seen that face? The boy stood in the doorway of Mrs Maisy's Tea House and looked about him in a manner of impudent superiority. The entire room was already attentive to Lady Fanshaw's outrage and enjoying the anticipation of Sybil's downfall. The boy barged in front of Lady Fanshaw and in a whisper to the waitress guaranteed to be heard at the back of the room.

"Miss Sybil Turpin?" Sybil turned without a smile, recognising the voice. The boy handed her a sealed message and bowed to the waist. He stood beside her while she very slowly read it and even more slowly finished her tea.

"Lady Fanshaw, may have this seat shortly; it seems I am summonsed," she looked at the awesome figure, "to court," she added.

The tea house remained silent and watched the discomfort of Lady Fanshaw, not entirely without humour. Sybil enjoyed the moment immensely but was angry and confused by the message from her absent guest.

Outside on the pavement she looked around, in the side streets, at the shop fronts across the road; there was nothing to support Richard's suspicion that she was being secretly followed.

Clem Applebee stood beside a superior carriage.

"The cab's paid for Miss Sybil and the master sends his apologies. If you was to wish it he will be happy to attend you at any time and place of your choosing."

"You may tell him," she hesitated trying to gather her thoughts and not to sound cross with the messenger, who she thought played his part very well.

"You may tell him to go to hell."

"Very good Miss," the boy was not at all deterred by this.

"You clean up well Clem."

"Thank you Miss. It's Clem Applebee now Miss."

Sybil smiled enjoying the boy's cockiness.

"Got to get back Miss 'for this clobber is found missin.'"

He grinned and was gone.

It was an altogether more comfortable trip back to the tavern. But the note in her hand was a mystery she could not fathom.

CHAPTER EIGHT
THE TALL CHAIR

"The Bank's been here on Princess Street since 1695," William Chasemeet announced. His raised voice, competing with the noisy gathering in the entrance hall became shrill and squeaky. Richard knew he was getting a well- rehearsed history of the building. The Director could hardly disguise his boredom having to entertain this young upstart. Richard thought, if he had not been introduced by the Duke the man would not have given him the time of day. Chasemeet lamented the cramped conditions in which they had to work.

Richard, half listening, looked up at the massive domed ceiling, admiring towering ornate arches. The hall itself must have been sixty feet in length and half that in height. Around three walls there were tall polished Mahogany desks dwarfing the customers who craned their necks to speak with the tellers.

The side facing Princess Street was a mass of high arched windows beneath which crowds of busy people passed back and forth through the doors in to the great hall. A multitude of different activities going on gave a chaotic impression. There were short chattering queues in front of some of the Tellers. Others stood about talking in groups, drinking beverages, or just reading from the news sheets. Out of sight beyond the barrier of desks there were open fronted cubicles separated from one another by six foot high oak panelling. Richard and Chasemeet stood on the raised dais at one end from where the bank's security guards stood watching all the activity in the hall.

The Director was dressed in the uniformly black collarless coat with deep cuffs, waistcoat, and breeches. It all signified he was a high ranking official of the bank.

Only the silky white stockings, lacy cuffs and constantly wafted frilly handkerchief, as if it was warding off something evil smelling, gave a clue to the conceited oddness of the man.

Richard, standing over six feet tall, stylish, dashing, by comparison was captivated by the scene in the great hall.

A gentle pat on his arm alerted him that his escort was moving on. In a room behind the great hall Chasemeet's servant closed the door and left them.

"So you are chosen to investigate a conspiracy Mr Hamilton."

"Heavens Sir, conspiracy or not, I have no idea at the moment." said Richard dropping himself down in the comfortable chair.

"Well how *would* you put it young man?" On Chasemeet's side of the wide mahogany desk the flooring was raised giving the older man an elevated view of his visitor.

"You know it well enough sir; Mr Walpole, the Chancellor, thinks there's a swindle going on. The South Sea Company, floated to trade in the Americas has become so powerful that it threatens to de-stabilise the government. It's already been gifted the national debt and whether the Jacobite's or the Spanish are behind it, no one knows."

Chasemeet smiled condescendingly.

"The conspiracy, if there is one, is whether there is an organised plot or it's just sheer incompetence."

"Sir Robert Walpole's views are well known to us. You should be aware that it has not stopped him personally investing in stock."

Richard knew this man could afford to patronise.

"You might care to purchase some shares yourself."

"How should one put the Chancellor's mind at rest Sir? How should we scuttle the rumours once and for all?"

Chasemeet smiled and his handkerchief danced around his face.

"The Company has already made the government seven million pounds better off and they are only asking for a five percent interest on the unpaid debt. In the meantime all those individuals holding government stock are receiving shares. No one loses. Hardly a plan likely to bring down the government?"

From his confident manner Richard knew he'd have to work harder to uncover conspiracy.

"Sir Robert Walpole sees conspiracy where there is nothing but goodwill. So where do you want to start your investigation?

"Strike me sir, I imagine a start by looking at the books of the

South Sea Company. See what history tells us of the dealings of directors. Who are the directors of the Company and what their gains were before the Government handed them the National Debt."

"It's all on public record my dear fellow."

The handkerchief was waving again.

Still no sign of concern.

"Then… I suppose I'd look at their bank accounts, to see the extent of their gain."

Chasemeet's expression changed; perhaps realising Richard was not the empty head he appeared to be.

I'm getting warmer, thought Richard.

"And then I'd look at the lives of the directors of the Company, what they have in common; political allegiances, where they club, foreign connections, that sort of thing"

The banker's countenance changed even more. Chasemeet looked red around his short skinny neck, beads of perspiration on the fleshy face.

"Then you are starting on a long and fruitless journey Mr Hamilton"; He was back in his stride.

Richard changed tack.

"The Duke's son worked here at the bank?"

"He did but for a very short time and in a very junior position. No doubt he would have leapt to the top with the benefit of his father's patronage."

Sir William began to shuffle papers, "You will have to excuse me soon young man, I have appointments…"

"Who did Thomas Sharingham work for, what was his job?"

"He worked under my tutelage and I wouldn't say as much to the Duke but I found him to be an idle fellow, not at all like his father." Sir William walked toward the door. "But now I really must foreclose," he was smiling again, "as we say to bad debtors."

"I hope you find something to put the Duke's mind at rest. I am sorry for his loss but I rather suspect the matter will be forgotten soon enough."

Richard was ushered out of the room and in to the hands of the servant who had been waiting outside the door.

Outside he leaned back against the portico and took a deep breath expelling it again noisily. He looking at the servant.

"He's a hard man, your master."

"Glory sir, you done better than most. I think he took a shine to you."

Richard raised his eyebrows.

"Shanks isn't it," he smiled at the man.

"Sorry Shanks that was rude of me. Must be a busy man your boss; had me in and out before I had chance to finish."

"They're all that way inclined sir," said Shanks. "Think it makes 'em look busy."

"Did Thomas Sharingham get on with him?"

"Heavens no sir. Mr Chasemeet hated him, thought he was too nosey by far. Young Thomas was constantly questioning everything done. The master didn't like that sort of thing in a pupil. I shouldn't be sayin' as much, but I liked the young man. He was so full of life and 'e might 'ave been the son of a Duke but 'e treated us servants of the bank like we knew more than him."

"Which you probably do Shanks," Richard smiled at the man.
"Tell you 'summat sir; some 'o these upper-class nobs 'ave less sense than my daughter Polly.

***

"It's a very smart green uniform with gold coloured piping round the collar and the sleeves. You get to wear a wig as well," said Richard.

"I can't work in a bank," moaned Clem. "I can't read or write."

"You can write your name now and you're pretty fly when it comes to money. Your manners are much improved too. Anyway, Shanks has got a daughter. I suggest you start there."

Shanks's daughter sold tickets at the Vauxhall pleasure gardens during the summer months. She also served food and drinks to the picnickers who hired the supper booths and very occasionally a young blade would ask her to dance. However Mr J Tyers esquire, entrepreneur and master builder of the pleasure garden was strict when it came to services of the more personal kind. Prostitutes were banned and although the opportunity for dalliances was ever present in the darker avenues of the garden, it was severely frowned upon.

Polly Shanks seemed so worldly to Clem Applebee.

" Course I'm only 'ere to get 'meself a rich 'usband then I'll be away from all this drudge."

But in the meantime she quite enjoyed Clem's puppy dog adoration.

"Clem stop that," Polly Shanks declared, you'll get me fired if Mr Tyler sees."

Clem had become a regular visitor to the pleasure gardens and he had found it was no effort paying attention to Polly. She was, he thought, the most beautiful girl he had ever seen. He stopped as Polly demanded but all it had been was an arm round her waist. Clem paid his shilling every evening and sat behind the music pavilion and waited for Polly to come round. He didn't enjoy the music very much but the atmosphere was exciting. There were always crowds of people sitting in the pavilions or walking up and down the tree lined avenues. There was a newly built Italian ancient ruin and a Turkish tent and Doric pillars. At nine o'clock sharp the concealed lights were lit and they illuminated the trees casting long shadows of inviting darkness.

After the toffs in their hired boxes were served with genuine mineral water at six pence a glass and red wine to wash down the awful tasting water they would settled down to listen to an orchestra.

It was then that Polly and Clem could sneak off. They would join in the promenade along the avenue or slip down to the canal to watch genuine Italian gondolas glide up and down, or creep away in to the darkness to fumble in one another's clothes. In the fumbling department Clem was a complete novice and Polly had to show him what to do. She took his hand and placed it under her skirt. Then she rubbed up and down and sighed with contentment.

All this, Clem thought, was very well and she got him free drinks. It must be like this in heaven he thought.

The orchestra played till ten thirty and then Polly's father collected her from the main gate.

One evening Polly was asked to dance by a stranger and she did so. With her lack of sophistication she puzzled when he offered her two shilling to walk with him in a path away from the lights.

Clem heard the screams first because he had been sauntering along behind. That was when he realised he cared about her; that it mattered to him who Polly was with and if she was safe. Clem found her in a distraught state, cloths all torn, she had been beaten badly around the head and was weeping uncontrollably. He gathered her up and carried her to the main gate where Mr Shanks took one look at his precious child and knocked Clem down before either of them could explain.

Eventually Polly Shanks did manage to tell her father that Clem had been her rescuer not the villain who attacked her.

By strange coincidence he found Clem on the pavement outside the bank looking very forlorn.

Shanks took the boy home where he was treated like a bit of a hero by Mrs Shanks. Polly was a little cool with him by now because she had found a job in a butcher's shop and taken a shine to the butcher's boy who was always covered in blood and played with sharp knives. It so happened that there was a vacancy for a servant in the Bank of England and eventually Clem wore a green uniform with gold coloured piping; looking very smart.

Clem came home at the end of each day complaining about the regular hours and then relaying the gossip between the servants.

"Mr William is the worst to work for, only Shanks will put up with him. He actually beat one of the servants who he thought was looking through his desk."

"Course I know it 'aint me *proper job* I'm only a doorman anyway but Shanks says I could be promoted."

Clem's excitement with his 'proper job' was self-evident. He relished going in to work and being responsible and coming home again with stories about what happened.

Richard was loathed to remind him why he was there.

"The 'ole bank's moving to a new building, they got all the plans laid out in one of the offices. It's gonna have as many rooms underground as above. It's where they'll store the gold. Won't be for some years; when they find the right place to build it."

"They're gonna to have their own military guard an all; special soldiers to guard the bank at night.

"I met the governor today," he said brightly, "well he walked past when I was doing the fire grate in the Chief Cashier's office."

"Guess who I met today," said Clem cockily.

"Only King George 'imself. We had to stand in a long line, like a guard of honour. Mr Shanks said he'd come to count 'is money; but he wasn't there very long."

"Did you speak to him Clem?"

Clem whistled. "Not likely, anyhows he don't speak English; he's jabbering away in some foreign talk."

Finally Richard said, "Don't forget why you're there Clem."

Directly after he wished he hadn't said anything.

"Found out where 'is nibs lives. One of the lads 'ad to take some stuff to 'is home so I offered to 'elp.

Big boxes of paper with writing on. Very posh 'ouse too."

And then after a full six weeks of employment Clem came home stripped of his uniform.

"Got the sack today,"

Richard raised his head from the news sheet he was reading.

"Got in a bit of a scrap in front of old Chasemeet. There's one cove, name of Cully, a servant but a real bully, always picks on others. Anyways I set him up. Slipped some papers off Chasemeet's desk in to his coat pocket. Sticking out they was.

"'What's that sticking out of your pocket,'" cries Mr William. "' It's for lightin the fire,'" says Cully, quick as a flash is Cully. I grabs the papers and hands them to Mr William. He's fuming; he looks at the paper, and sacks us both on the spot."

Sitting in the hearth of the kitchen Clem now readily thought of as home he continued.

"Once they'd stripped us of our greens I was kicked out the back door and the Watch came for Cully, but he knocked me about a bit before. Anyhow Chasemeet sees me bruised and covered in blood.

"'You spoke up,'" he said all smarmy, "'and paid harshly for your honesty. If you is looking for employment come to my home, I might be able to take you on.'"

"Well done Clem," said Richard, "but do you want to go in to the Lion's den?"

"Course I do, ain't that what it's been all about?"

The relationship between the two was now set firm. There was a little less than ten years between them but Clem was loyal to the older man. If able to explain his feelings he would have been troubled to describe the close friendship developing. Clem simply behaved as if Richard was an older brother.

The streetwise kid is growing into a man, thought Richard. Perhaps soon he will deserve to be Mister.

***

Sybil read Richard's letter for what must have been the tenth time. She read it aloud because she thought it might aid her understanding if she heard it spoken.

Dear Miss Turpin

I regret not being able to join you for tea.

I will confess that when Ned said you wanted to speak to me it was pure mischievousness which made me suggest we meet at Mrs Maisy's; however as I watch you in the window, not more than thirty yards away, I realise the fatuity of my action and dearly regret not being able to enjoy your company away from the tavern.

Information came in to my possession a short while before which suggested your life was in danger. I therefore took steps to follow you unobserved. You were shadowed on your trip today and as I sit writing there is still at least one man watching you quite carefully. You are in no immediate danger whilst I am close at hand but I am keen to discover who your spy reports to. I must therefore remain hidden.

Clem will deliver this message and he has arranged a carriage to get you safely back to the Tavern.

I owe you a fuller explanation but for the time being it would be better, for your sake, if you were not seen in my company. Rest assured I am not far away.

Your Friend

Richard

"Damn the man's arrogance." Sybil read it again pacing up and down in her room.

"'You're in no immediate danger whilst …' How dare he."

"So he thinks I need protecting. Much good he'd be."

By the next morning when she rose earlier than usual, the anger had gone. She walked down the stairs from her room and through the servery thinking to share her thoughts with Ned but he wasn't to be found.

She suddenly felt very lonely and friendless. She wandered in to the parlour, still dark. It was empty. Not even the usual stray drunk from last night for company.

The message was not reassurance from a trusted friend; more likely a ruse to destroy me, for his own gain, she thought.

She felt abandoned and with not the remotest idea what to do.

The tall chair beckoned her. It was a link with her childhood; even the good and the bad memories of tempestuous times. Her earliest memories were of Pa sitting there presiding over everything. Now *she* did the same. The tall chair was a great ugly piece of furniture which had become a throne; the presence of someone sitting in the tall chair meant everything was under control; it signified there was order amongst the chaos.

The chair had been made by a local furniture maker; to old man Turpin's own specification. It had two steps up to the seat and heavy arms which circled round as if embracing the sitter. Restless palms over the years had polished the arms to a shiny finish. It dominated the parlour and was a place of safety - a haven of safety.

The parlour was practically empty. Ned's dog Ratter lay sprawled beside the embers of the fire taking in the leftover whiffs of last night's spit roast.

The early morning light had hardly reached the dusty nooks and crannies of the room. On the floor in a far corner there was a scuffing noise as a body moved in drunken slumber. Sybil did not allow customers to do this but sometimes if it was one of her regulars they would be left to sleep it off rather than being kicked out in such a stupor that they would be a prize for the first thief. Guests, too drunk to move, might be carried to their rooms. Only strangers were deposited out through the front door and then only after making sure they did not have the price of a room.

Sybil didn't give the drunken bundle another thought.

She grasped the thick arms of the chair staring across the empty room, but looking at the table where Richard Hamilton always sat.

"This won't do," she said suddenly, "day will start without me."

Before any staff arrived, she left the chair and returned to her room.

The Hogshead was calling.

Up in the corner of her room there stood an upturned fifty four gallon barrel with an end removed. The barrel was her bath tub.

What she did next was behaviour so rare that it bordered on the insane.

She removed her nightclothes and climbed in to the barrel.

Slowly immersing herself in the cold well water.

It wasn't as good as the lake over at Spring Fields but it was good.

Eventually her head was under water and her long tresses momentarily floated then sank with her. There wasn't much room to move around.

Her staff that knew about this eccentricity and thought she was mad, and perhaps she was, but it was exhilarating and she cared not a drop for what anyone else thought.

There was a commotion in the parlour, people shouting; a boy hammered on her door.

"It's Ned, Mistress Sybil he's been hurt." Sybil hurried down to the parlour. Ned was leaning over the bar. Josie was leaning over him holding a blood stained towel.

"Whatever is it?"

I took hold of the tall chair to move it," he removed the towel. A large sailmakers needle had completely pierced the palm; its point protruding through the back of his hand. Blood was pouring from the entry and exit wounds. Josie supporting his wrist began to whimper.

"Bring him in to the kitchen, the rest of you back to work." Whilst he sat up to a table she began.

"I must remove it Ned," he nodded too shocked to speak. She wrapped some linen around the larger end to improve the grip. Ned held his own fingers down and Josie held his wrist. Sybil clasped the end and pulled sharply. The needle came out easily. Ned looked as white as sheet but it was Josie who fainted. Sybil held the needle up to the light in the widow. It was about six inches long and curved; it looked new. The point was shiny and sharp and as she unwrapped the linen Sybil noticed the needle had been covered in a green paste. She deliberately turned away from Ned and held it to her nose. The odour caused her retch and for a moment it sucked at her breath.

Sybil turned back to the table.

"I think we should let it bleed freely for a while. How did this happen Ned?"

"It was sticking up on the seat of the tall chair; wedged in a crack."

"But I was sitting in the chair not a half an hour ago. How...?"

She looked around the room.

"Who...? that drunken wretch in corner of the parlour." Sybil fairly ran out in to the parlour but the body had gone. She walked over to where he had been and smelt the odour of his body; she bent and picked up a button from the floor a distinctive black shiny button.

They held the hand in hot water to encourage bleeding, till Ned began to feel faint from the loss of blood. Then Sybil bound it up and sent him off to bed.

Josie had been quite neglected, but she picked herself up and went off to her husband.

Sybil was worried. This was a determined attempt to harm *her,* not Ned, but the worst of it was that the needle had been smeared in an oily substance. The only purpose for that, she thought, was to poison.

Ned slept for most of the day and whilst he did so. Sybil made a visit to the apothecary. She came back with a concoction of herbs including Chickweed to make in to a fomenting poultice which she and Josie applied to the wounds.

"As hot as you can bear it Ned," she whispered in his ear.

Sybil could do nothing to disguise her concern and her hands shook as she changed the poultice again.

Josie behaved as if insensible to the occasion.

"Pull yourself together Ned. He's always been a baby when it comes to a bit 'o pain."

But by the end of the day even Josie could no longer sustain false hope. Ned had begun to slip in to a coma.

Sybil talked to her, "It's serious Josie, there is poison in the wound, and we have to get it out quickly." Josie just shook, unable to comprehend.

By the next morning the hand had swollen like a balloon, the colour of a shiny tomato and it looked as if the skin would burst open.

It gave Sybil an idea.

Ned was delirious, he needed nothing for pain.

"We must cut it open Josie."

Sybil normally had no time for barber surgeons but in desperation she called one.

"We must lay bare the wound," he said.

"At least we can agree on that."

He did it competently enough with his knife. Sybil offered to sharpen the knife, and whilst doing so washed off the filthy debris of his last patient without him seeing. Surgeons had no comprehension about introducing infection from contaminated instruments, but it was only common sense to Sybil, even though the wound was already well and truly poisoned. Sybil assisted the man and thought he was competent enough, making long cuts through both wounds, exposing the suppurating flesh and giving it a chance to clean away the pus which poured from the wound. Ned still drifted in and out of consciousness and when he was awake the pain was intense. She gave him tincture of opium provided by the barber surgeon and this sent him in to long periods of more restful slumber.

"Never before," said the barber surgeon, "have I seen such a rapid progression of the noxious humours. It could almost be imagined that poison had been poured on the wound."

Sybil closed her eyes trying to shut out the man's excited chattering.

It was, she thought, just as he described.

By the third day the odour from the wound was overwhelming and black areas of dead flesh were more in abundance than healthy tissue. The sickly sweet smell of gangrene was evident and Josie could no longer stay at Ned's bedside. Her own time was coming shortly and Sybil was concerned for Josie's health and that of her baby.

When Sybil realised they were fighting a losing battle they discussed whether or not the limb should be removed. However up along the arm the veins stood out as prominent purple tracks and Sybil did not need to be told what this meant. The poison had already made its way in to the rest of Ned's body.

The awful truth was so obvious to Sybil; Ned would not survive. He was being slowly murdered whilst they all stood by helplessly.

He knew very little about the end when it came. At intervals, even in the semi-conscious state, he was violently roused in jerky spasms of pain and then he relapsed in to deep stupor.

Sybil and Josie sat either side of his bed, hardly able to stay awake for they had both been there beside him through the three days. Josie held him and listened to his mutterings, hoping to make sense of something. But it was all nonsense, he was too far gone.

After a very short while, when the breathing was so shallow that they had to listen hard for it, Ned took his last breath. It was a long lasting sigh and Sybil thought it signified that he was at last free of suffering.

Josie cried uncontrollably. Her tiny frame shook again and again. The outpouring of grief was heartrending. Sybil sat there drained unable to show how *she* felt.

Two deaths now and both, she felt, were related to her; but what made it so?

Do I have something hidden in Turpin's by Thomas?

How can I stop this killing?

For a long time she sat alone beside Ned holding the shiny black button in her hand. The one left by the sleeping drunk. She had been pressing it between her fingers. She looked at it closely; then held it to her cheek.

Richard O' Cerne's button. I'm sure of it.

The indistinct pattern; it's off his black coat.

An idea was forming in her mind. A plan to discover once and for all.

She had not seen or heard of the man since her return from Mrs Maisy's over two weeks ago, but making contact with him was not so difficult. Once she had decided to confront him the means of doing so appeared readily. By chance; as if he had been called, the boy Clem Applebee appeared sauntering along near the tavern.

She thought about the letter; and his comments angered her all over again.

'*You are in no immediate danger whilst I am close*'.

Such an overblown opinion of himself.

"Your life is in danger," she shouted out aloud and Clem turned towards her.

"What does he know?" She'd turn the tables on this arrogant fellow.

'Rest assured...'

Her anger boiled over. "Well I'm not... assured"

"Tell him I'll meet but on my terms." Clem stood back against the wall. Sybil's fury was evident, it overflowed.

"Tell him to meet me at Bilfon's field. You'll know where that is Clem. Back of Tyburn. Tell him to meet me there after dark. Tell him to have his wits about him," she said quickly. She looked at the boy who seemed reluctant to leave.

Finally he slipped away; hesitating as he turned the corner out of the yard, as if there was something he wanted to say but didn't have the courage.

As he disappeared in to the crowds Sybil stared out over the empty yard.

How can I ever replace Ned?

She need not have worried. Others close by, were also bent on finding a solution for her problem. Before Ned's body was cold.

From across the cobbled yard Strutt of the Cock Pit shambled over, his head always drooped as if he was looking for lost coins between the cobbles.

"Commiserations Miss Sybil," he wiped his ever-dripping nose on a sleeve. "If you're after a replacement for your dead Foreman...." he paused and lifted his eyes to stare.

"I'm available to 'elp you out."

"I'll keep that in mind Strutt."

She could hardly bare to look at the man.

The next offer of help was more welcomed. John Dutch, an Upright Man but one who had shown himself trustworthy.

"My Betsy was talkin, Miss Sybil, and she says I was to help, if you're wantin.'"

Sybil looked up at the tall man with the droopy moustache. He was another of the criminal gang leaders but one she had a fondness for. John Dutch was, she thought, an honourable man.

CHAPTER NINE
SEALED WITH A KISS

William Chasemeet's servant, dressed in a green livery similar to that of the bank staff stood at the door holding out an invitation to supper. Richard looked at the young man questioningly.

How did they find me here?

Only a few weeks after his visit to the Bank of England, Chasemeet had discovered where he lived. Despite Richard's best efforts his cover had been exposed. Did they also know about Clem's association with him?

Clem was presently employed at Chasemeet's private residence, and would be in danger if a connection was made between them.

A far greater concern was that Chasemeet had not hidden his dislike for Richard.

And it was mutual.

Richard was reminded of the droopy wet bottom lip which sprayed spittle every time he spoke. Why am I invited to his house when he could hardly bring himself to speak to me?

What was the man's motive?

Chasemeet lived in the select area of London beyond White Hall in a town house on Charles Street. It was a noisy one hour carriage journey for Richard. He picked up his carriage away from the rented accommodation in Cheapside, although such security measures were hardly worth the effort since his lodging was now known about.

Clem must be warned of the danger, but that would not be easy. Richard had already told him to stay away from their Cheapside lodgings, unless there was something urgent to impart.

The boy was on his own territory. Cheapside was his world. He knew this area of the city so well he could virtually disappear without trace only to reappear miles away like magic. Like a rodent he could scurry through back allies and over roof tops, through backyards and even inside lengthy adjoined roof spaces without the house dwellers ever being aware.

"Rats are noisy tonight," the householder might declare from the warmth and safety of a living room. That meant that Clem Applebee had passed through; just *like* a rat he would scamper through his territory unseen and almost unheard.

Richard smiled to himself. Boy's safer in the rookery than I.

Richard's thoughts went to Sybil, and he was still puzzled why the Tavern had become the target for so much sabotage. He knew about the ale being contaminated and the rat in the bread and the water. Whoever was behind it was making a determined attempt to put her out of business.

He knew very well she did not trust him, and it hurt his pride more than anything.

However if it was generally thought he was to blame, the real culprit might get careless; then Dick O' Cerne would be ready to make some useful connections.

In the meantime Richard could only dream of having a little familiarity with this remarkable woman.

His thoughts returned to their encounter at the lake and he dreamed a different ending to that meeting.

As the carriage sped on through the odorously noisy streets he leaned back and imagined a degree of intimacy wholly undeserved.

'Why Mistress Sybil I did not expect to find you here and in such a captivating situation. May I join you?'

'Well isn't that what you contrived,' she smiles as if he is not entirely unwelcomed.

'Don't you find the water a little cold? Your goose bumps are quite.... beguiling.'

'Not at all; but if you would pass me my clothes.'

'How clear the water is Miss Sybil, I can see right to the bottom, I can even see your toes.'

She blushes and he suddenly feel guilty at causing her discomfort.

'If you please Sir, my clothes?'

She stretches forward with her arm and he grabs her hand, but she's so quick. She catches him off balance and he tumble forward with much ungainly splashing. For a moment he is submerged but through the shimmering clearness he sees her distinctly.

So graceful through water; like a lissom nymph, I should think.

He forgets and takes a breath.

He surfaces choking and spluttering from the lake, and she laughs, and it sounds like the merriment a girl might have with an intimate friend.

Richard's fantasy fades and he is driven back to the reality of his present bumpy journey.

The sort of well organised household one might expect of a Director in the Bank of England. Chasemeet was a wealthy man and without the encumbrance of a wife and children he had surrounded himself in complete and utter luxury. It was a typical double fronted town house in an elegant tree-lined avenue. His neighbours, thought Richard, would be people like himself; bankers, lawyers and the like.

"My dear fellow,"

He was welcomed in to the library by Chasemeet. Still that slightly condescending tone as if the man was dealing with a subordinate, but there was a slight difference. He assumed a degree of intimacy between them. As if the knowledge of their shared undertaking allowed a familiarity which, Richard felt, was unwelcomed and completely at odds with their last meeting.

"So good of you to come and it will give me an opportunity to make amends."

"Make amends sir, whatever for?"

"An officer of the Bank of England in the performance of his duty conducts himself with a degree of detachment not calculated to encourage friendship and I am seriously in mind to repair my behaviour towards you."

"Lead on Sir, lead on." What a mouthful of rubbish, thought Richard.

The man's endeavours to show himself in a different light did not extend to his dress. Chasemeet's adjustment to being off-duty amounted to little more than loosening his ruff and a removal of his official black coat. The waistcoat was the same uniform grey and his pants and stocking looked as if he had been wearing them all day long. The real difference was in his fussiness and the manner in which he constantly danced attention; patting an arm, gathering Richard up and leading him towards the library.

It was a long, poorly lit room with pools of candle-light between armchairs. At the fireplace a servant tended the blazing fire.

To Clem Applebee's credit he gave no sign of noticing Richard.

The drab little man danced attention around him with such eagerness; his bottom lip dribbled alarmingly.

"I believe you have met Dr Medici Dearnought?"

A feeling of dread swept over Richard. This meeting had been contrived to disadvantage him.

He had walked into a trap.

He'd not seen the Doctor sitting reading in the back of the room and Dearnought had made no effort to *be* seen.

"We have indeed met," said Dearnought, "how good to see you again my boy."

To Chasemeet he said; "I shared with Richard one of those defining moments in a Physician's vocation when he is called upon to arbitrate on behalf of the almighty and ultimately, reluctantly sometimes, to execute his will."

"Indeed Indeed," said Chasemeet frowning.

"And I think he was greatly moved by it. Where you not Richard?"

"Yes well, no details if you please Doctor," said Chasemeet hurriedly. "I have no stomach for matters of your calling."

"You *were* greatly moved, were you not Richard?"

"Indeed I was sir."

Richard took a while to consider the facts. These two were acquainted, but what was their common interest?

Dearnought is the fixer he provides a service for Chasemeet and he is here to deliver.

Something…. My head perhaps; I'm getting to be a nuisance?

Chasemeet was aware of Richard's mission. Dearnought, by association, must also be aware.

"William cannot stomach matters of a clinical nature; so in the interest of his well- being we may need to curb our discussions on bodily matters."

Richard was relieved to hear this but was hardly listening. His mind was still calculating the purpose of this meeting.

If it were just a matter of my disposal, it could be done in the rookery at any time.

Far greater risk in bringing me here.

He wondered for a moment where in the household was his young friend. Clem had been sent away from the fireplace with a sharp word for taking an extremely long time to tidy the coals.

"Come and sit over here Richard. I had a consultation today with a quite remarkable woman. She wanted me to tell her the sex of her next child and when she should conceive to be sure of getting a male child."

Richard obediently sat next to Dearnought and without speaking conveyed his interest.

"It matters greatly that she gives her husband a son and with three daughters already she has real cause for concern."

If they don't just want to be rid of me they must be after something; information perhaps.

"Strike me sir, how can you possibly tell her that; It's like looking in to her future."

Dearnought leaned forward in his chair and his calm was replaced by an eagerness.

"I've studied her astral plain and the balance of her body's humours. You see Richard," he raised his arm; fist clenched in Richard's face, "all there is to know about my patient is contained within her mind." He pointed to his own fist.

"And her mind….," he looked directly in to Richard's eyes, "is a microcosm of the universe. If I study her life force so far as it has gone, it will signify what is likely to happen in the future."

Dearnought's calm composure returned but the point wasn't lost on Richard.

He's telling me he can read my mind.

The room was warm and Richard would have liked to remove his coat and stock. He allowed his eyes to droop. He listened to the soothing tones of the doctor and sought to find an antagonist on which to focus his mind. He had rehearsed such a manoeuvre.

He found himself focussing on Sybil, but it was not the right sort of distraction.

And there was something else; a familiar, foul-smelling, sickly sweet smell. Noticed before around Dearnought's company.

Intimacy with Sybil wasn't helping. She was no kind of antagonist.

He became aware of other voices in the room, but could not place them. They were standing around, discussing him.

"So you see gentlemen I tell my patient what he wants to hear and then his own astral aura will do the rest.............. ."

Need to focus…. on something.

"The body must be relaxed before I can explore his mind but it is all quite possible given his cooperation. He must allow me to invade his mind."

Richard rested his head back on the chair helplessly.

"We are almost there, but watch me carefully now." Dearnought leaned towards his subject.

"Richard, you are very thirsty. You are desperate for a drink. In front of you is a pitcher of fresh cold water. Pick it up in both hands and gulp it down Richard. As quickly as you can."

He did as he was told.

"Now look you have spilled it all over your clothes. Take off your ruff and wipe yourself."

Richard tore off his ruff and energetically patted his face and neck.

There was a gentle murmur of admiration from those watching.

"Now you may rest Richard."

Richard was still just in control; he had found his antagonist. Fearless Friar's repulsive face and body odour, leaning over him, breathing in his face.

Thank goodness for Friar thought Richard and he hung on to the nasty illusion.

Dearnought went on.

"You do not remember past events. You are Richard Hamilton and you have no recollection of your previous existence. You are here to serve me; to follow my instructions because you have the utmost admiration for my calling. All that happened in the past is clouded, distant and unimportant, you have become a disciple of Dr Medici Dearnought who you worship."

Richard allowed a smile after which he heard Dearnought again.

"You will sleep now until I wake you. When you wake you will obey my every word; now sleep Richard Hamilton sleep like a child."

This gave Richard a dilemma, for it had been many years since he slept like a child and he wondered how to contrive it to look authentic. The room was so warm and the glow of coals in the hearth helped considerable. He desperately held on to the image of Fearless Friar. He knew also to keep perfectly still for the doctor imagined he had him in a deep trance.

"You see the half closed eyes; that signifies he is well under my control now, but there is one final test which will verify."

The half-closed eyes was a ruse practiced to perfection and now it was very useful for it gave him the opportunity to watch the three men sitting in front of him.

"Very well William you may conduct the test."

"Richard," said Dearnought, "the woman you adore has just entered the room.

She closes the door quietly and is walking across to you.

You can hear the rustle of her clothes.

Smell her perfume.

She is leaning over your shoulder,"

Richard struggled to hold himself in check; he didn't know what was coming next but the voice was so persuasive.

"You feel the brush of her lips against your own,"

He really did feel the brush of her lips, but the next instant was gripped by revulsion. He tried not to recoil, attempting to control his loathing; realising what was happening.

William Chasemeet's tongue had forced its way in to his mouth. He strained to control every muscle of his face; all of which screamed at him to pull away. The bitterness surged up his gullet as he felt the man's tongue slide over the inside of his mouth.

"He has passed the test and you have your reward William. Now let him rest."

Richard wanted to cough and splutter till his mouth was clean. He was desperate to take a large mouthfu of his brandy and swill it round and spit it out but all he could do was sit as still as possible, loathing himself for allowing Chasemeet's saliva to run down his throat; choking him with its sourness.

They paid no further attention. He sat there ignored as if his presence as a party trick was spent. He was now an object of no consequence. He listened to their conversation intently. Clem Applebee, attending to the fire, came and went from time to time.

Richard listened as best he could; hoping to overhear something useful. It might at least make up for suffering the most unpleasant experience.

There were raised voices and disagreements between them. There was humour and calm discussion.

He slept and had no idea for how long but he woke with a blinding head.

"I am sorry for my bad manners Sir. Don't know what you must think."

"Not at all, I am gratified that you should feel so at ease in my company," Chasemeet had replaced Dr Dearnought in the chair opposite.

"I confess I may have dozed myself, it must have been too much of the grape don't you think. Medici had to leave; I do believe the man is never off duty."

"You will I hope apologise to him for me."

"Of course but I am sure there is no need. Any way I feel I have got to know you a lot better now so our meeting has not been wasted."

Richard went pale and the muscles in his jaw drew as taught as a bowstring. Looking at Chasemeet he fought back his thoughts.

That kiss has sealed your fate. I'll kill you, sometime; as sure as night follows day I will kill you.

Another problem troubled Richard. In the darkest recess of his mind another voice resonated. There had been someone else in the room, a fourth person. He tried to drag the memory to his conscious mind.

***

Sybil held the bundle she had removed from right at the back of her clothes cupboard. It was wrapped in a white sheet to conceal the contents from a casually inquiring eye. She laid a coat and breeches, cotton stockings, shirt and waistcoat on the bed. They were all coloured the darkest grey. Even the man's wide brimmed hat was the colour of darkness. From inside the hat she removed a grey silk scarf which she wound around her head. It had been many years since she had pinned up her hair in such a way that it was completely concealed under the scarf. It worked perfectly well. She smiled realising she had not lost the technique; only her eyes showed through.

Standing six feet tall and dressed for the obscurity of the night, she achieved a formidably sinister figure. A highway robber would have looked similar and would have been given a wide berth by casual travellers. Perhaps that was what her father wished for her; to be a dark knight of the open road.

In the old livery stables, once a busy place when the tavern was used as a coaching stop for the mail, there were store rooms and a brewery, but a   section was still in use for its original purpose. The horses of guests were still stabled here. There was a powerful smell of heavily soiled hay pervading. Sybil kept an ostler here who tended the visiting mounts and supposedly kept the stalls mucked out. She thought he was an idle fellow, a waste of space and he wasn't permitted near Sam Black's private stable. In a partitioned-off section there was a separate stall; the private accommodation of Sam Black. The horse was a sturdy stallion, bought for Sybil by her father when she was a child. Sam Black had grown old with Sybil but he was still exercised regularly and always excited by the promise of a run. In the receding evening light, he was led out of the side door of the yard backing on to other properties in Honey Lane. A little ally led east away from the tavern and on to fields and pastures which separated the city from the Moor Fields. In the gloom of the early evening Sybil was indistinguishable from many other solitary riders using the road and her appearance did not invite an approach from others. There was slow traffic until she crossed the Islington road. After that it was across country where Sam Black could gallop. They flew like the wind across Conduit Fields crossing Tottenham Turnpike before taking a circuitous route towards Bilfont's Farm. Dropping down on to Love Lane she turned on to the Tyburn road. It was very dark now but her night vision was good and she had no trouble picking out hedgerows and ditches. It was a long time since they had journeyed together for any purpose other than the sheer joy of a chase and it felt good. The pair of pistols in her saddle bags were a present from her father. Not many fathers would have kitted out a daughter with all the accoutrements for highway robbery. Sybil screamed into the wind as she remembered the exhilaration of the chase for a coach and the ever present danger of being shot at by a coach guard. Sybil had been a disappointment to Turpin for not adopting a career on the highway.

Old man Bilfont, who owned Tyburn, might have something she wanted but she had to reach the hanging place before she could be sure. The gallows was a triangular affair. Three upright posts supported three horizontal beams. There was room to hang eight people on each of the beams. The ground around the 'triple tree' was a large flat space of impacted dirt. On one side Bilfont had built a wooden gallery. It was a rickety affair. When full it creaked and groaned and threatened to collapse under a heavy load of spectators. On a good day hundreds of people would attend a hanging, many walking all the way up from Newgate where condemned prisoners started their final journey. It was considered a celebratory occasion with tradesmen selling food, drink and sweets. Peddlers sold gruesome toy models of the gallows. The spectators, if they could read, could buy a newssheet describing the gruesome crimes of the accused and, even before the hanging took place, they could read how the prisoner conducted himself in the final minutes of his life.

There was an old cart parked to the side, normally hitched to a pair of horses. It had been converted to provide a platform across its top. Bilfont normally kept the cart in his yard but on this occasion it was still drawn up to the side of the triple tree; left there since the hanging on Monday; no time to move it. Normally the bodies were taken down as soon as the hanging was over. Seldom did they stay on the gibbet for long after they had hanged. If not claimed by relatives, the first call was by the assistants from Surgeons Hall who were allowed to remove bodies for dissection.

There was one body remaining on the gibbet. He must have been a murderer, for his remains showed had been clothed in a tarred shirt and hung in an iron body shaped cage. It creaked and swung gently in the breeze and had already begun to smell despite the coating of tallow.

What Sybil planned was audacious; foolhardy even, but she was so driven by a determination; a kind of madness to win through and find the truth. Nothing less than having this man defenceless, would serve her purpose. She knew this place very well. As a child her Pa had often brought her up here to watch the spectacle of death and often to say goodbye to his old friends. For Sybil, Tyburn was an unhealthy place. The whole image of judicial punishment somehow being connected with entertainment was unnatural.

With some difficulty and a little assistance from Sam Black she manoeuvred the cart back under the gibbet. It never occurred to Sybil, for one moment, that what she was about to do, was impracticable. Although it was usually the horses which, kicked in to action, drove the platform away from the haltered prisoner, she knew there was a slight slope conveniently prepared to facilitate ease of movement. The cart would run easily enough. She found a spare rope. After a hanging they were usually prized by the crowd, being cut up and sold by the piece, but she knew where the hangman kept a spare. Sybil hung it alongside the iron cage and led Sam Black away behind the spectator gallery.

By the time Richard arrived the place of execution was deserted. But it looked curiously as if all had been prepared for a hanging. He tethered his own horse and walked around.

She watched him. As she had hoped, he was unfamiliar with his surroundings.

He's wondering why here. Of all places why meet here.

It wouldn't occur to him not to trust me.

Insufferable; patronising; worthless villain.

Out of curiosity he climbed on to the cart and mounted the platform. He looked at the iron caged corpse and visibly recoiled from the smell of rotting flesh. He looked around at the stand and she could see he was imagining how it must be on a hanging day. He raised one arm to grasp the rope high above the noose.

It was then that Sybil moved. In silence she floated like a passing shadow to stand, unnoticed, beside him. She slipped the noose around his neck and jumped pushing the cart at the same time.

It rolled so slowly away and Richard had no time to do anything but grab the rope with both hands to prevent the noose from tightening around his neck. He reach out with one hand to grab the stinking copse but it swung away. Richard was strong and it was no effort for him support himself with his hands; whilst he found a way to haul himself up. But there was no way up; the gibbet had been designed to prevent just that eventuality.

Sybil stood silently like a dark shadow her face still masked. Richard could see no more than just her shadow in the light from a clouded moon. He twisted and swayed around trying to find a purchase.

"This is for Ned Church my foreman and for Thomas Sharingham," she spoke. "When I was a child I was forced to watch people die here; I thought it was the worst possible way to be killed particularly when their hands got free and they hung sometimes for an hour before they tired."

"You've got this all wrong," he struggled furiously. "I didn't know about Ned Church."

Sybil was calm.

"I used to think to myself: you're only four feet from the ground if you could just stretch out you might touch it with your toe and save yourself, but they never did.

"My note, didn't you understand?"

"Understood perfectly. You succeeded in making a fool of me. What I don't understand is why. Perhaps you could tell me why you want to destroy me, why you want the tavern?"

"I don't but I have a task to do." His agitation was making him swing wildly.

"And now it is done Mr."

"Trying to protect you," Richard was far from calm.

"Fearless Friar says the same; trying to protect you."

Richard tried to loosen the noose but it simply tightened.

"Goodbye Mr Cerne or whatever you prefer to be called." Sybil stepped backwards to turn away.

"Thomas was my good friend," he was yelling now. "We were students together." Sybil stopped and stared up at the man hanging on the rope.

"Tell me more."

It was as if Richard suddenly realised he had met his match and would have to do a good deal more to convince this determined woman.

"I came to find out why Thomas was killed."

She drew her small knife.

They sat on a grassy bank, quite close together, on the edge of a field behind the crossroads and far enough away from the gibbet so as not to suffer the stench from the putrefying body.

"Were you really prepared to let me hang?" Richard looked closely in to her face.

She played with the knife.

"I was prepared for anything," she said mysteriously.

"So was I," he said smiling at her. "But this little friend," he pulled at his own sleeve, "would just not come loose." A blade appeared in his hand as if by magic.

"These gadgets are always going wrong." He looked at her with a glum expression and rubbed the rope marks around his neck.

She smiled at him nervously; with the relief and sheer madness of it all.

They talked for a long time; well in to the night.

Sybil shared her concerns about the tavern; the happenings there and eventually about her love for the man Thomas Sharingham.

Richard explained about the assignment he had been given and his meetings with Dr Dearnought and William Chasemeet.

"Thomas discovered a plot which threatens to bring down the government. He was killed for the knowledge he had. Dearnought and Chasemeet are involved but they are not alone."

"So what is the connection with the Tavern? Why is someone trying to sabotage Turpin's?"

"Perhaps there is no connection."

Richard was revealing his innermost thoughts now; as if they were partners, confidants, in the scheme.

"Perhaps the connection is that Thomas was killed on your doorstep because it was assumed he deposited something with you. Something he wanted to hide."

Sybil shook her head silently.

Perhaps it was thought he confided in you; that he told you something about the plot."

"I don't know."

"There may be something you don't even realise you know. Did he ever talk about his work or matters of concern to him?"

"There was never time for that sort of thing," she blushed in the darkness, thinking about her intimacy with Thomas.

Richard had a new respect for the maid of Turpin's but this admission made him think about his own feelings.

"I'm sorry, I'm pressing, and I've no right to do so," he touched her arm. "I don't want to… hurt you ….not again"

"Might Thomas have left something in the tavern?"

Richard nodded, "If you find anything? A list of names or letters or notes of a meeting."

She nodded.

There was a long stillness between them, each deep in their own thoughts.

Sybil finally broke the silence.

"What sort of agent allows himself to be caught on the gallows?" she asked mischievously.

"One so trusting that he'd not imagine being hoodwinked by a," he looked at Sybil, "a mere slip of a girl."

"Is that how you think of me?" She bit her lower lip and was glad it was so dark.

Richard shook his head. "No not really. But I am becoming one of your greatest admirers."

He leaned on one elbow and looked in to her eyes

"What sort of woman travels round the countryside, in the dark, dressed as a man and behaving like a highway robber?"

"One who has become accustomed to sorting out her own problems."

They collected their horses and made off. Sybil's thoughts returned to the problems of the tavern, how to replace Ned Church and how best she could support his widow who still carried his child.

There was a shared plan now; the outline of scheme which might provide some answers to why Turpin's was being targeted and who by.

Sybil had a feeling of relief. The hurt had disappeared and there was a sense of a burden being shared.

***

CHAPTER TEN
HIDDEN SECRETS

Nothing would be done in haste. The next few weeks were a busy time for Sybil. Ned's absence was a great loss in the Tavern and Josie was inconsolable. Sybil felt the loss of both. Losing Ned made her realise how much she had relied upon him. He was the only other person who could run the tavern. He knew about ordering, paying the tradesmen and keeping a watchful eye on the staff making sure they were not slacking or stealing. He had been totally loyal; he had been in the pay of no other master and his quiet unassuming manner made it possible for him to deal with the most difficult situations. Ned could anticipate problems and thus get on with planning solutions. He even had credibility with the tavern's lawless customers. Out in the rookery only the Upright Men ruled, but in the tavern it was Turpin's rules which counted and Ned like Sybil had been the authority of Turpin's.

But it wasn't just the loss of Ned. Josie was a victim too. She had always been a confidant; someone with whom Sybil could talk as she might to a sister. They chattered about women matters, dress and gossip amongst the fraternity of downtrodden women who made up the population of the rookery.

"It ain't fair Miss Sybil that's what it ain't," Josie had said recently. "Er ole man put 'er out on the streets 'cos 'e was too lazy to work; when she come 'ome e beat 'er till she turned. Now she's gonna 'ang for cutting is throat." They both knew the woman who would make the one way cart trip to Tyburn to hang from the gallows for the entertainment of the crowd.

"It's nothing to do with justice Josie."

Sybil had something else to get on with. She planned to search Turpin's from top to bottom. If there was something hidden she was determined to find it.

She started in the Den which had been her father's. There was an oak cupboard, set back in to the wall. She had never seen the back of it. So cluttered. It had never been used for clothes; more a junk cupboard. It remained full of paper; invoices, rolled up maps, the walking cane old Turpin favoured, smelly clothing, stubs of candle, ledgers written in by her father; she recognise his ugly scrawl. She pulled it all out on the floor and thought it might be a good plan to burn the lot.

The futility of searching for something Thomas Sharingham might have hidden gradually occurred to her. Thomas would never have had the time to hide something in this room.

There was nothing of value. Her enthusiasm deserted her. She dumped it all in a sack to burn.

It was a deep cupboard and she could hardly touch the back.

Her finger tips brushed over the solid oak back and she nearly missed the flat headed iron pin. It was a nail, except that, gripped between her finger nails, it pulled out and became a handle.

She pulled and a piece of board came away. Sybil lit a candle and beyond the false back old Turpin's secrets were revealed.

There was one ledger; more like a diary, with entries in Turpin's hand.

Why was this more precious than those in the front of the cupboard?

Sybil read her father's printed scrawl. He had written down scant details of events over the past five years. It was a recording about his dealings with folk. Some were his employees, visitors, local worthies, public figure, Upright Men.

Why did he do this?

It was a massive indictment on his criminal life style. Yet it showed a side to the man she never knew existed. Her father had kept a diary.

She wandered down into the yard, still thinking about her father. Remembering a childhood deaf and dumb friend Freddie Trewfell, she was drawn towards the Brewhouse where Freddie's father, was still in charge. It was here that she felt closest to the boy. Obadiah was nowhere to be seen. In the corner of the work area, behind a wall of empty hogshead barrels, there was a table and chair. There were sacks of malted barley and hops tidily placed on racks to keep them off the stone floor. On another shelf there was a cask of yeast. On the table Obadiah had chalk and a slate boards. He could not read or write but he could mark up the passage of time for his brews. Each brew had its own slab of slate covered in marks, incomprehensible to anyone but the brewer. Sybil sat in the chair looking for something.

She found it in a drawer. A wooden ball about three inches in diameter. Hard wood and polished by many hands. It was an ornament now but it was also a memento of her childhood. She took her turn to polish it.

"Hello Freddie," she whispered holding it close to her face. "Help me."

From her partially hidden corner she heard the sound of voices.

She listened; it was the cockpit man Strutt and her ostler. They were muttering together over one of the stalls. From her father's secret papers, she knew a good deal more about Strutt now and realised he was a man whose dealings with her father were deep and criminal.

Hard to hear what was being said. She sauntered out towards Sam Black's stall, still polishing the wooden ball in her hands. Seeing her approach Strutt hurried away.

The boy followed her into the stables.

She struggled to remember his name, wanting to address him properly.

"What were you talking with Strutt about?"

She faced him.

The boy stopped quickly. His face coloured red. His lips moved but no words. He was shaking his head.

"Nothing Miss Sybil," he finally managed.

Sybil opened a stable door and looked inside.

"Are they all as fowl smelling as this one?"

She opened another stable door.

"Do you want to continue working here?"

He nodded.

"Then muck out all these stalls before you leave tonight. When it's done come to me and I'll check them." She looked at the boy. "What's your name?"

"Bluw Miss."

"I remember…: your Pa went to the gallows."

"The boy nodded."

"Can you afford to lose your job then Bluw? Your Ma's got a lot of mouths to feed."

The boy nodded again.

"Come to me before you go home. And stay away from Strutt."

When time permitted she called for John Dutch again and requested a meeting with the mysterious Dr Dearnought.

"I want to speak with him again John, will you arrange it?"

Always, she recalled, that faraway look whenever the name of the doctor was mentioned.

"It can be done Miss Sybil if that is what you want."

Just the hint in John Dutch's clipped voice that he did not approve.

The old blood hound continued. "You have always been good to my Betsy and me Miss Sybil; I, we, would not want to see you harmed."

"What are you telling me John; that Dr Medici Dearnought is dangerous?"

John Dutch inhaled Sybil's fragrance of violets and, as if it appeared to clear his mind he spoke sincerely.

"I serve the man because I must, but that don't make the doctor a good feller Miss Sybil,"

She had never seen him like this before; it suggested a divided loyalty. It hinted that John was not entirely a willing servant of the doctor.

"You must give him this note John; but don't let him question you about my reasons."

Her next action was intuitive, given an earlier conversation with the man. Sybil sought him out later in the day, away from his followers in the crowded bar and gave him a little twist of paper.

"You and Betsy can both take this if you wish John. But not too much; it's a tonic." He gave her a funny look.

"On Betsy's finger, like before?"

She nodded and smiled. "It's a tonic John."

No certainty that he understood and she did not care to explain. It contained Dill, Ginger root and an exotic root from the Americas, well known for its aphrodisiac properties.

The task of appointing another foreman seemed fraught with problems. There was no one to discuss it with. Several of the applicants, she felt, were backed by characters like Fearless Friar. Obadiah Trewfell had put his own name forward and she had to manage his hurt feelings.

Sybil felt angry with her own indecisiveness. She felt angry with Richard Hamilton.

"The man has addled my brain," she said to the long mirror in her empty bedroom. When ever she stopped to imagine who she could see in Ned's job she kept seeing Richard. That self-deprecating manner and the smile: and, secretly watching him climb out of the water in the not-so-secret pool - those broad shoulders; such a handsome body.

They had agreed not to meet in the tavern, except as adversaries. Richard was certain there was an organization responsible for all the incidents which had occurred and also a single person controlling it. It would not do for anyone to think they were working together. They had worked out a way to communicate. Clem Applebee was the link. Although he never came in to the tavern, he could often be found in and around the tavern and seemed to turn up in the yard or at the back entrance by the stables just when he was needed. He became the link between them and Sybil looked forward to the little notes she received.

In the evening, long past his going home time young Bluw the Ostler came to find her sitting on the tall chair in the Parlour.

"*Well* boy?"

He stared up at her, whispering his words. He was unfamiliar with this part of the Tavern.

"Finished?"

He nodded.

"Has Strutt been giving you jobs to do?"

The boy nodded again.

"Go home now; we'll talk again in the morning."

She beckoned him leaning forward out of her chair. He stepped closer.

She whispered, "Stay away from Strutt."

***

Dear Miss Sybil

You will be pleased to hear the rope marks are healing well. I have finally mastered the small knife in the sleeve and provided I keep a straight hand when activating the trigger it slides conveniently in to the palm. Should I ever find myself in a predicament similar to our last meeting I am confident of delivering a better performance.

I have taken the liberty of looking at some of the candidates for your replacement foreman. Two of the contenders are definitely in the pay of Upright Men. The best of the bunch seems to be the fellow calling himself Jacobs. At the Rising Sun on the north of the river, he has a good reputation for hard work and a no nonsense approach to his work. He comes well recommended to me. The only drawback might be his missing arm and I suspect that he enjoys, testing the ale he serves. I have watched him in action and he is very capable but has a little of the bully in him. He is the best of the bunch. Perhaps you might give him a trial to see if he suits.

Your Servant

Richard

He makes me laugh Sybil thought.

***

Sybil went down to the stables the next morning. The stalls were spotlessly clean; fresh straw in every loose box. There was no sign of the Ostler, yet he was around somewhere. She walked on down the row to visit Sam Black.

"What are you doing in here boy?" Bluw was scraping the floor; Sam Black was nuzzling him – they were obviously well acquainted.

"You know the rules," Sybil was angry. She raised her voice. "This is out of bounds to everyone including you."

Bluw scampered away without saying a word.

She looked around the stall. He had been busy in here. It smelt as sweet as ever and Sam Black was content.

She and Freddie Trewfell played together around the stable block. It was a favourite spot. She leaned back against the wall whilst Sam Black ate fresh hay from a manger which itself looked as if it had been recently scrubbed clean.

Hide and Seek amongst the stalls was a great game and they both knew every nook and cranny in the yard. On the floor above the stalls there were rooms for guests. Stairs and an outside veranda served as access to the rooms.

The stable was one of the few areas of the Tavern that Thomas Sharingham would have been briefly left on his own.

This is where he could have hidden something.

Above Sam Black's stall, there was a store room and above that, a hatch gave access to the loft.

She smiled to herself. Doubtful she could still get through the hatch as she had when a child.

Where is Clem Applebee when I need him?

***

A week after Richard's letter, another less welcoming one came for Sybil signed by Dr Medici Dearnought.

Dear Miss Turpin

The Dutchman has given me your message. I understand your concerns about Richard Hamilton and I would very much like to help you if I can. It would be best if you came to see me, so that we can discuss this matter. In the meantime I suggest you avoid his company. I already have intelligence which leads me to believe he may have been responsible for the death of your foreman Ned Church. If you would be comfortable to do so, I propose we meet in my rooms at Curzon Street.

Your Friend and confidant
Medici Dearnought

***

Sybil was wary of Dearnought, but this was something she had to do. Richard knew nothing about it and he had warned her to beware the doctor's mesmerising eyes.

Lately she had reason to doubt her own judgment towards the behaviour of people around her. It caused her concern; whether she could trust her own judgment.

There was at least one matter she *could* put right.

"I'd like you to help me look after Sam Black."

Sybil thought Bluw looked just like her childhood friend Freddy Trewfell; baby face, blond hair, blue eyes.

"He seems to have taken a liking to you."

Bluw grinned and nodded furiously. They walked towards Sam Black's stall.

"There was something else Bluw," Sybil had waited till they were in the stall and Sam Black stood between them.

"It's about Strutt."

Bluw's face became serious.

"I don't want you to take orders from Strutt. If he asks you to do anything, I want you to come and tell me," she smiled gently. "You won't get in to trouble. I promise"

It was apparent from her father's diary that even he did not trust Strutt.

***

"Miss Turpin," He disarmed her with his smile which, despite the disfiguring scar giving him a lopsided look, she warmed to.

She avoided his eyes; at least just a glance at his face, curious to observe the crystal clear, piercing black eyes she had been warned of. They sat in a drawing room and he talked about everything except the subject on her mind.

"You'll have noticed a number of patients as you came in: all are wealthy enough to wait whilst we talk together."

His manner and warm smile, enjoying his own humour, gave Sybil the feeling that she was his foremost concern, no one more important; that she was granted all the time in the world.

"My most deserving patients are in the hostels, I would not keep them waiting for they are most worthy of my time."

Richard had warned her about his work with *fallen women*, as Dearnought called them, and she had to be careful not to give away how much she knew."

"I was sorry to hear about the demise of your man. It must feel to you as if someone has a vendetta against the tavern?" He smiled and patted her hand as if to encourage her.

"Doctor Dearnought…,"

"Please dear lady, may I presume to call you Miss Sybil and then you'll feel comfortable to use my first name."

There was always that edge the conversation; he made no effort to disguise. The superior opinion he had of himself; it was plainly patronising and she was thankful for it. It served as a reminder of just how unpleasant this man really was.

"Dr Medici" she started and he smiled unctuously at her chosen address.

"I must discover what Richard Hamilton wants in the Tavern. I am sure he is responsible for the problems. The poisoned well, contaminated food and now the death of Ned."

He listened patiently.

"What do you think he is seeking; something from my father's day perhaps?"

Dearnought shook his head gravely. "Almost certainly something from when Thomas Sharingham visited."

"But what Dr? Thomas left nothing behind. I hardly think he would have trusted leaving anything in Turpin's."

"Let me…, send someone to help you."

The hand was patting Sybil's again. She decided an outpouring of emotion would be a good response.

"I just don't know doctor," She shook and wailed at him, her head bent, looking down in to her lap. Sybil felt her performance was going well, after all there was an element of truth in everything she had said and the frustration of Ned's loss was still with her.

But it was about to get more difficult.

"Look up my dear." Dearnought lifted her chin with his finger.

She offered her tearstained face. He frowned and then held her with piercing deep blue eyes.

But he failed to penetrate her mind.

Her tears and the emotion, she felt, stayed between them like a miasmic barrier. She was safe from his power but hardly realised it was so.

"You are a woman of great strength of character Miss Sybil," He was now sitting back at ease in his chair. If you were ever free of the burden of Turpin's I predict you would succeed and be an asset to any enterprise you might engage yourself with." Medici Dearnought's voice went on. It was entrancing Sybil thought; no matter the circumstances he had the skill to relax her and make her feel good about herself. "Leave this matter with me. I shall see he bothers you no more."

"No more killing sir," she pleaded, "I will have no more deaths at my Tavern."

"As you say Miss Sybil," he sounded like a concerned parent.

"But let me ask something in return."

She was silent.

"That you visit some of my hostels and see how you think I might better manage my work with the poor and unfortunate women of the streets."

***

Leaving the doctor's private rooms Sybil was glad to see the light of day again. She wasn't so familiar with this genteel part of the city but as arranged she made her way in the direction of Hyde Park and mixed with the well-bred gentry promenading along the walks.

No doubt in her mind the street urchin travelling some distance in front, had permitted her to see him and she was content to follow. A lady walking alone cannot stop, turn, or dally, it was behaviour which would be misunderstood, so she relaxed in the custody of her young guide. She arrived on the edge of parkland where Richard was waiting.

The sudden joy seeing him again felt like a burden lifted. The image of Medici Dearnought faded and was replaced by an excitement hard to disguise.

When it *finally* happened the manner of their meeting was so restrained; yet it felt like the height of a passionate affair. She curtsied, he removed his hat, bowed and they sat, a short distance apart, on a wooden bench over-looking the lake.

"You smell like a lady's boudoir," she said quietly to the handsomely disguised young man; whilst trying to keep the excitement out of her voice.

Richard replaced his hat and replied.

"From the French I believe, literally translated, a room for sulking in, but I was trying to please you my Lady," he answered with a smile.

She told him everything about her meeting with the doctor.

He listened without commenting.

After a while Richard suggested they move and promenade along the walks; like other couples were doing. It was a walk through tree lined avenues where the meadow grass had been cut short and beds of flowers had been planted.

Richard took her arm and placed it through his.

She relaxed. It felt blissful; right up there with swimming in her secret pool and riding with Sam Black.

"You see like others are doing,"

Sybil frowned. Was he implying she didn't know how to behave?

Secretly she enjoyed promenading like other normal couples.

Sybil's confidence grew; She managed a nod and smile of acknowledgement when another couple passed by.

Out of the hearing of others his manner became more intimate.

"It would serve no purpose if I were to ask you…..?"

"None at all," she interrupted. "Leave it all to you?" She shook her head, "I can't do that."

"Sybil, he's an evil man."

"I won't be left out Richard; you must understand that."

They both glanced up to see that Clem Applebee twenty yards ahead had entered in to the spirit of the occasion. With one hand on his hips, the boy was swaggering along imitating the gentry.

"I'll kick his backside," said Richard.

"Don't do that," said Sybil shaking her head. "He's rediscovered his childhood."

Richard had his doubts, but it gave him an idea; a solution to a problem worrying him.

"I do believe you are better disposed towards the boy?"

Sybil smiled at Clem's antics and nodded.

"*Would* you take him back in to the tavern?"

There was a long silence. Richard reckoned he could hear her thinking.

"Send him back to me then," she said suddenly. "He could help me with the hunt for evidence."

Richard nodded.

"Keep him nearby. He'll know where to find me at any time."

"You think I'm in danger then?" Sybil turned toward him.

"Dearnought is a middle man, but a dangerous one, a fixer for corrupt wealthy clients. But he isn't the brains behind this criminal scheme. I must play along with his game to get to the mastermind."

"There seems to be a lot I don't know about the criminal scheme?"

"Better if you don't know," he said softly.

As they promenaded along the path Richard did a daring thing; an outrageous breach of social etiquette. He reached out an arm and slipped it around her waist.

It went unnoticed, except by Sybil who moved closer and felt her heart beat faster.

***

It was a week before Medici Dearnought made contact with Richard again.

The Doctor assumed a degree of control over him and his attitude had changed significantly. He no longer made a show of admiration for Richard's free spirit. He pretended no interest in Richard's opinions. He still invited his company but in his presence Richard felt treated more like a favoured servant. He responded accordingly; behaving as if he were in the doctor's power; asking Dearnought's opinion when he would rather have run him through with the steel blade of his Frobisher.

"Well dear fellow I think you should change your lodgings," said the doctor.

"I have spare rooms in Curzon Street."

"Oh I couldn't possibly impose."

Damn the man.

"I insist; your accommodation is enough to make you feel glum and on any account I have an idea that you might care to employ yourself on my account Richard."

"Of course Medici anything I can do to help," through his gritted teeth.

Dearnought had stopped listening.

"I have many business interests across the city and need a person I can trust to inspect them regularly. A loyal fellow like yourself." He patted Richard on the shoulder.

Richard's struggle to control his anger went unnoticed.

Dearnought described his business interests as palaces of pleasure, where patrons could gamble, seek the services of a prostitute or simply partake in rather more passive entertainment.

"Naturally you will want to sample the goods on offer," Dearnought chuckled at his own humour and then, warming to it further, "let's say it is obligatory for you to sample the goods on offer; Ha ha."

"Should I like that Medici, do you think?" said Richard hesitantly. Dearnought laughed so much at his own joke that his wig slipped sideways.

"Dear me yes but I wonder if you have the strength to keep it up. Ha ha ha ho ho."

***

Clem arrived at Turpin's through the back yard.

"I've come to help out Miss,"

"Do you mind Clem; coming back I mean?"

"Lordy no Miss. I do all sorts now; coming back is easy," he hesitated as if trying to get an idea straight in his head. "Bit bothered about Master Richard coping without me though."

Sybil smiled inwardly. What a change in the boy.

"Thing is Mr Applebee. I have a spare room up there," she pointed to the store room on the balcony. "If you like we could tidy it up and you could use it when you want."

"What…. my own room in Turpin's?"

Sybil nodded. "You could just come and go when you like."

They walked towards the balcony stairs.

***

The Madam sat at the table opposite Richard. She had laid out all her books for his inspection. She had the look of an aged hag yet Richard guessed she was no more than thirty years. Tidily dressed too, and the shawl looked like a quality garment or it had in its day.

It took him a moment to realise that she had been a beauty, but she breathed the sweet odour of Gin. In fact Mistress Geneva pervaded everything in the little room. Her bloodshot eyes and cheeks were sunken, hair dishevelled and she gazed at Richard through pale lifeless eyes which hardly focused. On the table an uncorked stone bottle and a grimy cup. A wooden box stood beside it and she pushed it toward Richard.

"It's all there every penny of it,"

Richard looked at her intently.

"I don't do a turn," a spark of defiance in her voice, "but if you want someone I'll call a girl; I am sure you're allowed to take your pick of the house."

He shook his head. She was well spoken this one and he wondered about her story. Mostly the brothel keepers were hard rough types. He puzzled how she managed to control her girls. He looked at the account book; the entries all written in a neat cultured hand.

Richard had visited high class houses across London where gentlemen of means, it was not cheap, could gamble, fornicate, take a massage or simply spy on others doing likewise. It was not cheap prices started at three guineas.

"I'm not always in this state," she said as if it was suddenly important that he should know. "Just sometimes," Her voice trailed off, her eyes closed and she held her head in both hands.

"You don't seem suited to this," she looked at him sharply but a knock on the door interrupted.

A young nymph put a head round and peered up at Richard with bedroom eyes. She handed the Madam a card still looking at him. The card was read with some care. The Madam went across the room to a wooden panel on the wall and slid back a tiny shutter giving view to another room. She peered through then nodded to the girl.

"Six guineas," she said without emotion.

"And take Millicent with you," she commanded.

To Richard "You'll find nothing to complain about in this establishment Mr,"

She poured herself more drink.

"You didn't answer my question."

"I'm not here of choice," she replied hardly able to keep the derision out of her voice.

"Tell me about yourself," he sensed that here was someone who might talk to him.

"And get thrown out on to the streets," there was defiance in her eyes.

"You just don't seem the type," he pressed her gently.

"The type," she stared at him angrily.

"You really don't know do you; you have no idea how it works." She leaned across to Richard and with the palm of her hand she held his cheek whilst she looked closely in to his eyes. "You've not been touched by the man, so why are you here?"

"Touched by him?"

"You must know what I mean, that's how it starts with the touch of his hand, and then he looks into your soul and takes something of it away."

"He hasn't touched my soul but he tried."

"Then you should leave whilst you still have the free will to do so," she sipped at her cup of gin.

"What's your name?"

"I was Dora Melplash. Until mother died; until the good Doctor Dearnought stole my inheritance and," she faltered, "and now you'll tell him and I'll be out on the streets."

"No you won't. I'll not tell Dearnought anything."

He could tell she wanted to trust him.

"He was treating my mother until she died; I think he killed her with his potions. She bequeathed him our house and most of the estate—for the benefit of his charity."

"The Homes for Destitute Women?" She nodded.

"He said, 'I am sure it was never your dear mother's intention to see you imperilled by the terms of her will.' "I started work for him in one of the homes."

"And then?"

"I became more and more under his power. No free-will to refuse him.

When finally the spell was broken, I woke up to discover I was here."

The true horror of Dearnought's business empire became clear to Richard. The man seduced vulnerable women to steal their fortunes. Then at a time of his choosing, he committed murder to collect the fortune. His empire extended to the 'Palaces of Pleasure', such as this which Dora Melplash ran for him. Across London there were also the hostels for vulnerable women and Dora was able to enlighten him about their connection. The hostels were an outward face of respectability and gained the man his reputation as a benefactor; a saviour of lost souls. However the most frightening aspect was his ability to ensnare those around him and bend them to his will. With his magnetic power to capture the minds of vulnerable people he controlled his victims; to make them behave in a way which would serve his sinister purposes. Dora had been such a victim and although she was no longer held. She was still a slave trapped by a different evil.

For Dora it was too late. Even having regained her wits she was a prey to the malignant curse of Mistress Geneva. A wicked adversary. Gin was thought by the population at large to be a panacea for all the illnesses and diseases known to man. The oily sweet smelling liquor could cure everything from scurvy to the plague. It warded off old age and it was declared to be an aphrodisiac. From eye disease to the cure for dropsy; there was nothing it could not do. The clear pungent spirit which dripped from the distillers vessel burned the gullet and seared its way through the organs of the body was prescribed, even by doctors of good repute. It was the wonder drug; an elixir for a better life.

CHAPTER ELEVEN
THE REFUGE

"Oh where is that bloody man when I need him?"

Josie Church had been screaming with labour pains for the past half hour. Her wretchedness had turned to anger towards Ned who had left her to endure this on her own.

"We've to manage without Ned, you know that very well," said Sybil mopping her brow.

There were two neighbours in the room with Josie and Sybil and although it was customary to have three or four gossiping women to act as witnesses to the birth, Sybil thought she had enough and anyway she wanted women who would be useful. One of them had built up the fire and the heat in the room made them all perspire. It was airless but everyone knew that the odours from the river were the cause of disease, so she had closed the shutters and they just suffered. Boiling water was brought up in a cauldron and having first checked that it really had boiled, the pot boy was told to leave it on the landing. The room chosen for lying-in had been thoroughly cleaned for the occasion; scrubbed from top to bottom in fact and Sybil had left nothing to chance. She had picked the best room in the tavern and turned a guest out in the process.

"Mark my words you're going to have this baby normally," she'd said to Josie,"

The midwife arrived at the door. It was still very early in the morning; several hours before sunrise.

"Wait," screamed Sybil before the midwife had chance to enter the room.

"Let me see your hands."

The large creature with a red warty face was stopped from bustling in to the room where she expected to take charge.

Sybil had already vetted her before she was selected and knew that her licence to practice from the Bishop was up to date. This gave very little clue about her competence as a midwife. Sybil had further checked on the woman's credentials by visiting several mothers who'd used her recently, but still she would not let her in.

"Hold them out for me to see."

The woman held out her hands and blustered indignantly.

"Turn them over."

She looked at the fingers. There was dried blood under the woman's cracked and broken nails

"Go and cut your nails and scrub those hands."

The midwife inhaled deeply and seemed to fill the doorway

"I'd rather leave than be spoken too like that," she turned to go. Sybil grabbed her by the shoulder and twisted her round.

"Have you been at the gin?" She leaned forward to smell her breath and then called Jacobs her new foreman.

"Take her down to the scullery to clean up and see she comes straight back." To the midwife she whispered.

"You'll be well paid for your work but mark me well, there'll be nothing if we lose either mother or baby."

Sybil had given in to Josie's demands for all the foolish mumbo jumbo required at the birth. One of Ned's old shirts was tucked under her pillow to ensure her husband shared the pain. She had even found her friend an eagle stone for good luck and slipped it in to the bed; much against her own better judgement. Sybil's own feelings were that success had more to do with skill than superstitious nonsense.

The contractions came faster after the midwife returned to the bedroom and tried re-establish her control. Josie gave way to her instincts and encouraged by Sybil, she roared as the pain of contractions took hold. Sybil stood by unwilling to trust anyone. The two gossips stood either side of the narrow wooden bed, tuttering to one another over the patient. The straw in the mattress had been renewed for this event and Josie was propped up with plenty of pillows.

As the contractions increased in strength so did Josie's cries. The gossips moaned in sympathy matching the volume of noise. More like a cattle market, with all the baying of beasts thought Sybil.

Bag in hand the midwife approached the bed and stood defiantly before her patient. The nine months of pregnancy was considered as a period of illness, and in the mind of the midwife only her expert skill could cure the poorly afflicted patient.

"Well get on with your business," Sybil spoke sharply.

The midwife rolled up her sleeves and greased her hands and arms with duck fat. Advancing toward the patient; her authority was established. As the gossips held up Josie's gown, a cursory examination and she announced I must cut,"

"No," cried Sybil staying the woman's hand, "wait."

Sybil knew she was on dangerous ground now but it was pure intuition which governed her thoughts and actions.

Josie was panting now but there was no sign of tiredness just a determination to deliver. She loudly cursed her husband for not being there and screamed at the gossips for the opposite reason. She raged loudly at everyone in sight including the midwife and Sybil. She was, thought Sybil, a fighter.

"Natural course," hissed Sybil under her breath to the midwife.

Silently with a look of thunder the midwife stood challenged and not liking it one bit. Moments ticked by and Sybil wondered how long she could wait.

"I must cut now," said the midwife defiantly holding her little sharp knife, the only tool she was allowed to use but that which was often the means of destroying life rather than saving it.

"No," said Sybil again, "stay."

Finally Josie gave birth and it happened, easily, gently with each contraction; the baby arrived of its own free will amid the cries of the gossips who behaved as if they had been personally responsible. When the midwife cut the cord with her instrument there was grim relief and satisfaction was shared. Josie had delivered herself a new little Ned. Despite everything she had done it herself.

***

Clem had cleared the box room and made himself a snug little den. He stood outside the room, on the balcony, leaning out across the yard when Sybil came up the stairs.

Together they watched the activity below. Several residents sat smoking pipes on benches. It was no doubt the smell of fresh baked bread which encouraged them to linger rather than be about their business in Cheapside. The well was a meeting place for servants and the gossip was all about Josie's new baby. From the brewhouse crashing noises were testament to a problem Sybil had; persuading Obadiah Trewfell to accept some help. In the stable, Boy Bluw, as she had begun to call him, was letting everyone know he was about and working hard.

"I need help Clem,"

"It's Mr Applebee now Miss," he managed a cheeky smile.

"So it is Mr Applebee.

Jacobs the new foreman walked across the yard and glanced up as he walked towards the parlour door.

"You met the new man?"

Clem nodded. "Mr Richard's man," he said innocently.

Sybil smiled to herself. That's what I thought.

"Will you help me find something Clem?" Sybil looked at the young lad seriously.

"That what Mr Richard told me to do Miss."

"Let's start above the hatch in your room."

***

William Chasemeet was a man much troubled.

It was not a matter of his confidence to manage finance; a requirement of his position as a director of the Bank of England.

The Duke's introduction, when he had stated: 'He is the Bank of England' might have been an exaggeration, but it acknowledged that Chasemeet was a much respected financial strategist in that shady area where government and finance clash.

When the Lord Treasurer Robert Harley had been looking for vast sums of money to bail out the government, it was to the acclaimed tactician William Chasemeet that he came. Chasemeet engineered the process which floated the South Sea Company, which later took on responsibility for the entire National Debt.

The foppish, tittering, , handkerchief waving, lip-wobbling William Chasemeet was the architect behind the trading company's deal; thought to be the infallible solution for a government desperate to fund a war with Spain.

Chasemeet's *trouble* was his infatuation with the fine-looking Richard Hamilton.

It disturbed his sleep and interrupted his daily work. It dominated his home life.

When first introduced by the Duke of Sharingham, a seed of desire was planted.

At Dearnought's house, when the old bachelor had tasted from the fountain of youth he had become besotted with the young man.

However his artless desire for Richard was mixed in equal measure with a growing guilt for the deception he had been part of.

***

"Bit of light coming through the tiles; not enough to see properly." Clem was balanced on a ladder with his head through the hatch in to the roof space. "It 'in't what you call tidy."

He thought of himself as a bit of an authority on the roofs of the rookery, having traversed most of them at some time during the course of his thieving career.

"Boxes of paper; looks like old ledgers."

Sybil, standing at the bottom of the ladder was itching to see for herself.

"Let me take a look?"

"Looks like the rats been nesting in it."

She changed her mind.

"Bring down the rubbish nearest the hatch." If Thomas had hidden anything up there it wouldn't have been far away."

It began to arrive rapidly at the bottom of the ladder.

Clem's snug den was now piled high with dusty ledgers, junk in boxes of what could have been stolen goods; purses, note books and Sybil sat on the floor and looked at it despairingly.

"This stuff has all been there since father's day."

Clem passed down a satchel, expensive looking, well-oiled leather; not been there long.

"This is it,"

Sybil drew out the contents. She recognised Thomas's handwriting immediately.

"We must get these to Richard quickly."

***

The longer Richard worked for Medici Dearnought the more he discovered about the evil and corruptness of his business empire. Every imaginable deviant behaviour was available in the Doctor's Palaces of Pleasure. The proprietors of the establishments were constantly on the lookout for new business opportunities. Wealthy customers of repute were sought to become the victims of blackmail.

Wherever Richard went the doctor's name was known and feared but the shadowy figure was seldom seen and never personally involved. A proprietor discovering the presence of a wealthy visitor of social standing would simply befriend the victim, encourage him towards increasingly perverted behaviour, and report to one of the doctor's trusted overseers. The extortion would then be carried out by others.

Richard now an overseer himself well understood how clients became sucked into the criminal world. He made his visits at night when the Palaces of Pleasure were busiest.

He approached a building on the dockside by a back alleyway between ramshackle wooden houses. It was a place he had not visited before. All the structures close to the river were packed together in such a haphazard way it was impossible to discern one from another. Candles flickered in some windows but the fading daylight made location difficult.

From a dingy yard a carriage and pair suddenly raced recklessly out almost trampling him underfoot. He heard shouting from within the carriage and a reply from the coachman. It was too smart a coach to be a resident in this stinking area of dockside.

He was expected, and the proprietor had the business accounts out on the table for his inspection. There were lists of transactions and the takings were logged in a journal. The names of employees, the working girls, and anyone taking a wage from the place were listed. Richard had learned to calculate the amount of business to be expected and proprietors were rewarded when their performance exceeded expectations. If they were caught cheating the penalty was sudden and brutal.

"Belcher at your service Mr 'Amilton Sir," he croaked and made the parody of a bow. This proprietor was short and dumpy with a bright round face and a disarming smile which suggested that here was a hearty fellow, genial and disposed to always do a good turn.

Not so.

He was a loathsome fellow who enjoyed sampling the pleasures of his own establishment and a ruthless master to his girls. He wore a long unbuttoned waistcoat which came halfway down his white stocking clad legs. It was a garish red quilted affair, out of which protruded a shirt which struggled to cover a fat belly. On the shirt front there were the remains of several meals. He wore a scratch wig, too big for his head which slipped down over his eyes.

"Now while your are ere Mr 'Amilton I'm to offer you every pleasure of the ouse. Those are my hinstructions; my girls are at your disposal."

"Thank you Mr Belcher but I must get on." Richard settled himself at the table.

"Some small glass of something warming perhaps," said Belcher rubbing the palms of his hands together. When it came, it turned out to be a brandy and was brought to the table by a girl who Richard thought little more than a child. The face was painted, the hair immaculately styled, and she was dressed as a fashionable courtesan. The child smiled at him propitiously.

"What do you think, 'aint she a rich little beauty?"

Richard was sickened.

"I call 'er Princess Sharena; course there's no touchin' this one. Just for show this one but ain't she a little beauty though?"

Richard wondered once more how long he could keep up his pretence. How long before he was caught out for setting seeds of discontent as he went about this business in the Palaces of Pleasure.

"Indeed Mr Belcher, very…"

He drank a little of the Brandy and continued checking the accounts.

There was surely enough proof now to get Dearnought convicted but was there evidence to connect him personally?

He closed the books wearily a while later and rubbed his eyes before finishing off the brandy.

"Now just take a look in ere before you leave Mr 'Amilton; a little surprise." Richard stood up ready to offer another of his frequently used polite refusals.

"This sir is what makes *my* establishment in the top league Mr 'Amilton."

He led Richard through a door in to another wood panelled room. It was so small there was hardly room for the one chair which faced a wall. Belcher held a finger to his lips and beckoned Richard in closing the door. There was a small hole in the wall through which a stream of light shone. Belcher peered through it and turned whispering.

"Take a look at the Peep Show Mr 'Amilton, this is what brings the customers in."

It was weariness which prevented Richard from declining. He put his eye to the hole in the panelled wall to view a brightly illuminated room.

"Shilling a time; they'll pay"

Waves of nausea overcame Richard as he sat to look through the spy hole at Princess Sharena performing.

"I've room for six customers to watch at the same time. Now 'aint that something Mr Amilton?" The deference in Belcher's voice was gone and he cackled like a crow on a chimney.

Richard was gone; unconscious. His last thought was a memory of the carriage which had pulled away so quickly from the back of Belcher's establishment. Or rather it was the driver sitting on the top of the cab that he heard and recognised.

"*Which is what I have been 'oldin this last 'alf hour, and what you will be catching your death,*" He heard the voice of Sir Ronald Able-Makepiece's coachman's once again.

***

At the rented hovel which he and Richard shared, Clem Applebee waited for his master to return. It was as cold in the house as it was outdoors; a bitter wind. Eight hours passed and he still had not returned.

Clem had messages to give him and something else now, from Sybil. Something he felt was important.

In the early hours when still pitch black outside there had been knocking on the door. A solitary figure, shrouded in a hooded cloak stood on the doorstep. Clem spied on the figure from an upstairs window and saw alongside him another person.

It was Chasemeet's head man. The very same person who had beaten him about the ears and kicked him out several days ago. Clem's employment as a servant at the house of Sir William Chasemeet had lasted for one day. In the closed household community, his behaviour had set him apart from others. He had found it impossible to kowtow to other senior servants and had ended up fighting...... everyone.

Clem felt badly let down by Richard.

Walked away, that's what he's done.

It seemed to him that no sooner had he made a friend than he was discarded again.

Don't trust no one; then it don't matter what.

Know where you are on the streets.

He knew how to survive in the alleys and back yards of the capital city.

Being in Mr Hamilton's employ had its benefits too. It gave him more

street credibility, but he still had all the nous of a street urchin. He could always find food and shelter amongst the poorest kids in the rookery and that is where he aimed for now.

Know where you are with your own.

Derelict site; he nudged his way closer to his old tribe. At least a dozen of them; waifs and strays from the streets usually camped out in the open topped cellars of the destroyed buildings. Now he shared the warmth of an open fire with them.

"Who's that fine cove you're arsin around for Clem?"

"It ain't like that, he's a respectable gent; pays me too"

There were jeers from around the fire,

"Oow respectable is that then?"

"What'll you have to do for him to pay you?" said another and then whispered something to the boy next to him and they sniggered.

Clem, half the size of the bigger boy walked around the fire. He kicked him in the shins and when he bent over he punched him in the belly.

"He taught me how to fight."

And as the boy buckled Clem grabbed his nose and gave it a vicious twist.

"Then he taught me how to read," another punch in the stomach, "and write," another kick."

The boy swung a punch which Clem easily missed.

The boy kicked out and Clem caught his foot and lifted it high.

"See. He taught me how to win."

On the ground now, Clem leaned over him. "And he's given me a proper name. I'm Applebee now, that's what you have to call me; Applebee."

The next morning Clem was on the roof of Turpin's stable yard, waiting. His room in the Tavern was still available, but he had reverted to the roof tops. His fight with the street urchins had set him back. Clem had discovered he was not part of the old tribe any more, and that was difficult to handle.

Sybil stood watching him for a while. Then she beckoned him over.

"He's only been and gone that's what," Clem said angrily. "I waited for 'im all night to come back and he didn't"

***

In a house along the road from St Barnabus Church there is a large wooden fronted building standing back from the main road. It is shunned by the local people who believe it is no more than one step from the workhouse.

"We're a refuge for women," declared the stern faced matron who met Sybil at the door.

"They come to us beaten and bruised; sick and starving." Sybil was being given a guided tour of the establishment. In single rooms a number of young women were resting, some had beds, some simply laid on straw mattresses on the floor. All had the forlorn expression of women with no hope. Seeing Sybil's reaction to the somewhat unclean conditions the matron went on.

"We're an unpopular charity. Were it not for the good Doctor, we should have closed down long ago."

"What happens to them after?"

"Some end up back on the streets," said the matron in a matter-of-fact manner, "but others are found a regular position. Paid employment," she added."

Sybil nodded; it all looked impressive. She was shown a bathroom and kitchen and store room well stocked with food.

"Does Doctor Dearnought visit very often?"

"Whenever there's a girl ready to be placed. Come and meet your namesake." She produced a thin smile for the first time since they had met. Matron raised her voice and called out along the passage, "Sybil." A young attractive girl ran toward her wiping her hands on an apron.

"What are you doing child, not getting yourself dirty before they come for you."

The girl bobbed a curtsy. "No matron just 'elpin feed the girl who came in last night."

"Final interview with the doctor first and then off you go," the matron looked proudly at the girl.

"Tell Miss Sybil about yourself," she said over her shoulder, "while I get a room ready for the Doctor."

"Got a position in a 'ouse miss," she bobbed again, unable to keep still for her excitement.

"Do you know where you're going Sybil?"

She shook her head.

"Shall soon though."

"Have you met the doctor before?" The young girl became a little coy and nodded to Sybil.

"E said I 'ad the prettiest face 'e'd ever seen. Said he'd 'ave no trouble finding me a suitable position."

"Did you like Doctor Dearnought?" She nodded and hesitated.

"He's got funny eyes Miss."

"How did you come here Sybil?"

"I was a ladies maid in a big ouse off the Chelsea Road. Then the master took a fancy to me and next thing, I'm out on me ear." They stood in a large bare dining room. From the window Sybil could see a tiny yard littered with rubbish. Along a path a back gate led out to a side street and as they stood talking the gate opened and Dr Medici Dearnought came up the path. The girl jumped up and down clapped her hands together with excitement and rushed off shouting.

"E's 'ere matron, the doctor's 'ere."

Sybil stood watching as the doctor prodded the back gate closed with his silver topped cane and walked up the path. Why, she thought, does he choose to come in by the back door? She shivered at the thought of what plans he might have for her namesake, young Sybil.

"Miss Sybil, here you are," he said gathering her hand and touching it to her lips.

"And what do you think of our little haven of respite from the wicked world?" The words oozed from him like syrup and she struggled not to shiver at his touch.

"First I must meet with the young lady, but then perhaps we can talk a little?"

Sybil smiled nervously.

As Matron closed the door on the pair Sybil heard the girl's excited voice asking so many questions. They were in the room together for more than an hour during which time Sybil pressed the matron with questions about the home.

"Do you ever see any of your young women after they are placed? Is there any contact with them after they leave your care?"

***

Clem Applebee was stretched out along the top of the wall his back leaning against a slated roof. The air still smelt fresh at this early hour of the morning; Less polluted than it would be later when the rookery came properly to life. Up here it seemed to help him think things out. He could see for miles across the tops of buildings. From St Mary Le Bow he could look across to St Saviour's, and on to London Bridge. North, to Honey Lane and Turpin's Tavern. To the Southeast he could see across the river as far as Harrow Dung-hill. It was good place to be on a fine day, hidden from the view of almost everyone who might wish him ill.

That was how he felt today; that everyone wished him ill. It seemed the whole world was against him. One true friend had gone. That was the trouble with people, he thought; they crept in to your life, made themselves important to you, then disappeared. Richard Hamilton had done just that.

Just at the present Clem could no more express such thoughts than he could fly off the roof, but the misery sat on his shoulders like a great burden.

Richard had become important in his life. Like a big brother. He looked down the length of Cheapside towards Threadneedle. The stalls were already appearing along the sides of the road.

The smell of the Thames was always present, like a large open drain carrying away the human waste of the city; it was relentless with them. Londoners thought it normal for the air to be tinged with the stench of the murky river water. It was as part of everyday life as the night-soil men visiting houses to empty cess-pits, carrying them in a barrel through the house, and emptying it all in to the river. And if the householder could not afford to pay - throwing the contents out in to the street.

While street traders were still fussing around their stalls, early customers were appearing. The noise level steadily increased as the stallholders got into good voice. The aroma from a tray of freshly baked fat pies wafted up towards Clem. The carrier was hardly visible beneath the tray.

There was plenty of choice for breakfast and the mingling smells of cooked food drifted upwards, making it increasingly difficult to resist. But he lingered on and continued to think about the poorly state of his wretched life.

Don't believe he could have been taken against his will.

He felt angry again.

Just can't trust grown-ups.

The fat meat pies move steadily up the street and above the cries of other street vendors Pie Boy's voice was clear and inviting. He knew Pie Boy and knew exactly the route he would take before returning to his father's shop on Elbow Lane. Clem lifted himself from the top of the wall and stretched lazily. With the ease of a cat he made his way across the roof and dropped silently down in to Turnwheel Lane. He had a penny in his pocket and he knew the pies were tuppence each. Some other way of getting one would be needed. Pie boy stopped at the corner of Chequers Yard, rested the tray on the well top, and slipped in to the ally for a piss. This little junction of lanes was hardly busy but a cart passed by and behind it a small flock of sheep was being driven up Trump Lane towards the knacker's yard. A few residents of the area where out for some early morning shopping. Clem slid down the side of the lane and crept silently towards the well. Pie Boy was a belligerent lad grown fat and slow on his father's pies. He was also watchful being a regular target for street urchins. Clem lifted a fat warm pie from the tray and put it in his pocket. Pie Boy turned and in the hurry pissed all over his trousers.

"Hey, stop thief," he shouted.

Other heads turned. For an ungainly lad he was quick. Clem dived in to the flock of sheep and crawled on all fours up the lane amongst them. It was not just about being caught red-handed but also being recognised and grabbed later by the Watch. Clem slipped easily in to another ally. There was no hue-and-cry. At that time in the morning no one had the appetite for a chase. There were even a few smiles from passers-by who quietly enjoyed Pie-Boy's discomfort. Clem found himself a quiet corner away from the crowds and squatted down to eat the pie while it was still warm.

"You," said the young woman fiercely pointing her umbrella at Clem. "You stole that pie; it was half-eaten now but Clem was disheartened by this interruption to his breakfast. He shook his head unable to speak and looked dolefully at the woman. Even her testimony would be enough to have him put away. The penalty for repeat offences of even such a minor crime was very severe. Particularly when you were a street urchin. He sat cornered in the ally and made no attempt to move. The umbrella held by the woman began to waver and as Clem looked hard at her face Dora Melplash spoke.

"I've seen you hanging around Mr Hamilton?"

"Not me Miss," said Clem shaking his head furiously.

Miss Melplash wavered and Clem thought he would have no trouble slipping away from this woman who ever she was.

"I know where he's been taken," she said.

***

Sybil was standing in the hallway when Dr Dearnought emerged from the room with her namesake. She stood aside to let them both pass. Matron smiled graciously. The coachman opened the carriage door for them and the young girl passed through without saying a word to anyone.

Was she, thought Sybil, suppressing her excitement to impress the doctor with her good manners? Where was the bubbly excitement of the girl who had entered the room a short while ago? At the carriage door Dearnought turned and came back as if just remembering his offer to speak with Sybil.

"My dear Miss Sybil," he hesitated looking up and down the deserted street, this is hardly the place to speak, but there is a matter which, seeing you here again makes me feel impatient to share." Dr Medici grabbed her hand and held it firmly looking urgently in to her upturned face.

"Might you ride in the carriage with me, a short way? When we have deposited the young lady you might permit me to explain."

Sybil was curious to engage her young namesake in conversation again and there would be the opportunity to see where the girl was being placed.

"She is very quiet," said Sybil watching the once bubbly young girl who now sat vacantly in the corner of carriage her eyes empty, staring directly ahead.

"Is she completely well?"

"How singularly appropriate of you to be concerned," the doctor leaned forward and placed his hands over Sybil's.

"I have come to admire, most intensely, the vitality of your personality."

"Dr Medici," she pulled away.

"Relax my dear," he said quickly. "The girl can follow none of our conversation.

I have begun to know you very well; you are not only a very attractive woman but I detect in you a strong and dynamic soul. And I know you have come to admire similar qualities in me. I am rich already; very rich in fact and successful; and, you will forgive some immodesty, powerful and influential."

His eyes poured over her and she felt them penetrated her very soul.

"Sir, stop please, I find this disturbing ….," Sybil's eyes looked for help towards the girl. But the Doctor continued; carried away with his own eloquence.

"I have never before considered there might be a like-minded person with whom I could share my ambitions."

Sybil looked towards the covered window, wishing there was a perspective of the outside world on which she could focus. It had all gone too far, but how to extricate herself. The carriage lurched and she fell sideways pushing against the girl in the corner.

There was a whimper of protest.

"Sybil, my dear are you quite well?" the young girl looked at her namesake but there was no sign of recognition in her eyes.

"Dr Medici I am too concerned about her, perhaps you might take us both to Turpin's where I can care for her."

Medici Dearnought was silent and Sybil could tell he was exasperated.

"Miss Sybil," again his voice was quietly spoken but there was venom which was frightening, "I do not offer you my hand lightly."

Before he finish she grabbed his cane and rapped on the roof with all the force she could muster, the carriage slewed dangerously as the driver endeavoured to respond.

Momentarily Dearnought was transfixed. Sybil grabbed the girl and dragged her out of the door of the carriage before he spoke again.

"An arrangement of any sort you might find agreeable."

Without turning Sybil kept moving for he was more intent on pursuing his clumsy attention to her than stopping her departure.

"You misunderstand me sir, nothing would possess me………,"

Dearnought grabbed her arm pulling her round; his face crimson and seething with anger.

She was so close that she could see his scars pulsate and his odorous breath was suffocating.

By now the young girl was on the street standing, immoveable, dazed, and vacant.

"Understand me Miss Sybil; I will not be easily deterred…"

"You should be sir." She grabbed his cane again which had fallen to the seat and rapped on the roof again.

The distraction worked, he released his hold.

"If you are not with me," he shouted as she disappeared in to the crowds, "you are against me."

Sybil held on to the girl and they ran. Eventually the unmistakeable absurdity of the situation hit her; she smiled up at the distant figure of an enraged man leaning out of the carriage door as it sped away.

"I rather think I am."

The street was busy with people and even Medici Dearnought could do nothing more but she did not underestimate the significance of the threat. Sybil had just made a powerful enemy.

CHAPTER 12
LONDON BRIDGE

"The trouble is, my dear William, you wear your heart on your sleeve," Medici Dearnought was relaxed, his elbows on the table a glass of wine beside his plate. He had a lot of experience in keeping contempt out of his voice and the only noticeable departure from his normally well-polished manners was the inclination to fidget with his new cane. His thumb ran constantly over the ebony crown as if to polish it.

"I don't suppose I like the man any more than you Medici, but that's no reason to dispose of him; it's all this killing," he looked pitifully at the Doctor.

Dearnought smiled placing his hand over Chasemeet's.

"William, the man is set against us, he threatens to spoil our little plot; he cannot be allowed to go on. I have tried to engage him but he is resolute; he pursues a mad course of his own. Now taste this oyster pie, is it not the best thing ever?" They ate silently but Chasemeet merely prodded the food around his plate aimlessly. "Anyway, Hamilton has none of your *inclinations*. I find he has designs on Miss Sybil Turpin."

Chasemeet dropped his fork with a clatter and held clasped hands to his face.

"Oh not that slut from the Tavern?"

Dearnought laughed loudly.

"Did you think, after his accommodating performance with you the other week, that he shared your perversion?"

"You can be so hurtful Medici,"

Dearnought sat back holding his glass in front of a candle "To think this wine was liberated from a French vessel not a week ago."

He sipped from the glass and looked at the man across the table. "Were it not for your intellect where money is concerned we would have little in common yet I try not to let your depravity get in the way of our relationship."

"We all have our uses Medici. There is no need for you to be so high and mighty."

Dearnought said nothing. He had cultivated a friendship with Chasemeet; feeding his deviant habits and then coercing him to collaborate. The man had served the Brotherhood very well and Alpha had been pleased. But regardless of Alpha's views Chasemeet had served his purpose and soon would be no longer be needed.

He was weak and too easily ruled by his heart: and he knew too much. Alpha might be the leader of the Brotherhood of Honourable Benefactors but Dearnought felt no allegiance to anyone. He was his own master and had no compunction about eliminating the man he called friend or anyone else who stood in his way.

"Do you like my Frobisher, William?" said Dearnought resting the shaft of his cane against the other man's knee. "I'm having the ebony top replaced with gold."

"It's only a stick Medici, what is there to like about it?"

"It's far more than that William. I shall call it Mistress Hades." He flicked the crown and six inches of shining steel slid soundlessly out of the sheath and the blade twisted a degree as it locked. It scarcely pierced Chasemeet's hand but a tiny spot of blood appeared and the point was made.

***

Richard fought to keep his brain working even when he knew it was hopeless. His last vision through the peep hole had been of the girl Belcher called Princes...., dancing around in the little room watched by, he imagined, a hundred greedy eyes concealed around the walls.

The whole thing had been so repulsive that it goaded him now; it became an antagonist to the overpowering waves of nausea and unconsciousness.

His final vision was of Sir Ronald Able-Makepiece's coachman outside the Palace of Pleasure. His spymaster had been visiting the place?

But for what purpose?

***

Smoothly Strutt pulled and twisted the neck of the bird killing it instantly.

"No good to me. No fight in it see," he grumbled.

Jacobs the new foreman leaned on the low wall which surrounded the pit. He did not look impressed.

Fearless Friar was watching. He looked over at Jacobs.

"Killin' machine that man," he pointed to Strutt. "He'd be a good man to 'ave at Tyburn if you was short on rope."

He cackled at his own humour.

"He 'aint so good at keepin the pit clean. Stinks to high heaven."

Jacobs shouted at Strutt. "Smell the stink of this place in the parlour. Puttin people off their grub."

Strutt and Fearless went quiet.

Inside the pit the floor was deep in blood stained droppings and the debris of rotted carcasses.

Jacobs turned to go, but turned back and pointed at Strutt.

"You get it cleared out fore the morning."

They both watched him walk away.

Strutt agitated by the criticism began nodding his head slowly; his long bony nose pecked like one of his cocks; the thin cruel mouth scowled in the direction of Fearless Friar.

"Not long now Strutt," Fearless looked across the pit at him. "You done good but don't lose it now."

Strutt disappeared and came back dragging Bluw by the ear.

"I seen you're good at muckin out." He tossed the boy over the wall and the two left, deep in conversation.

***

Richard woke to find himself lying on a wet stone floor. It was pitch black and his head throbbed. Waves of searing pain pounded in his temple. Every heartbeat brought another pulsating searing agony. He lifted a hand to his head but it would not reach. He was manacled about the wrists and the chain was linked to his ankles. By bending his knees, there was enough loose chain for the hands to reach up. He pressed his fingers in to his head as if to massage the pain away.

He could hear nothing save for the pounding inside his head. He felt his face and judged from the growth of hair that he must have been out for at least twelve hours, possibly longer.

Slowly came the realization that the pulsating roar of rushing water was not inside his head at all. The noise if not the pain came from elsewhere. Not in the cellar, if that's what it was, a cellar.

More like a cell, he thought.

No window.

A door, there must be a door. He felt around the walls, dragging the heavy chains. It was more a crawl-way; no door just a stone arch, high enough to creep through on his hands and knees. The roaring got louder and the stone floor was covered in at least a foot of water.

He knew where the water came from. It was Thames water no doubt about it. The stink of the river was recognisable.

High above his head there was the noise of iron grinding on stone. A wheel was turning somewhere close by.

Finally he realised the truth. The noise was the turning of a waterwheel. He was being held in a chamber somewhere near London Bridge next to the water wheel. He recalled Sir Ronald Able-Makepiece's words.

"This is where they punish their own," he had said. "They wind the wheel up and tie their victim to it, then wind it down again slowly."

It hadn't thought that drowning would be such a slow death but by lowering the wheel a little at a time they could extend the agony for an hour or more. At first the victim would be able to hold his breath and would attempt to do so for longer and longer periods. As the wheel came up and over, the water would drain out of the victim.

Every ducking would only be long enough to cause the pain of near bursting lungs before relief and the dreadful anticipation of the next revolution. Richard felt the breath catch in his throat and he gasped to make himself take a deep breath.

He was being held here in the cellar to await his turn on the water wheel.

***

On the Duke of Sharingham's palatial estate the tranquillity was about to be interrupted.

"Calls himself Chasemeet; says he must see you urgently, your grace."

The Duke of Sharingham looked at his footman.

"William Chasemeet….; all lace and frills?"

"That will be him your grace."

The Duke's country seat was a good distance out of the city. A measure of the banker's determination, not be followed, was the effort he had made to get himself here. It involved hiring a carriage, some distance from his home and from the bank. It was a two hour journey and he had insisted on a diverted route.

Chasemeet was aware of the risk he was taking. As a member of the Brotherhood of Honourable Benefactors he knew the penalty for action he was about to undertake.

"Find myself needing your good council your grace," Chasemeet's usual arrogance was not evident.

"Can't be a matter of finance Chasemeet; you of all people would not be coming to me for that." The Duke had no intention of making this easy for the man although he had a feeling he knew where the conversation was leading.

The man looked wretched. He hesitated and stuttered and the lace handkerchief was waving frantically all over the place.

"Information has come to me…."

He stopped and started again.

"Your man Hamilton sir…. may be in danger. He may already have been…. taken."

"How do you know that?"

"I cannot say your grace…."

"Explain yourself Chasemeet…. Quickly if you please."

"You're man…," he looked desperately at the Duke. "Richard Hamilton."

The Duke as head of Prime Minister Walpole's secret service was a man worn down with despair by the baffling intrigue of the South Sea Company. For so long the scheming and secrecy had been impenetrable. He knew that a very select group of people, mostly well connected through government contacts, were making vast amounts of money out of greedy investors. The government had implicated itself by giving the Company responsibility for Britain's entire Nation Debt.

All this contrived, supposedly, to raise funds for Britain's war effort.

It was a scam.

Robert Walpole knew that, and so did the Lord Treasurer Robert Harley, whose idea it had been ten years earlier.

The plot was beginning to unravel slowly but it had become a very personal affair for the Duke. His sacrifice had been considerable. Thomas his only son and heir had been taken, and he blamed himself for it. But there was something else. Something less well understood but evident since his visit to Turpin's. It caused him discomfort of a different kind. His meeting at Turpin's had brought back long forgotten memories of a time when his own youthful, high-spirited behaviour was not so different from that of his own son Thomas.

Different only in so far that there had been a dalliance with a married woman.

"Let me try and help you Chasemeet …."

"You're a paid up member of the Brotherhood of *Dis*honourable Benefactors?"

"That makes you implicated in the plot against the State."

"You're not in it for financial gain; at least that much is evident."

"So you must be benefitting in other ways?"

Chasemeet wrung his hands and groaned.

"You are finished Chasemeet. So please don't waste my time."

***

Richard tried to focus rationally on his present predicament.

If he was being held near the water wheel he must be inside one of the cavernous stone piers which supported the arches of London Bridge. He reasoned that where he stood was probably at water level. The tide rose ten feet and so it was possible that at high tide he would be far below sea level.

Using his hands he established that one of the walls of the chamber did slope upwards and away from him; the inside of an arch he thought. The chamber had two walls parallel, twenty feet apart. High above him, about thirty feet or so, a weak light filtered through an ill-fitting wooden hatch. There was the faintest sensation of fresh air from somewhere, driven in, he thought, by the movement of the twenty foot high water wheel which continued its relentless grinding roar.

Using his hands to feel the way he concluded that the chamber was used as a store house. There were lengths of hollowed-out Elm logs stacked against a wall. He knew these were used as water pipes.

He knew the water wheel worked by raising Thames water into a wooden storage tank high up, level with the top of the water wheel; from where it achieved sufficient head of pressure to be piped to a large number of houses in the district. Besides the water pipes there was a carefully stacked pile of planks. If the timber was brought down here, he thought, there must be a device for removing it again. A ladder would not serve to lift the timber. The logs alone appeared to be at least six feet in length.

He had no broken bones or bloody injuries so who ever delivered him to this place must have used the same method to lower him down. Sometimes the light from the hatch above his head increased and he thought this must be when a door was opened emitting light in to the room. From the frequency of movement above he figured out that the room was in fairly constant use. Perhaps it was the office of the Watchkeeper; the person responsible for good order on London Bridge. He might well be in league with his captors. On any account there was no use shouting for help his voice would never be heard over the roar of water and the grinding of iron on stone. During one of the more illuminated periods he was able to see that the axle of the water wheel ran through both walls of his prison.

***

"You mean you've seen 'im without his clothes on?" said Josie.

"Only from a long way off; the sun was behind him so I could hardly see anything of him," and as an afterthought she added, "I'm sure he couldn't see me."

"There's a sure way of knowing if he did see you," she grinned mischievously.

Sybil looked questioningly.

"Was is tin whistle up or down?"

They both shrieked with laughter. This was girls talk, laughter, and chatter like naughty children.

Sybil cherished such times with her friend.

"You're blushing," declared Josie.

Sybil lifting loaves of bread from the oven on a long wooden paddle suppressed a smile and Josie pushing the piping hot bread to the back of the bench began to hum quietly in a sing song fashion.

It wasn't missed by Sybil who turned to baby Ned wrapped in a shawl and propped in a wooden carriage.

"Your mother is awful, she is, brings the worst out in anyone."

Both of the women had a rosy glow but no one could say that it was not the heat of the oven.

The smell of freshly baked bread would soon bring other tavern staff drifting in on some pretence or other but for the moment the two women enjoyed a shared intimacy.

"He's disappeared, that's the truth of the matter," Sybil became serious, "and Clem feels it personal,"

She also felt that like Thomas Sharingham, Richard had squeezed his way in to her affection only to disappear again at the very moment when feelings of liking were changing to something more heart-breaking; more difficult to ignore. Perhaps it was as well he had gone; perhaps it was a good thing.

"Jacobs is quite nice," said Josie breaking in to Sybil's thoughts.

"But you're not on first name terms yet?" replied Sybil looking at her friend.

"I shall 'ave to find a father for this'n," she said looking over at the baby.

"Don't rush in to anything; you don't need to. There's a place here for you as long as you want it."

***

The passage of time was difficult to judge, but at one point, Richard thought, it might be during the night, the noise of the wheel stopped. Curious he thought, without the noise, the darkness seemed darker; only the relentless roar of Thames continued.

From time to time he heard the sound of raucous laughter and voices.

He felt surprisingly detached from the immediate danger, wondering how his captors would contrive to remove him from the chamber; he reasoned that his own cooperation would be necessary.

Sitting, back against the dripping wall his mind dwelt on the only two people who knew he was missing.

One was a boy who he'd grown close to. He'd made Clem a promise and the boy was rapidly earning his title of Mr Applebee.

But that will be an empty promise if I don't get out of here.

The other person on his mind was a different matter entirely.

With the Maid of Turpin's there was much to admire. She single-handedly ran the most notorious Inn in Cheapside and did it with such style.

Their relationship had come far, and he knew her a good deal better. Those piercing blue eyes were no longer such a mystery. Sometimes they revealed much about the woman who seldom smiled.

Richard looked for her now, and found himself giving voice to conversations he'd had.

"Were you really prepared to let me hang?" he said to the stone wall running with water.

"I was prepared," she'd said mysteriously.

"You think you'll be running Turpin's for the rest of your life?" he had asked.

"It's what I do," she'd said. " I can think of many things I'd prefer to do; but it's my father's legacy to me. And if I give it up...."

There had been a long pause while she thought about it,

"I'd rather it was because I choose to do so. Not because I have no choice."

"Would you like to get married and have children one day?"

A rather too personal question, but she hadn't objected.

"I'm not very good at choosing men."

It had been as if she was talking to herself, as if Richard wasn't there.

"They either end up on a journey to Tyburn or dead,"

Then she did look at him, "and that's all the same thing."

"You took me to Tyburn and I returned," he said staring at the dank wall of the cellar.

However it was none of that which set Sybil apart from other women he had known. It was her ability to compete and often outdo what he said or did.

He smiled to himself. If she was the master of a ship, it'd probably be a privateer.

***

Sybil had not seen Clem Applebee for several days and it had been over a week since Richard had gone missing. She had tried to immerse herself back in to the routine of the tavern. The rooms were all taken and the parlour was as busy as ever.

She was back in the tall chair in the evenings pitting her wits against one or other of the regular criminal fraternity but there was an unresolved problem.

Finally she decided.

Having left Turpin's in Jacob's safe hands, Sybil planned to take off with Sam Black. She had not been able to get Thomas's hidden documents to Richard but felt they were important enough to deliver them elsewhere.

The mornings were dark later now but by the time she was ready to go the sun was up and she was impatient to leave the Tavern behind her. Striking north from Honey Lane she crossed London Wall skirted Bethlem Hospital and out on to Moor Fields.

Within the hour she had crossed the Artillery Ground and was making her way across the turnpike on to the open country. She gave Sam his head and with the slightest touch the stallion responded. She was riding on rough track used by the drovers bringing sheep and cattle in to the city, but there was hardly a soul around to check her speed. Open country sped by and there was nothing to avoid bar the ditches on the side of the drove. She wore her grey outfit and rode in the saddle like any man; but her golden hair was the giveaway for it was tied only lightly in a band and streamed out behind her like a trail of flame. She was completely at one with Sam Black who seemed to sense her mood and gave her mile after mile of unstinting loyalty in the only way he knew how.

The pair had been close since Sybil was a child and Sam Black asked nothing from their friendship except to carry her, when called to do so. She had only to whisper into his alert and flickering ear for her childhood friend to respond with every sinew of his being. They passed hamlets of tiny dwellings without stopping and the road changed from time to time and when she finally slowed to a canter Sam Black was blowing hard but still willing to carry her on no matter how far. There was a stream on the outskirts of a small gathering of cottages and they stopped to rest. Sybil did not recognise the area she was in and a greeting to a figure working not far from the road was ignored. She led Sam Black in to some pasture to graze while she sat on the bank of the stream. Beyond the scrub of the roadside there were small but poorly attended fields and ahead at a crossroads the scrub turned in to a densely wooded copse.

Sybil's thoughts returned to Clem. The boy had been feeling the absence of Richard and it showed itself in his defiant behaviour.

"I don't believe he's left," she had said.

"It's your doing anyway," he'd shouted, unable to control his hostility.

"You like him don't you Clem," Sybil looked at the boy his face was taught with emotion; hardly able to hold back the tears.

"He don't mean nothin to me." Clem had pushed his food away angrily.

Sybil raised her voice, something she seldom did.

"Well he does to me Clem, that's a certainty."

The boy frowned at her.

"What," he'd said without looking at her.

"Someone's trying to force the Tavern to close down and Richard's on my side."

Doing nothing was not an option for her. There was only one other person who might be able to help. The leather satchel was hidden on the saddle and she was determined to deliver it.

Sybil had no natural fear of others; another legacy of her upbringing in the tavern. Turpin would have despised fear. She could use a knife and a gun; she knew how to fight using the element of surprise and above all she had the wit to avoid trouble.

The solitary figure tilling in the field stood watching but gave her no cause for concern. She had a presence which arrested the attention of others and stopped some people in their tracks. It was a quality which she rather took for granted.

The heavily built lad, dressed in ragged cloths, walked across the dusty field towards her and stood, very close, staring as she sat on the bank.

He looked suspiciously at her; a figure who dressed like a horseman but had all the appearance of someone rather more feminine.

Sybil smiled at him, wishing at the same time that he would put his tongue away and close his open mouth. She beckoned him closer and pointed to the ground a few yards from where she sat. He held a long wooded hoe easily in his left hand. It crossed her mind that it was a weapon, but there was something innocent about the lad which made her doubt he would harm her.

"Where are you from?"

After a long delay the answer came back, as if the question had finally penetrated.

The hoe was slowly raised and pointed the way across and beyond the copse.

"What's your name?"

The earnest young face stared at her and struggled to reply.

"Ee..d," he replied.

More effort as his face contorted and strained.

"Eed-iot."

Sybil suppressed her surprise and was rewarded with a smile.

"Eed," she said and the lad with eyes as dark blue as her own and hair the colour of straw nodded his head with such enthusiasm that she thought it might fall off.

Sybil offered some of her fresh bread and he took it without letting go of the hoe. They sat apart sharing each other's company. He ate hungrily but his eyes never left her face.

Suddenly he stopped and stared. From behind, she felt a staff press down the back of her hand on to the ground and with such force that she cried out with the pain. She was pinned to the ground, unable to move and then she heard the cackle of Fearless Friar who appeared beside her.

"Well this is a pretty sight; the mistress of Turpin's and an idiot boy."

"I'd rather his company than yours Friar."

"Oh would you so; and idiot boy likes yours too," he cackled. "So let's help him."

Sybil didn't understand until she looked at Eed again. Two of Friar's men held him and had untied his pants. His shirt was lifted. She restrained a sob with the realisation that she may have unwittingly led him on.

Eed quite unable to follow the conversation, fought against his captors.

"Let's help the Idiot boy have his way," said Friar.

Two of them held her down and the others dragged the boy over by his hair. He was pushed heavily down on top of her.

Eed was shaking his head and moaning.

"No, no, no." he cried. "Bad it is, bad boy."

Friar lifted her skirts and held the boy down. He struggled all the more.

The boy stopped struggling, and Sybil closed her eyes. For a moment she felt his hands on her arms.

Then there was screaming; Eed had broken free and he wielded the hoe with such strength. The shaft knocked Friar to the ground and then the blade sunk in to the back of a skull and then another. Eed the boy, fought like a brave man.

Three of Friar's men went down killed instantly with the hoe.

Just as quickly a knife slashed across his throat and Eed dropped like a stone as blood gushed from his neck.

CHAPTER THIRTEEN
CAPTIVE IN TURPIN'S

Richard, anxious not to be carried away if the water level in the cellar rose, wedged himself amid the bundles of Elm logs. He slept fitfully, but the dream was not pleasant. He was manacled to the water wheel and it turned slowly and relentlessly.

The logs he sat on began to feel hard and he eased himself around to find a softer spot. The hollowed out water pipes had one tapered end. They were tied in bundles. The rope might be something he could put to good use. However, when he had been taken, all his pockets had been emptied and shoes were removed. He had nothing which might be useful to help effect an escape. Except of course; the small knife blade still in its spring loaded casing hidden in the sleeve of his coat.

"Damn useless knife, still doesn't work." He pulled the sheath out of his sleeve and examined the metal casing. The spring was a poor affair, supposed to shoot the blade down towards his hand when it was release. He pulled the blade out and used the point to detach the steel spring. It came away and he held it in two fingers. He felt for the primitive lock on his manacled wrist. He twisted the tempered steel in the key hole with little hope that it would do any good.

He grinned thinking that if Clem was here, he'd deal with these simple locks in a trice.

Suddenly he felt a movement and the lock fell open. The spring made short work of the other three.

Richard worked out that the water wheel stopped at night; and just after, there was the noise of boisterous behaviour from the room above the wooden hatch. Normally, just before it stopped for the night, a platform was lowered. It stopped with a crash as it hit the floor and there were shouts from above attracting him to food placed on it. It was just a sturdy wooden platform with a rope at every corner. He took the mouldy bread and ate it hungrily. Then the clanging of iron wheels signalled that the platform would rise. He reasoned that the power of the water wheel was used to raise and lower the platform. A simple gear system enabled them to alter the direction of the platform. No water was sent down so he sucked at the moisture from as high as possible up the walls where he thought it was more likely to be condensation than river water but it still tasted foul; sewerage in its purest form.

On one occasion, after the platform had come and gone and the wheel had stopped, there was the sound of great drunken enjoyment from above. He heard the grill being removed again and a voice he recognised shouted to him.

"River rat," Fearless Friar called out. There was raucous laughter and an order, "Come to the light." He dragged his chains over, keen not to give too much away. "You can share some of this ale," a harsh voice shouted, "we've finished with it." More whoops and cries. He stood looking up at the faint light as three streams of urine poured down on him. He stepped back and angrily looked around for a means of fighting back. Since a child he had been a good shot with a well-balanced stone and the floor was littered with them. Richard selected one the size of a small fist he balanced it in his hand and lofted it towards the light with little hope of hitting anything.

There was a scream and a string of oaths. The stone had found its mark. A shin perhaps or even one of the heads peering at him from the small hole. He quickly stepped back in to a crawl-way, just in time to miss the shower of heavy objects thrown from above. Anger had made him react in a hasty way. His captives would retaliate. But then again there seemed that he had nothing much to lose.

Several of the objects thrown were pieces of iron bar. Useful he thought if he could think of something to do with them. Richard collected them together with no particular idea in mind. He wondered if there would be more vengeance raining down on him and decided to stay in the crawl-way rather than in the chamber under the hatch. A good decision as it turned out for the rest of that evening and night a selection of unpleasant objects were gifted to him from above including the contents of someone's bowels.

***

Sybil was bundled across the saddle of her stallion. Her feet and hands were tied. The simple act of breathing was painful, as Sam Black was perhaps aware of his mistress's discomfort, trotted calmly across open ground led by Fearless Friar. There were only four of Friar's gang left since Eed had dispatched the rest with his hoe.

They had left the boy to bleed to death and taken off.

Sybil was consumed with remorse. She felt the boy's death was entirely her fault.

She had no idea where she was being taken, but they seemed to be making their way back towards the city. Her head was on a level with Fearless Friar's bad breath and beyond the nausea it caused it also served to keep her alert.

They would come back in to the city passing Tyburn and she wondered if she would be returning to Turpin's trussed up in this manner.

"Takin you back to Turpin's," he cackled and his fetid breath almost asphyxiated her.

"Only it's ad a change of ownership since you was last there and there aint no place in the management for you Miss Turpin." He cackled and they all joined in.

At Tyburn they stopped and her question was answered. The wagon used to transport human remains back in to the Surgeon's Hall in the city was parked on the far side of the field. Old man Bilfont the farmer had the concession on the transportation to and from Tyburn. It was no problem purloining his cart. Sybil was bundled in and covered with sacks and straw.

There was heated discussion about the loan of the cart before they departed but Fearless Friar's needs usually prevailed. Sam Black was ridden off at great speed before they departed. Sybil's concern was for the welfare of Sam Black and the satchel of papers.

Their progress towards Cheapside attracted little attention until they reach the slum of the rookery where heads were raised inquisitively, but it was never sensible to show too much interest around the business of an Upright man.

The procession was noticed by Clem from a rooftop. John Dutch also saw the distinctive waggon draw up inside the yard of Turpin's and when the tall wooden gates were closed behind it, something that only ever happened during the night, it was clear to all that the old order was gone.

Whilst Sybil was held, all the servants were warned it was business as usual or she would suffer.

Bluw the ostler had taken Sam Black to the stable. Jacobs' loyalties were well known and he was roughly beaten and held in the brewhouse.

***

When food was delivered to Richard, the hatch opened and after a short pause the platform started down. It took about two minutes to reach him and usually arrived just before the water wheel was stopped for the night.

He concluded that the operator had no way of knowing when the platform reached the bottom other than by feeling when the rope went slack.

This evening he tested his theory by placing four of the Elm logs, end on.

The roughly tapered end was designed so it could be hammered in to the hollow of the next log, when being laid as a pipeline for the water supply.

When the platform arrived it stopped dead as it reached the four logs. It stayed at head height. He reached out to inspect the underside of the platform. As expected it was flat but with a large hole in the centre.

Could be used to attach an extra length of rope, he thought, which when threaded through would make it possible for the platform to be used as a crane. He reached over the top with his arm. The normal diet of dry bread had become a welcomed event even if he had always to scrape off the mould and soften it with water before it was edible.

No bread this time. Instead something furry slipped away from his hand and squeaked. He pulled away instantly but not before he felt a bite. He shuddered with the revulsion of it. Someone had tied a large grey rat to the top side of the platform. His involuntary scream was heard from above and there were raucous cries of laughter as the platform began to rise.

He sucked at the tiny bite mark on the back of his hand and spat it out. Drawing blood was the best he could do to clean the wound. There were rats all over the floor of the chamber; it was not unusual to feel their weight scampering over him when he was resting. They were inquisitive creatures but did not normally bite.

Richard sat propped up against the wall. He tried to focus his mind. The platform was undoubtedly the way out of this hell hole but how could he get up without being seen by his captors. His mind was playing tricks again. Despite the best intentions he could not concentrate. There would be no food now for another twenty four hours and he felt dispirited. He wondered why they bothered to feed him at all if he was to end up on wheel. Yet something was delaying his gruesome departure; what was it?

He was getting weaker and every day meant the likelihood of survival from an escape attempt would be less.

Even now his mind kept wandering. He closed his eyes and he was swimming naked in that natural pool of cool and refreshing spring water. The sun was on his back and he glided effortlessly across the surface opening his mouth to satisfy his thirst. He could see the woman hiding behind an overhang of the bank; partially hidden; just golden hair and her fair complexion giving the game away. She was watching him and he pretended not to see her. Then he felt the soft touch of her hair brush across his face. He awoke with a start thinking how much better was the memory than what actually happened. Then he leapt up and banged his head on the overhanging stone work as an inquisitive brown rat fell to the ground. Richard smiled at the futility of his dream and wondered if he would ever feel Sybil's hair against his face. It had been nigh on three months since he had followed her to the pool.

By the time the platform came down again the next evening he was as ready as he would ever be. Having a plan to occupy his time had enabled him keep focussed. There were enormous risks but if he added up all the possible things which might go wrong he might just sit here and wait to die.

What if they discovered him at the top of the chamber?

What if it stopped before the top?

What if the platform was drawn up so close to moving machinery?

He shuddered, but doing nothing was not an option. The only thing that reassured him a little was that they seemed to want to keep him alive.

As it always did, the noise of the water wheel slowed right down before the lowering gear was engaged. Then he heard the clunking sound as the keeper of the wheel engaged the wooden cogs which would lower the platform. He could see the silhouette of a broad shouldered figure leaning over the trap and the man spoke. The voice came down to him with a hollow echo which reverberated around the chamber like a malevolent and evil apparition.

"Eat well turd, won't be long now."

"What about some water with the bread?" shouted Richard, trying to be as conciliatory as he knew how.

The reply was the expected one.

"'Elp yourself turd. There's plenty down there."

The platform trundled down and as it came to rest on the four upturned logs Richard snatched the bread off the platform and stuffed it in his shirt. He threaded one of three loops of rope through the hole in the centre of the platform and hooked it on. Into the harness hanging under the platform he slipped his legs and waited.

The voice called again from above. "Hey turd, show yourself."

Richard's heart sunk, he had been caught out. He slipped out of the loops of rope. "I'm here," waving the stick of bread.

"Here's some water for you." Richard could see what was coming as the man above opened his trousers and a stream of piss poured down.

"Thank you," he said, "remind me to return the favour some time."

He sheltered under the platform.

Roars of laughter came from above. "You'll have all the water you want soon enough."

He heard the screeching noise of gear wheels being engaged before the platform took off again. There was no time to get himself back in to the harness again. He just grabbed at the ropes and waited.

Slowly the platform lifted off the Elm logs. The water wheel mechanism slowed and hesitated as it took the extra weight of the man hanging underneath and Richard became anxious that the entire mechanism would halt. It was an unreasonable worry for the entire pressure of the river Thames drove the wheel effortlessly onward and upwards. Hanging under the platform he twisted and turned uncontrollably trying to slip his legs through the loops.

Slowly the platform, with its load, moved relentlessly, unstoppably upwards. The sound of the wheels grew louder and Richard waited anxiously under the platform for the sudden stop which might loosen him from the precarious hold.

He could see nothing above, but the relentless roar of the water and the screeching sound of wood on iron became unbearable as it got closer.

The platform gently stopped and the sound diminished to a repetitive whooshing roaring, and slowly this also reduced as the wheel itself was lifted out of the water and it slowly ceased to turn. He was directly under the turning mechanism but suddenly there was a loud bang and the two doors of the hatch were closed leaving him in complete darkness once more. At least he thought they intended no inspection of the platform; no one suspected.

Richard had no idea how long he would have to hang on in the precarious harness beneath the platform. He had no opportunity to examine what was happening above and when he reached out he could only feel the dripping stone walls of the chamber. Above him in the room he could hear the voices of at least two men. He presumed they were settling in for another night of drinking.

***

The grim reality of being captive in her own Tavern had caught up with Sybil. She was held in a cellar beneath the building in which she had lived for her whole life.

How could she possibly not have known of the existence of this chamber, deep beneath her own home. It had a makeshift bed and it looked as if it had been lived in at some time in the past.

She had been carried down, blindfolded and in a sack.

Josie had brought gruel in a bowl and some fresh bread every day.

At the door Strutt looked on.

"No talkin to 'er, else she'll go wi'out."

Josie couldn't have talked if she'd wanted too, Sybil thought. She wept and wailed in the most heartrending way.

Sybil held her gently and murmured quietly in to her dishevelled hair, as if consoling a small child.

"Be strong for me Josie," she whispered. "I need you to be strong."

With hardly a pause the sobbing eased and Josie whispered, "Bluw found the satchel and hid it. Clem thinks he knows where Richard is."

Then on cue, the heartrending sobbing started again and Strutt turned away, it was too much for the cock fighter.

"I'd wring both their bloody necks," he muttered.

Every time she visited, Josie conveyed snippets of information to Sybil. A routine was established and Josie showed a talent for mummery which surprised Sybil. Whenever Strutt got suspicious the two enacted their drama which forced him to retreat grumbling and swearing towards the cell door.

"The Tavern is full of Friar's men."

"Friar sits in your chair as if he own it."

"Said he'd eat baby Ned yesterday if he didn't stop 'is crying"

Jacobs got away and took young Sybil with him."

Sybil struggled with the hopelessness of her situation.

The cellar was set up as a prison and must have been used in her father's day for that very purpose. It had a high brick arched ceiling. It was pitch black but she could tell from the echo of voices that it was a massive structure; perhaps running the length of the Tavern.

By the third day of captivity her bindings had been removed and Josie had furnished her with a pail of water for washing and a small sharp blade. Neither of them thought Sybil could fight her way out but it gave her some comfort. Josie explained that access to this underground labyrinth was from inside the Cockpit. That explained why Sybil had never discovered it herself.

She began to explore her prison. It did extend to the far end of the tavern and an iron bound door suggested it went even further.

Sybil had plenty of thinking time and Richard featured heavily. Memory of his visit to the secret pool had faded but there had been other encounters and he was established in her consciousness, for better or worse.

As a secret agent he was a liability, she thought, with his bizarre gadgets; and Miss Maisy's Tea House; what was that all about?

It gave him a vulnerability which she felt tenderly about.

She just wished her life was not so dependent on him.

***

Richard hung in the two rope slings beneath the platform for what seemed like hours. Every part of him wanted to relax and sleep.

The ropes cut in to his legs and his arms ached from holding on. Sleep would be a fatal mistake. He had twisted an arm through a rope to prevent himself from falling backwards and like a tourniquet it stopped the blood and sensation to his hand. He established a routine whereby he eased the pain of one leg and one arm at a time; but it ceased to help as he grew weaker. He swung himself around feeling all the time to catch hold of something.

 He felt for the knife which he could use to cut himself away but that was never a serious option.

Eventually the sounds of the two in the room above ceased and Richard allowed himself to believe they either slept or had gone away. He reached above with his hand for the edge of the platform and pulled it down but the hanging harness was not long enough and the platform could only be wedged under his elbow, but there it stayed. All the while it swung wildly around bumping in to the sides of the shaft.

The four corner ropes supporting the platform were tied to a single thick rope which disappeared through a hole between two hinged trap doors. When raised in to the room above the platform lifted the two doors which then dropped back in place after it had passed through, much like he had seen as a child in the flour mill in his home village.

He could smell fresh air from his perch beneath the platform and he breathed deeply. It might only be the odour of the stinking Thames but it smelt good and he imagined he could see the sky and stars. Deep breaths filling his lungs, refreshed his brain, and he began to plan again.

Can't stop here.

Must move on.

Do something or I will simply be lowered back down on to the floor tomorrow.

That was too much to bear. Eventually the platform tipped till it was vertical but now the harness which looped around each calf beneath the boards was pulled tight. The loops held fast and scraped skin away leaving raw flesh to bleed.

He grasped the thick rope with both hands but was bent double around the board, hardly able to move a finger or a foot.

But now he could release his harness.

Either cut himself free if he could reach his knife or unhook the harness from where he had secured it above the platform.

He lay quite still on top of the platform. The wild swinging had stopped; he was motionless directly under the hatch. There was nothing to see through the holes in the hatch.

The sound of rushing water through the narrows in the bridge was helpfully noisy. The grey light of early dawn began to penetrate around the edges of the hatch. He imagined people above him were stirring from their beds and the bridge which was home to many Londoners was waking to a new day. If he lifted the doors now he knew he would not have the strength to fight his way out.

He still held the knife; it was covered in his own blood because hacking himself free had involve digging in to his own flesh. It had been a painful business.

He closed his eyes briefly and sleep came instantly, but it took him to the water-wheel again, being lowered deeper in to the Thames until it was too dark to see.

Then he heard a cocky voice he knew well.

"Told to deliver to the watchman of the bridge."

Richard imagined the boy standing defiantly.

"That's all I know."

"Well that's me, now give us it and push off." growled the other voice.

"Owd I know it's you," Clem Applebee stood his ground.

"Cos I'm telling you that's why."

"Yea but I was told to wait for a reply."

"Who told you? Who sent you?"

"Some woman sent me, said you'd know,"

Clem was ever the innovator.

"Woman you say, what was she called then tell me that?"

"What's all these wheels and ropes for."

"Mind your business or you'll be on the wheel yourself, now bugger off."

The voice was raised and angry and someone was standing on the top of the trap doors.

Richard had been slow to realise this was not a dream. Clem *was* in the room above.

"What's this rope for."

The platform started to swing wildly again and Richard hung on for grim death. There were sounds of a scuffle and someone fell heavily on the hatch. Richard had no idea who it was but it was heavy.

It might be Clem.

Through the rope hole he stabbed gently with the point of his knife. There was a roar from above and the body leapt away from the trap. The water wheel was not turning so the platform could not be raised. The doors could only be lifted by hand and they were far too heavy.

"Can I watch you start the wheel?" said Clem but the man was roaring with pain.

Richard pushed hard against one of the doors but it hardly moved. If he shouted it would tell Clem he was there but might endanger him.

There were lighter feet on the platform and small fingers were trying impossibly to lift one of the doors.

It was now or never. Richard put all his weight against the same one and it lifted an inch or two. Clem was peering in to the gap.

"Ere there's a big hole down here."

"And you're going down it."

The watchman grabbed the other hatch door and lifted it easily with one hand. Richard was instantly blinded by the light but he could see enough. The man's other hand had Clem and was about to thrust him through on to the platform.

A foot came up directed to the watchman's throat.

"Clem Applebee," said Richard, "I hope you weren't rude to this gentleman?"

"No sir I was just asking him how the ropes and wheels all worked."

The watchman was holding his throat and making strange noises. Richard crawled off the platform and stood over him. He could see puzzlement in the man's face.

His prisoner had achieved the impossible. Crawled out of the cellar thirty feet down. Clem's face was one enormous grin and between them they pushed the helpless body of the watchman on to the platform.

"Never been so pleased to see you," he grabbing the boy around the waist.

He slammed the hatch door down.

"This is how it works Mr Applebee," said Richard slicing his knife in to the thick rope.

"The platform comes up and down when the water wheel is turning; but there is a quicker way."

The blade severed the rope and the watchman's voice echoed around the chamber as the platform plunged to the ground. Richard took the piece of dry bread from inside his shirt and lifting the hatch once more threw it in.

"In case he gets hungry."

***

Sybil sat on the makeshift straw bed with her back to the wall. It was cold despite the blankets Josie had brought.

Should have let him hang at Tyburn, least it would have spared me his fine talk.

But she was miserable.

I'm sounding like Clem, she thought, but he had *me* to cheer him.

She picked up a handful of gravel stones and threw them, one at a time, against the wall opposite.

And when the last stone is thrown this 'captivity' will end, she thought.

It was beginning to feel that the end was nearby, but how did it shape her future.

Suddenly the stones were being returned with amazing accuracy.

Each finding a target on the wall behind her.

"Nothing better to do, I suppose," said Richard calmly, arms folded, standing in the shadow of an arch.

CHAPTER 14
THE BROTHERHOOD OF
HONOURABLE BENEFACTORS

Sybil gasped, jumped in the air and threw the remaining handful of stones at the image in front of her; as if to discover if he was real or not

"Sorry I'm late."

Richard held up his hands proving he was real. They embraced and Sybil wept; and couldn't stop.

Without releasing his hold he whispered into her hair.

"I've waded through mud to get here, so I smell a bit…; but then so do you."

She slapped him hard about the face and Clem sniggered and sighed loudly.

"You as well," and Clem was gathered up in the hug.

"How… Where…" She hardly knew what to ask first.

"John Dutch is the answer,"

Richard was still enjoying the embrace even though it was shared with Clem.

"John Dutch knew about the tunnel."

"We've got to get you out of here," he whispered.

"I'm not leaving till I've got Turpin's back," she said defiantly.

Richard looked at her steadily. "I thought you'd say that….So I have a plan."

Sybil raised her eyes to the vaulted ceiling; but before she could say more they heard the rattle of keys. Strutt was coming.

Richard raised a finger to his lips and pointed Clem towards the other side of the door.

"Not so cocky these days, Missy. And you can scream to yer art's desire down 'ere, and you wont be erd."

He stood in the doorway as Josie walked towards the bed with a bundle of clean clothes and a tray of food. She stopped when she saw

Sybil's lifeless body on the straw mattress. She screamed and Strutt crept one step through the doorway.

Richard and Clem lifted the Cockfighter through the air and hooked him, by the back of his coat, on to a high meat hook protruding from the ceiling.

"This might be a good time to get answers to some questions?"

Richard shook his head, "he'll make too much noise."

Sybil thought and then shook her head, "I don't think so."

"You hear that Strutt, Mr Hamilton thinks you'll start shouting if I hurt you?"

Strutt had a gag in his mouth but the noises he made did not give them reason to believe he would cooperate.

"Can we turn him upside down on the hook?"

Richard looked puzzled, but went along with the plan. Strutt was now hanging from the hook on the wall with his head waist high.

"Now this is a bit complicated. Clem can you make sure Strutt doesn't make a sound. If the gag is spat out just push it back in with that pole."

Sybil approached with her sharp knife.

"Mr Strutt will understand what we are doing because he does it to the birds in the cockpit. He cuts their combs, wattles, and earlobes off. It makes them fighting mad."

She sharpened her knife on a piece of brick and lifted one of Strutt's earlobes.

"Unless you want to tell me who murdered my foreman Ned Church?"

The knife drew blood and it flowed in rivulets down his face.

"Just grunt when you want me to stop Strutt."

In the parlour Fearless Friar leaned back in the Tall Chair. He enjoyed being master of Turpin's. It was not as busy as usual for a Friday evening. A few people lounged around on the tables. Despite the warmer weather, the fire was blazing and the spit was tended by a small boy. There were fewer candle lamps lit and all but one of the cubbies was empty. A new doorman slouched over a table nearest the door; the stave had been replaced with a pistol which rested on the seat. There were far more doxies crowded around one of the cubbies cheering themselves with gin and chatter. No business.

Ratter slept with his nose as near to the spit as he could bear.

The lively atmosphere of the place was missing but Fearless was unconcerned. It was all his now; by default he had inherited and already adopted the mantle of ownership as if it had been passed to him by the hand of old man Turpin himself.

Fearless allowed only his band of criminals in the tavern. Other Upright men were excluded.

He climbed down from the chair and swaggered across the parlour towards the girls who separated as he approached.

He pulled one by the sleeve, and whispered into her ear.

Her reaction to his malodorous breath was noticed. He snarled and pulled her into an empty cubby. She screamed and tried to pull away. Behind the curtain there was a scrabble and more screaming and the girl learned as others before had learned, it was not a good idea to show their feelings.

Fearless came out from behind the curtain adjusting his trousers and wandered into the Cockpit. A crowd stood around the circular pit leaning over the low wall. They poked the hanging basket with sticks as it swung backwards and forwards across the pit. Pathetic cries were heard when a stick made contact with boy Bluw sitting in the cage trying to make himself smaller.

"Sport is it lads, is that what?"

Boy Bluw, the Ostler had done something to upset them and was being made to pay.

***

Outside in the Parlour, the door swung open to admit a big fellow. He looked around at the empty Parlour.

"You born in a barn or summat?"

John Dutch turned to the doorman and smiled.

"That is a very bad way to be speaking to a customer and even worse to the Maid of Turpin's." With one hand the doorman was lifted from the trestle table and deposited out through the door.

Jacobs behind John Dutch passed him on down the street to the night soil cart.

Sybil's prison cell under the Cockpit had a tunnel which, unbeknown to her, was a secret route for bringing contraband goods from the docks. It had also served as an escape route and means of disposing of unwanted goods. Most of the Upright Men would have known about it and in Turpin's day it would have been used frequently.

"Whose is makin all the hullabaloo down there," Fearless Friar was tiring of tormenting Boy Bluw.

"Sounds like Strutt," he gestured for someone to look. The hatch was lifted and two of his heavies clambered down the stone steps in to the cellar.

Fearless had been savouring the moment when he would take the Maid of Turpin's for his chattel. That would be a crowning achievement of no ending pleasure. It was only a matter of time before she succumbed, and he thought himself a patient man.

He hoped that Strutt had not damaged the goods.

In the cellar Strutt was no where to be seen. In the corner Sybil Turpin was motionless. Fearless hurried over to the blue woollen dress kicking around on the straw bed. He growled and pushed the others aside in his rush.

Strutt's gagged face and nodding head peered at him and struggled to get up from the bed. He was covered in blood but he still had his ear lobes.

Just.

Fearless Friar kicked at the noisy part of Strutt in shear frustration.

Fearless was never a speedy thinker, but he led his gang by managing to stay one step ahead. Realization slowly dawned, he looked around and noticed that he and his crew were all in the cellar together and the Maid of Turpin's was nowhere to be seen.

Leaning over the waist high wall of the Cockpit, Sybil, Richard, Clem, Jacobs and John Dutch listened to the noise in the cellar. Every time someone climbed out he was roughly returned to the bottom of the stone steps.

"If you were thinking of filling it in; now would be a good time," said Richard.

Sybil smiled and shook her head, there might be some more to gather up.

She pulled a borrowed cloak around herself.

"That was a very expensive woollen dress."

Richard looked at her admiringly and spoke quietly, "It came off with little trouble."

She looked at him dismissively, "on my terms Mr Hamilton."

"They 'aint discovered we've stopped off the other end yet," said Clem.

Boy Bluw had been released from his captivity and hurried off to find the satchel to return to Sybil.

***

The Brotherhood of Honourable Benefactors was gathered. Twenty men sat round the table, each man's head covered with a lose fitting black silk hood which hid his identity.

For Richard it brought to mind convicted criminals from Newgate to Tyburn awaiting the noose. A hood was always offered although the crowds preferred to see a hanging without the head covered.

He could understand that the Honourable Brotherhood might take comfort from being shrouded in such a way; anonymously concealed from the world they were cheating. But he enjoyed the comparison with guests waiting for Tyburn.

Richard had studied Thomas's satchel of papers and was well informed about this organisation and its members. Thomas had done the dangerous work and had paid a heavy price.

He felt closer to Thomas after reading the documents. Their lives, he thought, had become intimately connected, and not just by the assignment. They had also shared an attraction towards Sybil Turpin. Richard had discovered, through diary notes that the Duke of Sharingham had been aware of Thomas's liaison with Sybil.

There was only a little talk between the characters around the table. They sat soberly, each in front of a name place bearing their Greek pseudonym.

They waited.

Only the chair at the top of the table before the title of Alpha was empty.

Richard's had taken the name of Epsilon. He had taken the identity of Palfrey, the jolly, plump, well powdered owner of a shipping fleet.

Palfrey, merely a greedy shareholder, had been only too pleased to cooperate when offered a bunk in a prison hulk, rather than one of his luxury ships.

But the plot was not without danger. There was no guarantee that he would go unrecognised. He knew the voice, and the characteristics of the man but he had no sure way of knowing if his deception would deceive anyone.

Richard survived the nodded greetings between members on arrival, and the absence of any sort of idle chatter was to his advantage.

It was to be a matter of one watchful step at a time.

When Alpha arrived at the top of the table a servant assisted him in to the chair. The room quietened and the hooded brotherhood became attentive. Heads stopped moving and all eyes turned towards the man who they were so dependent on.

He pressed his twisted bony finger tips together in a kind of prayerful manner.

"It is time gentlemen," The condescending voice hissed at those about the table. Alpha's head moved around engaging each of those present in the room.

"Your patience is soon to be rewarded."

A spell was broken by Alpha's words and now there were murmurs between neighbours.

Alpha had given his menacing approval for them to relax. Everyone present, except Richard, would remember the brutal assassination of Kappa.

Everyone knew they were party to a worldwide criminal hoax and Richard supposed they took comfort from one another, but there was still fear in the room; Richard could feel it.

This was not a meeting of equal partners.

Alpha had given his permission for them to relax; so they did. Alpha had spoken.

The South Sea Company has become a household name over the past few years. Even the working classes had been investing in its stock; the aristocracy, the Church and Parliament. From ladies maids to King George himself; all were seduced by the promise of untold riches.

Those who should have known better thought the Southsea Company was far too big to fail.

The entire country has succumbed to the greed. In fact much of the civilized world has been watching the London Capitals Market. In Switzerland £150,000 had been invested recently. The story was the same in Germany, Holland, and France.

The Company had already loaned the government seven million pounds in return for a monopoly on all trade with South America. Around the table these wealthy financiers had watched their shares increase in value five hundred times.

Soon the share price would crash. No amount of trade with South America would help.

For Richard, fear was of an entirely different order. Alpha's utterances were the proof of what Thomas had led him to suspect. But now with the certainty of knowledge, the danger had become immense. Alpha was unmistakeably his spymaster. The government's spy-in-chief, Sir Ronald Able-Makepiece, the man who had sent him on this mission, was himself the mastermind behind the plot.

Sir Ronald was running this enterprise. It was no wonder that Richard felt he had been impeded every inch of the way. All the while he had been reporting the progress of his investigation to Sir Ronald.

Richard wondered how much the Duke of Sharingham knew. He had certainly warned to watch out for an insider.

"In the papers before each of you there are instructions. Be sure to follow them to the letter. It is imperative that you each cash in your shares at precisely the day and time assigned. Failure to do so will likely ruin the entire enterprise. There is no room for failure gentlemen."

Richard was conscious that one pair of eyes in the large room was watching him most carefully. One person sought to pierce his disguise. Whilst Alpha's head moved to and fro watching all around him, one of the hooded figures carrying a gold topped cane was very watchful. He slowly raised his head to the figure opposite whose silk hood was motionless. The man was silent and still, staring across the room. Richard recognised the cane. It was his own Frobisher.

"Phi does not share the excitement," Alpha's voice cut across the room.

"Not so Alpha, I am well pleased with the news you bring,"

The unmistakeable figure of Medici Dearnought gave nothing away but there could be no doubt.

"I was watching Epsilon," said Dearnought, spoken in that beguiling tone.

Now, amongst the twenty there were three drawn in to conversation whilst the rest chattered idly. Alpha's fleshless fingers pointed towards Richard. There was an expectation he would speak.

He had prepared for this moment and launched himself in to the Palfrey character.

"Lord above sir, but we shall be so rich. I am fairly overcome with the excitement of it all."

He bounced up and down on the seat and gave out a long hacking cough which racked his rotund body. He took a handkerchief from his pocket and pushed it under the hood; he cleared his throat loudly and spat mucous in to it.

Richard played the part of Palfrey to perfection. Epsilon the long-winded, boastful ship owner could no more contain his enthusiasm even with a racking cough which threatened to carry him off at any moment.

"Let's all hope that Epsilon does not expire before he has chance to collect his reward."

Alpha at least was taken in by Richard's disguise. Around the table there were guffaws of laughter at the mean joke.

But what of Phi, was he deceived by the Richard's play acting?

Alpha spoke again.

"Why even Phi, always so restrained, even he might be persuaded to relax and sink a celebratory drink with me?"

Phi looked far from convinced by Richard's show.

Across the table he leaned forward and spoke in a whisper so that only Richard might hear.

"Think on this Epsilon. You're just not that good, and I will have the better of you yet.

He shook his head slowly, the deep penetrating eyes ineffectual under the silk hood.

"You might think that Phi, but I'm coming after you next"

One other hooded face at the table watched the exchanges between Dr Medici Dearnought and Richard Hamilton. He was a man much troubled by recent events; a man who presently had difficulties deciding where his loyalties lay.

***

There were buildings on either side of the thoroughfare across London Bridge. Shops, houses, and accommodation of every description clung to the narrow crossing. The structures leaned against one other for support. Whenever the old bridge looked in danger of collapsing, the city authorities built another sterling on the river bed to give a bit more support; in so doing they reduced the space available for the river water, which in turn increased the ferocity of the rapids through the narrows.

Richard felt he knew the Bridge very well now and it hadn't all been pleasant.

No one lived in the building above the cobbler's shop. Richard had been recognised as he entered the shop and presented a token collected from the window display. He wondered, smiling to himself, if anyone was ever authorised through by being told to pick up the cat in the window that still slept soundly. The cobbler had glanced up and nodded Richard through to the upstairs room.

He stood with one foot on the low stone seat in the window overlooking the white racing water. Alone in the bare room his thoughts were not on the magnificent view. So much had happened since he had first become acquainted with London Bridge. He leaned out to his left and could just see one of the water wheels beneath which he had been imprisoned. He remembered his spymaster's warning that the rookery executed their own on the water wheel and he was glad to have narrowly avoided that particular end.

From the opposite window, down river, he watched a large ocean going vessel casting her moorings and being towed out in to the mainstream by a number of small tenders; each with four rowers bending oars against the current.

He imagined how good it would feel to be leaving on her.

Bound for the Americas no doubt.

But that wouldn't do; there was unfinished business.

There was also a certain young woman. He hoped Sybil was safe in Turpin's. Clem, Jacobs and John Dutch were there keeping a watchful eye out. He was not her keeper and in the Tavern Turpin's rules applied

The task he had been charged with was almost done. There were still loose ends and some of them were a tangle. His thoughts about Sybil Turpin were a tangle of a different sort.

Footsteps on the stone staircase drew his attention to the door.

"You failed to meet the reporting schedule," Sir Ronald Able-Makepiece stood in the doorway; he looked grim, red faced and angry.

"It was jeopardising my safety." Richard turned. "Someone was getting to hear about my reports to you and making life difficult."

Sir Ronald glared at him from the doorway.

"It must have been your own careless behaviour."

His soft spoken voice was, as ever, sinister and menacing. Richard thought the man could be discussing the weather and it would sound like a death sentence.

"We both know that's not the whole story, Sir Ronald. Perhaps it doesn't matter now. My mission is almost complete."

"You have succeeded?"

Sir Ronald might have wanted to sound encouraging but it was still condescending.

Richard nodded and threw a bundle wrapped in oilskin on to the table between them.

Sir Ronald leaned forward to take it.

"Have you opened it?"

Richard looked at him steadily.

"Yes I have. It explains everything."

"Your task was to discover the connection between Turpin's and a so called plot to bring down the government."

"No, what you really wanted was for me to retrieve lost documents, so incriminating that they would bring down highly placed individuals. Well I've done that for you."

Richard turned his back on his spymaster and gazed out of the window." He heard movement behind him but didn't turn.

"Your secret's in safe hands now, Alpha."

Sir Ronald hesitated.

"Foolish boy."

"I wasn't supposed to succeed, was I?"

"Quite right, but it doesn't matter now, it's too late."

Over Sir Ronald's shoulder a large pistol was aimed at Richard's back. The coachman's arm never wavered.

"Sit down Hamilton; let me explain something to you."

Richard stepped back and sat on the stone seat below the window.

"You were not supposed to live this long. Dearnought was to remove you but he tried to be too clever; thought he could turn you, by one means or another."

"What's in it for you Sir Ronald; is it wealth or the politics?"

"You wouldn't understand Hamilton. Suffice to say destroying a corrupt Wig administration and their puppet Sovereign is a prize worth fighting for."

"Sounds like treason to me sir. Think you sympathise with the Jacobite cause as well?"

"You surprise me Hamilton. If your future did not look so bleak I might have persuaded you to join us."

"You make it sound like a principled war?"

Able-Makepiece was unstoppable now.

"The cause of Catholic sovereignty will not be achieved without bloodshed."

"So there we have it Sir Ronald."

The voice came from outside the room.

"You *are* a rare breed; a principled servant of the crown who aspires to anarchy for his cause"

Just then Sir Ronald's coachman was knocked to the ground and the room was filled with militia.

The Duke of Sharingham stood in the doorway.

"But of course, Sir Ronald you have been light on principle and heavy on anarchy.

The Spy master looked from Richard to the Duke, but he said nothing.

"You're under arrest for treason, murder and a good deal more I suspect."

"Well done Richard."

They sat at ease in the same little room above the cobbler's shop.

"You have more than completed your assignment and are free to leave this matter as it stands."

"No…, there is someone far more evil than Sir Ronald who must be stopped."

"The Doctor?"

Richard nodded, "He's without a doubt the most evil man I have come across."

"And the Maid of Turpin's?"

The duke spoke her name with surprising gentleness.

"Sybil," said Richard. "She's the innocent in all this."

"I would prefer not to see her harmed, if that was possible."

"Richard raised his eyebrows,"

"Find her for me Richard; I would like to speak to her again." The Duke left without looking back.

***

Events had moved rapidly since Richard's escape from captivity at London Bridge, and it had to be so. He realised that success was dependent upon being able to keep one step ahead.

It was twelve hours since Fearless Friar was rounded up in Turpin's cellar. His stinking band of thugs were still battened down and Richard had ensured that no word of their captivity had leaked. He had penetrated the Brotherhood and Sir Ronald Able-Makepiece had been detained.

The final events were about to unfold.

***

Dearnought's coach raced through the countryside. A brilliantly moonlit night made the journey faster but gave the doctor little chance of relaxing. He had decided it was time for Doctor Medici Dearnought to disappear. He still had supreme confidence in his own ability. There was no sense of defeat because everything the man did was calculated and unfailing. The Palaces of Pleasure, brothels by any other name, had been a major financial triumph. Distributed across the city and patronised by the rich and famous, they were a massive source of income and a constant opportunity for blackmail and bribery. His reputation as a successful physician had brought him celebrity status amongst the wealthy classes. His homes for wayward women had given him recognition as a philanthropic social reformer and benefactor to the poor.

He had made himself untouchable.

In his criminal mind Dearnought's greatest achievement was the domination of the criminal class in the city of London.

It had given him total supremacy in the criminal underworld. The ruthless exploitation of the weak had brought him great wealth.

The growing celebrity status had a down side. Dearnought was shy of public recognition.There were increasing numbers of prominent people in the City who had good reason to rue the day they allowed the celebrated Medici Dearnought into their lives.

The infamous doctor had become weary of his own success and craved the opportunity for another challenge.

He had one matter of regret and it concerned the Turpin woman. Dearnought was accustomed to getting his own way in everything he set his mind to. He could not remember a time when he had been refused anything, even as a child.

Can't remember having been a child? He thought.

Perhaps, being unusually self-critical, his overtures towards her had been a little clumsy.

'A like-minded person with whom I might share my ambitions;' he re-examined his words to her and nodded approvingly.

Dearnought was accustomed to just taking what he wanted, not having to ask for it.

'Come to admire your vitality and dynamic soul, and I know you admire similar qualities in me.'

But she hadn't; she'd refused him.

Stupid girl.

'If you are not with me, you are against me'.

That *was* clumsy.

He had so admired her determination; so unlike the poor weak creatures he normally coerced to his will; courtesans with whom he took his pleasure. He had imagined what it might be like living with Sybil Turpin and it had seemed perfectly right.

Being in her company at dinner, she, at the end of the table attentive to his every need; Intimate moments together when he'd share his visions of power and domination.

Desire also; Medici Dearnought had to deal with desire and it was an unusual   emotion. It was a feeling he hardly understood. So irrational, but he imagined how it might have been. He gently pressing his lips against her silky skin and she returning his affection with all the passion he imagined her capable of. He felt the bittersweet comfort in his loins at the thought of Sybil lying beside him.

The coach hardly slowed and Dearnought saw that he was expected; the large iron gates were open. His servants would have been waiting patiently outside the gatehouse for the sound of his approach so that the carriage could continue uninterrupted up the long drive. He expected nothing less. He banged on the roof for the driver to stop.

"I'll walk from here," he shouted. Put the horses away and leave. I shan't need you again tonight."

Dearnought's thoughts returned to Sybil Turpin as he walked up the long, weed covered gravel drive.

She'd be burned to a cinder by now along with Sharingham's man Hamilton. That had been his instruction to Fearless Friar. Destroy them both and burn the tavern to the ground.

He walked towards the house in almost complete darkness. The moonlight hardly penetrated the tall dense trees which crowded the drive. Dearnought was angry.

She wouldn't bend to my will so I destroyed her; but there could have been so much more.

"Why did you make me destroy you," he called out in the darkness.

He knew the answer already. She had got under his skin. She had turned the tables on him and that would not do. The thought of her burning aroused conflicting feelings in him.

In the library; a single flickering lamp had been left. The shuttered windows giving entry to the garden had been closed but he opened them again and sat looking out across the lawns bathed in moonlight.

"*Stupid girl,*" he shouted to the overgrown garden.

The thought that he had made a mistake would not leave him. He watched as a cool breeze gently moved shadows of the trees. He poured brandy from the decanter and drank deeply. His eyes began to play tricks on him.

What would he do if she was to come?

CHAPTER FIFTEEN
DEARNOUGHT AT HOME

Sybil and Richard took the side entrance out of the tavern into Honey Lane. It was ten o'clock in the evening but the streets were already deserted. The night air was clear and it smelt clean; even the moon was visible. Getting away unseen through the empty cobbled streets at this hour was still a challenge but Sybil led both horses at the start making use of every bit of soft ground till they were out of sight of the tavern.

She was once more dressed in male attire; an outfit more suited to that of boldfaced highwayman.

"I'm beginning to enjoy seeing you dressed in breeches," said Richard. "but it's worrying."

"It's not worrying me," she smiled under the hat and silk scarf covering most of her face.

Sybil had offered him her stallion Sam Black and she borrowed a visiting mare for herself. She was a sturdy creature selected from mounts belonging to guests of the tavern. Towards the outskirts of the city they spoke barely at all needing all their concentration to negotiate the debris and potholes in the streets.

They hardly met a soul and no passer-by would put himself forward to pass the time or wish them a safe journey. The watchman would not challenge; knowing only too well that it might invite a life threatening argument he was unlikely to win. Along the toll road, towards Hackney Marsh, the two riders were a menacing sight, flying through the countryside.

Once out of the city they were obliged to take a more measured pace again for the road was soft and rough surfaced. Heavy rain for nearly a month had caused coach wheel grooves several feet deep. It would be the easiest thing in the world to break a horse's leg in the rutted track.

On the turnpike towards Epping, Sybil reflected on why she had not hesitated to follow Richard Hamilton on this epic mission. There was a mutual sense of purpose; of being at a turning point in this bloody business. Richard had shared his determination to stop Medici Dearnought and she wanted to be there when it happened. Like so many others who had come into contact with the arch-criminal, she had been marked by the doctor's evil touch and watched the way in which he had manipulated the lives of innocent people for his own good. Sybil felt she had to be present to erase the experience.

***

There was also a lone figure making the same journey by a different route. He might have been less well equipped for the trip but no less resolved to travel and make some reparation for a shameful misdeed.

William Chasemeet was a much respected figure in banking circles but a poor creature, ridiculed by people who knew him and the butt of humour for his foppish, effeminate ways.

He travelled alone driving his own carriage but with a determination to put right an awful wrong.

Since before his meeting with the Duke of Sharingham, Chasemeet had been afflicted with remorse for a wrongdoing to Richard Hamilton; he had been coerced by the doctor and manipulated by Sir Ronald Able-Makepiece.

All this gave him reason to believe that Richard Hamilton was in danger and it was his doing. It was true that the brief contact with Richard had touched him deeply. He felt a growing affection for the man; well hidden as always behind his normal pugnacious behaviour; his protective shield. His hostile manner stopped people getting too close. It usually served him well.

However for 'dear Richard' there was an infatuation which grew. And as it flourished so did his guilt.

William Chasemeet was not a man of action. Racing across the countryside to Medici Dearnought's country house in a Pony and Trap was a nightmare.

A mile from his destination the Trap overturned.

A wheel broken; he had to free the pony and continue on foot. His determination did not waver.

***

Sybil and Richard arrived at Dearnought's residence, on the edge of the forest. The gates were firmly closed and padlocked for the night. The lights were still on in the gatekeeper's cottage so they dismounted and walked up along the road away from the drive.

"Do we have a plan?" she asked hopefully, knowing, and not liking, Richard's inclination for working things out as he went along.

"Sort of.'"

He held her arm. "You wait in the garden while I find a way in around the back. I need to take this man uninjured; or at least alive."

"He has staff who won't just sit and watch you do that," Sybil was wary not to dishearten him.

"So have I," he whispered mysteriously; "somewhere."

He looked around hopefully.

Half a mile on Richard found an overhanging tree and with little effort they both climbed from their mounts on to the top of the wall and down into the dense undergrowth of the garden. No light penetrated through the canopy of trees and it was a matter of guess work to feel their way back towards the drive.

Sybil held on to Richard's coat tails; that way they kept in touch.

The trees cleared to be replaced by scrub, and the moon illuminated massive bramble bushes which prevented direct forward movement.

"Are you sure we'll still meet the drive?" Sybil exclaimed after they had been struggling for fifteen minutes.

"Hard to say, but we've little alternative but to keep going."

Down a steep bank he increased his pace and Sybil had to let go.

She was a fit young woman and found no difficulty in keeping up but suddenly she went head first in to brambles, falling face down. She screamed and then there was silence.

"Where are you? What a noise you do make." She gritted her teeth at this but could not move an inch being held painfully by sharp thorns which impaled her in a hundred different places. Richard hacked away with a knife and gently, with his arms around her waist, he drew her from the brambles. She leaned back against him and lifted her head upwards. Now *he* was held; captivated by her face, eyes tight shut, glowing from the exertion, smudged with mud and tiny pin pricks of the blood covering her cheeks. He knelt behind her and tried to wipe the blood away with a dirty finger.

That wouldn't do, so he did the most natural thing. He leaned forward and his tongue washed away the blood and the mud and she did not move.

Her eyes still tight shut, she whispered; "Have you missed any?"

"Just here and there," his tongue flitting across her lips.

"Once more," she sighed, inviting him with open mouth. She put her arms around his neck and there they stayed.

After what seemed like a pleasurable age she stretched and murmured.

"You do that very well."

Her arms dropped.

"Don't move your left hand," His tone was urgent.

"The back of your hand is resting on the open jaws of a mantrap. If you press the plate the jaws will close around your wrist." She looked urgently in to his eyes, but he could not move for she was leaning back against his knees.

"Do something," she pleaded.

"I'm thinking." He felt around with both hands for a log or something wider than the thickness of her wrist.

"Now gently lift your arm if it touches metal stop." She lifted her arm slowly. When it was clear he dropped the log on to the trap and the jaws sprung shut snapping the branch in two like so much matchwood.

Richard lifted Sybil gently to her feet.

"This way I think," keeping firm hold of her hand.

***

Medici Dearnought sat staring out at the moonlit wilderness. He had never before in his adult life thought so long and hard about one woman. He struggled with the possibility that he might have made a mistake to order her destruction. It was a rare experience for the man. That a decision he made might have been wrong.

In the flickering dark shadows of the garden wilderness a slim youthful figure appeared and detached itself from the backdrop of the shrubbery.

Dearnought recognised her directly. The way she swayed across the grass.

He hurried to the doors, doubting his own eyes. Could it be false; an image in his mind, so earnestly desired that against the odds it had become a reality. Such things he had read about.

Then as she came closer he felt first such relief; it *was* the Maid of Turpin's.

He wanted to embrace her there and then. He imagined doing so and crushing her with clumsy arms so that that her perfume of lavender and camomile filled his head.

"Thank God," he said aloud, "you're alive."

The figure stared at him silently.

"You would have burned me like a witch," Sybil said quietly.

Dearnought backed in to the room and she followed.

"That's how I think about you," she continued. "A destroyer of women."

Sybil walked towards him.

"But you could be my witch; there is still a chance for us?"

"There is no *us*." She held a heavy horse pistol, in each hand. "I think that you are the most evil of men. And you are finished now."

"It was a mistake, I would not let you be harmed again, whatever."

Sybil couldn't believe what she was hearing. "You left me in a sack to be burned."

"I promise you everything your heart might desire; a life of luxury," he had moved back into the gloom away from the flickering candle lamp. He raised an arm towards the wall and before she could shoot she heard a heavy grating sound as the doors and window slowly closed and locked.

"Now we are quite safe from interruptions. It's my security system; it locks and bars every exit to the room. No one can disturb us."

"So much for your proposal," Sybil still held the pistols steadily.

"I doubt you came alone?"

"Richard is outside with others of the watch you will not be able to leave."

"Neither can you: please sit down and let me look at you properly Sybil,"

***

"I don't care if you're *governor* of the Bank of England. You still can't come in. Scruffy lookin' object"

William Chasemeet raged at the gatekeeper.

"Evil deeds are planned in this place and I must stop them happening."

He was covered from head to foot in mud.

"If you're not gone, I'll open the gates and set the dogs free."

In despair Chasemeet let go of the iron gate he had been clasping with both hands.

"I have money," Chasemeet waved paper notes at the man.

"Let me see."

He put an arm through the bars of the gate.

It was grasped firmly and pulled so that the man's face was pressed painfully up against the ironwork. The other hand had struck out and was similarly held.

Chasemeet looked as surprised as the gatekeeper to see two more figures either side of him.

"Shall we open the gate now," said John Dutch. "before your arms break off?"

Clem Applebee lifted the notes from the gatekeeper and returned them to his old boss.

***

Richard had circled the building looking for a way in. The back of the house was in complete darkness. The garden a wilderness and in places the undergrowth encroached up to the building; long thorny brambles snared Richard as he crept around. He realised it was a hopeless task. With an arm out, feeling for the wall he progressed slowly.

Suddenly he was walking on timber boards which he thought might be the entrance to the cellars. With a crash he was through the rotted wood of a door and dropping helplessly. Stone steps broke his fall, but he continued downwards landing painfully. Richard sat for a while gently testing that his arms and legs were all still working. The damp smell was reminiscent of earlier cellar experience.

I could begin to have nightmares about cellars, he thought.

Suddenly there was a rumbling like the sound of approaching thunder. The whole cellar vibrated as if heavy stones were being moved. Behind him a slab slowly lowered down the wall resting for a moment on his shoulders until he leaned forward and it continued to the ground, trapping the tail of his coat.

In the quiet he heard the soft sound of voices from the room above.

When I told her to stay in the garden, I should have tied her to a tree, he thought.

On the walls his hands felt the ropes connected to stone weights and he guessed that behind the façade of a decaying old building, Dearnought had built himself a fortress. Richard had seen such mechanicals before and knew to expect a complex system of counterweights and pulleys throughout the house.

He was reminded of an assignment in Spain several years before when chasing a turncoat diplomat from the British embassy. The man had been the lover of Dona Teresa Alvarezo whose appetite for love was only exceeded by her beauty.

Richard was captive in her villa for several weeks, anxiously trying to escape; not entirely anxious all the time. He smiled to himself at the memory.

Her house had been full of secret passages and rooms which changed shape, doors which disappeared; even the stair cases moved. He knew that to immobilise these mechanicals it was necessary to cut ropes connected to weights in the right order, otherwise the moving doors, shutters and partitions would stay shut. In consequence they would either be locked in or locked out.

He must find himself some light.

***

"I was determined that no one else would have you if I couldn't."

Dearnought sat looking relaxed in an armed chair. Behind him a tapestry screen covered the wall. He rubbed a hand over his scarred face and looked over at Sybil.

"You are a strong-minded woman; ruthless even, and I saw in you someone who'd be sympathetic to my cause."

Sybil rested the pistols on a small table and sat beside them in an upright chair across the room from the man she had come to find.

She was determined to stop him by whatever means she could. Her mind went back to the girl, her namesake. The young Sybil was to be taken into slavery, introduced to whoring in one of Dearnought's palaces of pleasure where soon enough she would be destined to stay for the rest of her pox-ridden life.

"You are wrong doctor I have no stomach for the kind of ruthless evil you practice. You thought because I run a tavern for thieves and criminals, that I am one of them. Nothing could be further from the truth."

"My dear Sybil you are wrong about yourself," Dearnought spoke to her as if she were a friend.

"You *are* like me. You're intelligent and that's how you wield control."

Sybil stayed alert at the small table, her hands not far from the pistols.

If Richard intends to intervene now might be a good time, she thought.

"I cannot control your mind as I can others; and that's something I respect."

Sybil reasoned her best chance of staying alive was to keep him talking, giving Richard the opportunity to find a way in.

"You're a cunning-woman; and I've have heard about your successes with potions and cures."

"Is that why you would burn me in a sack? Perhaps the truth is that you think me a potion-making witch."

"The age of enlightenment is upon us Sybil," he spoke now, as if talking to a child.

"Or perhaps you haven't heard; people don't get punished for being witches any more."

Sybil remained silent.

"You're different; there's no denying it and my seed would give us heirs well enough gifted to rule the world."

"I think your seed should be destroyed so that mankind never has to suffer such evil ever again." Sybil could not help herself, she felt so repulsed at the thought of this man's embrace.

Dearnought stood up, "then I must leave you here Sybil. I'm tired of this place; I plan to start anew,"

He laughed quietly at first and then louder. "If you're not with me…."

Sybil reached for a pistol as Dearnought retreated in to the darkness of the room.

"Help yourself to my brandy. I'm sure Hamilton will find his way in sooner or later."

She fired at his shadow but heard only the smash of breaking glass.

"I can't be harmed my dear," the voice came from a different part of the room.

They both heard the rumble of thunder from beneath their feet.

Sybil turned and watched as the French windows became un-shuttered and opened wide.

She was still as the moon shone in once more, silhouetting her in the doorway.

From the darkened end of the room Medici Dearnought raised a pistol and took aim very slowly.

How William Chasemeet, waiting outside the shuttered windows, became aware that the silhouetted figure was being targeted, no one knew. Afterwards Clem said he heard his old boss call out.

"Dear man," he had called frantically.

The banker stepped forward in front of Sybil and took the ball directly in the forehead. He dropped like a stone.

It was aimed at Sybil's heart.

Chasemeet fell back against her. He never knew it was Sybil's life he had saved.

In the cellar Richard heard the first pistol shot and the sound of crashing glass. He feared for Sybil but was unable to get in to the library. He had mastered an understanding the mechanicals controlled by weights, pulleys, and wrist-thick ropes and managed to open the shuttered doors to the library.

Standing in the cellar looking up he could now see a long narrow passage, probable the height of the house.

Having lit the space, as best he could, one side of the passage was a wooden partition extending from the library to the rooms above. It had staging at different levels and ropes hanging from high above in what must have been the roof space.

He marvelled at the ingenuity. Dearnought had designed himself a route for exiting rooms and entrancing others at will and undetected.

This was the answer to how Richard could get in to the library.

There was a second pistol shot. A door opened above his head, and Dearnought leaned out grabbing a rope with both hands. It began to lower him slowly, until Richard stopped the man's downward movement by pulling on the other end.

Dearnought was suspended, unable to move up or down.

Richard grasped the longer of the ropes and began to do the only thing he could.

He wound one rope around the other, weaving them together like a massive plait.

Dearnought became secured in the bundle.

Richard climbed up the partition until he reached the cocooned Dearnought.

"Hang around for a while doctor. I'll be back for you shortly."

In to the library he came out from behind a screen and was instantly set upon by John Dutch and Clem.

At the darkened end of the room he took a beating before Clem realized he was not the enemy.

EPILOGUE

"Where are they then?" asked Josie looking across the table at Jacobs.

They were sat in the parlour, in a cubby, sharing a quiet conversation. The curtain was open so that Jacobs could keep an eye on Clem sitting in the tall chair. Clem Applebee lounged with all the confidence of a seventeen year old left to oversee Turpin's customers.

"He was ordered to call on his very high-up boss, and he took Miss Sybil with him."

The parlour was filled with locals and there were a few travellers who still tended to congregate at the long trestle table in the corner nearest the Servery. It was still felt to be slightly safer than being in amongst the local thievery.

The embers of a fire were keeping the hog roast heated but it was receiving little attention. Given the weather, customers had little appetite for sizzling hot food.

"Don't see much of her right now,"

Jacobs smiled at Josie, "Is that a worry to you lass."

Josie blushed.

"Not when *you* speaks of it like that."

"You don't worry about the mistress she knows what she's doin."

"But we've been there before see. And it weren't a happy time."

The Cockpit had gone for good, but the secret discovery of a cellar and passage to exit the Tavern was kept. Turpin's was still a Tavern where disreputable people frequented and an alternative escape route was still an asset.

"I've known Mr Hamilton for some years and I'd trust him with me life,"

Jacobs went quiet for a while. "Fact is, I 'av trusted him with me life. He wouldn't let anything 'appen to Miss Sybil."

He reached out to cover Josie's hand with his own.

"Let's see where their romancin' takes them and then we'll know."

"So that's what it is then Jacobs, romance?"

He looked at her steadily.

"If I had two arms instead of one I'd put them both round you and hug you to pieces."

Josie pretended a frown. "If you were to do that to me…, I should like it very much,"

Josie blushed at her own boldness.

***

Sybil and Richard had been shown in to the Duke of Sharingham's Library. It was not a social call they had been summoned. They stood in the tall glass double doors looking out over the estate. The Duke had not arrived, but they could see his coach approaching them through the avenue of trees half a mile away.

Sybil sighed and reached out to touch Richard's hand.

"You're nervous about this?"

"There's something. I don't know what it is. Why both of us?"

The Duke arrived breathlessly having come directly from the Palace of Westminster.

"Hope you have been looked after? I have just come from Sir Robert Walpole. He is well pleased with the outcome of our operation." He stopped as if to catch his breath and stared at Sybil without speaking, for what seemed like an age.

"Where are my manners; Miss Sybil welcome to my home," he gathered both her hands and held them to his lips.

A most familiar gesture Richard thought.

Richard had already decided she looked stunning, and apparently so did the Duke.

The sat around a small table placed under the window.

"I am sorry you lost Dearnought. I know he was a particular loose end you wanted to sort. How did he escape you?"

"I was careless. Having wound him up in a rope, I had to leave him in a hurry. When I came back he'd cut himself out and vanished."

"He was a thoroughly evil man," the Duke said looking towards Sybil.

"He was known as Dr Death in the city. He's left us much to put right for the young women he enslaved."

Richard leaned across and touched her arm.

"Sybil is making it a personal crusade to rescue them."

"We've made a start," she said enthusiastically.

The Duke smiled.

"You have some well-deserved leave coming Richard, but first I wanted to get you here to thank you personally.

"Turned in to something of team effort your grace,"

Sybil looked away; she felt ill at ease, coming here, to be thanked for… what?

The Duke nodded.

"Yes I believe that to be so; and that's *partly* why you are both here so that I can thank you…, from Thomas as well."

The Duke went quiet.

Sybil sighed inwardly. She didn't want to be part of a discussion about Thomas.

Then suddenly she realised that it was the Duke himself who was discomfited the most. He was struggling to continue.

"You'll appreciate the father still mourns for the loss of his son. But I have the added burden of being responsible for his death and that sits badly with me.

"Your grace surely …" Richard tried to interrupt.

"No listen Richard," the Duke held up both hands. "I do have both of you to thank."

Silence hung in the air; a different problem for each of them:

The Duke wished to say things from his heart which might burden the young woman.

Richard wanted to explain the way his friend Thomas had bravely put his country before his own safety.

Sybil feared having to talk with a still grieving father about his son whom she had loved.

The Duke finally spoke, but slowly, with difficulty. All the assertiveness and self-belief seemed to have left him.

"Sybil if you will permit me to share some confidences." He looked towards her as if waiting for permission to continue.

"Thomas came to tell me of his love for you and that he wanted simply to…"

Words failed the old Duke.

Sybil pressed fingers to her mouth but it didn't stop the tears flowing.

"When he told me, I was full of righteous indignation for his stupidity in thinking he could just throw up his birth right for the sake of a… It wasn't till later I realised there could never be a match between you anyway."

"Stop," pleaded Sybil. "Please stop."

The Duke shook his head.

"There is something else my dear child. After first meeting you I *thought* he might have been your half-brother: And now I am certain of it Sybil; you are my daughter."

Sybil was shaking her head but so was Richard.

"I wasn't sure until a moment ago."

He took her hands again and held them gently in his own, palms facing up.

"You have the Sharingham hands," he was smiling now.

Richard leaned over.

"Her thumbs?"

The Duke nodded.

"For the last three generations the daughters of the family have had thumbs which articulate in that unusual fashion."

Sybil's thumbs *unusually* bent backwards at the top joint.

It was Richard who finally broke the tension.

"I knew it," he looked at Sybil and smiled. "I knew you had style, since Miss Maisy's Tea Room."

Sybil said nothing she just sat staring at her hands

***

At this time of the year Sybil's secret lake was a fine place to be. The water was still cold but the sun warmed the shallows.

It was half an hour off the main road and they had to lead their horses for most of that time. They sat on the bank of the pool, the horses tethered in the shrubs well hidden from the road.

"Your secret place," said Richard. "Show me your hand again."

She held them up pressing her thumbs back.

"The Sharingham thumbs," he said admiringly.

"Don't laugh at me," Sybil said pulling her hands away.

"I think he wants to get to know you better."

She shook her head without speaking.

"Duke's been *good*; offering you help with your plans for Dearnought's victims.

He's an honourable man Sybil. I believe he sincerely wants to make amends.

"He's nothing to make amends for. I don't blame him for anything. And anyway we are worlds apart."

"You have the Sharingham blood running through your veins. And that makes you very special, whatever you decide to do."

"All I know is how to run a Tavern in Cheapside."

Sybil looked at the man beside her. She wanted to fall in to his arms. She already knew how good it felt.

But where would it take them. Richard could never be fulfilled just running a Tavern in the rookery. She looked towards him.

He was watching her intently.

"What….," he started and then hesitated.

"What would a fellow have to do to earn the affection of this lady?"

She was taken back by his forwardness; but eventually leaned forward and touched his cheek with her open hand.

She turned away from him and looked at his shimmering image in the still water.

"He already has the affection of the lady... He will be missed when he leaves and goes off to war again."

She picked up a pebble and tossed it in the pool and turned the moment around with her humour.

"Particularly since she worries about his capability as an agent of the crown."

She grinned mischievously and doubted he would see that the humour held an element of truth.

"I have a present for you." He removed an oblong shaped wooden box from the saddlebag.

Sybil released the lid and removed a finely carved wooden puppet. The joints were all delicately cut and perfectly shaped. The head and face had simple plain features.

He smiled, "It was the call-symbol, Sir Ronald assigned to me."

"But the strings have all been cut?"

He nodded.

"I think that was intentional; a sinister message if you like."

"Can't imagine anyone cutting your strings," she said jokingly.

Richard smiled. "Well that's where you're wrong Miss Turpin."

"Knowing how well you like to swim?"

"Now you're teasing."

They both knew he swam like a crab.

She kicked him gently with her bare foot and he rolled backwards in to the shallows.

There was much splashing. She leaned forward to pull him out and the inevitable happened.

Sybil was tugged in.

Both were weighed-down in their wet clothes and hell-bent on playful mischief; but this time Richard changed the mood; gathering her in his arms.

"This is where I should like to be… without strings."

THE END